Boy Trouble

Boy Trouble
© 2012 Mark A. Roeder

All rights reserved. No part of this book may be used or reproduced by any means, graphic, electronic, or mechanical, including photocopying, recording, taping or by any information storage retrieval system without the written permission of the publisher except in the case of brief quotations embodied in critical articles and reviews.

This book is a work of fiction. Names, characters, places and incidents are products of the author's imagination or are used fictionally. Any resemblance to actual events or locales or persons, living or dead, is entirely coincidental. All trademarks are the property of their respective owners and no infringement is intended.

Cover Photo Credit: Teresa Levite on Dreamstime.com.

Cover Design: Ken Clark

ISBN-13: 978-1470062477

ISBN-10: 147006247X

All Rights Reserved

Printed in the United States of America

Acknowledgements

I'd like to thank Ken Clark and James Adkinson for all the work they put in proofreading this book. Without their dedication this book would be a grammatical nightmare.

Dedication

This book is dedicated to Ken Clark for the enormous amount of work he puts in not only proofreading manuscripts and designing covers, but also creating and maintaining markroeder.com. Thank you, Ken, for all of that, and for being my friend.

Percy
Bloomington, Indiana
Tuesday, September 1, 2009

I froze. For several moments I could do nothing but stare at the boy who had rapped on my door—a boy dressed all in black from his shoes to his leather jacket. His spiked hair, the spiked collar around his neck, and the spiked bands on his wrists gave him a belligerent air. His blond hair and blue eyes stood out in stark contrast to his black eyeliner and Goth attire, but his expression was grim.

"I'm here."

"Yes, and..."

"I'm Caspian... your... nephew," he said slowly and with great disdain as if he was speaking to someone who was too stupid for words.

"Caspian? You're... I... Come in."

Caspian pushed past me, looked around at my antique furnishings for a moment, and frowned.

"So do I have a room or do I have to sleep on the couch?" he asked.

"I prepared the guest room for you. Of course, you'll want..."

"Where is it?" he interrupted.

"It's right over..." I began.

"Just tell me," Caspian said impatiently before I could begin to lead him to his room.

"That one," I said, pointing to a door.

Caspian shouldered his backpack, grabbed his duffle bag, walked into his room and slammed the door. I just stood there for several moments with my mouth gaping open.

Oh! My! God! What have I gotten myself into?

I gazed at the closed door for a moment. I started towards it, and then hesitated. My nephew obviously wanted to be alone.

I changed directions and headed toward the kitchen to make myself a pot of tea.

My mind was reeling as I put the kettle on the stove and turned on the blue flames.

THAT is Caspian?

I had last seen my nephew when he a precocious three-year-old racing around my brother's living room flying a model space shuttle. My brother, his wife, and Caspian lived across country in California, so visits were rare. If I'd known... but, there was no point in dwelling on the mistakes of my past. My brother and his wife were dead, killed in a house fire from which Caspian had narrowly escaped with his life.

I'd been expecting Caspian, but not the young Goth who had knocked on my door. I hadn't spoken with my brother often, but he'd never mentioned that Caspian had adopted a new lifestyle. I'd pictured Caspian as a preppy, California surfer boy. What appeared on my doorstep was an utter shock.

I turned off the stove and poured the steaming water over the Edinburgh Blend tea bag I'd placed in the pot. I set the kettle back on the stove and sat down.

My brother had been dead less than a week, his body cremated, his ashes scattered. There were no services as per his request and I was left reeling with the news. I'd agreed at Caspian's birth to be his guardian if need be and the time had shockingly and abruptly arrived.

I poured a cup of steaming tea. There was a boy behind his closed bedroom door who had been completely uprooted from his life. His parents were dead, his home destroyed, and he'd been torn away from everything and everyone he knew—all in a week's time. What must he be thinking? I had lost a brother I saw rarely. Caspian had lost... everything.

Caspian and I were strangers. I'd sent him birthday and Christmas cards and gifts every year, but I hadn't been a part of his life. Most of a continent had separated us. Now, with only a few feet of physical distance between us he seemed far away still.

I resisted the urge to get up and knock on Caspian's door. He would come out when he felt like it. He needed time to himself, time to adjust, time to settle in to his new home. I knew nothing about raising a fifteen-year-old boy. My only parental experience was my years as a camp counselor. I'd worked with kids at Camp Neeswaugee for more years that I could count. At least that was something. I doubted it would be enough. This boy wasn't going home after a few weeks. *This* was his home now.

I carried my tea into my office and sat down at my laptop. I knew there was little chance of getting any serious writing done, but there were always emails to answer, always endless details connected to publishing my books that required my attention. The amount of time I spent on the non-writing tasks of publishing never failed to amaze me. Still, I counted myself lucky to work hours of my own choosing in my own home.

Sometime later I heard footsteps in the living room. I looked at the old mantle clock my father had given to me long ago. It was nearing five p.m. I'd been at it for more than two hours. I often lost track of the time when I as working. I stood, pushed back my chair, and found Caspian holding one of my antique stoneware jars. He replaced it when he noticed me.

"Sorry for handling your stuff," he said, clearly without meaning it.

"You can handle anything you want here, Caspian. This is your home now."

"It's *your* home, not *mine*. My home is a pile of ashes."

"This is *our* home, Caspian."

His only reaction was to spear me with a glance that told me he'd just as soon smack my face as look at me.

"You hungry?" I asked.

"Yeah."

"What do you like to eat?"

"Steak."

"Okay, steak it is. How about Texas Roadhouse?"

"What's that?"

"A steak place—lousy music, great food. You don't have Texas Roadhouse in California?"

"Maybe. I don't know. Never been there."

"Then let's go."

Caspian shrugged and followed me out the door.

"What the fuck is this?" Caspian asked, staring at my car.

I stiffened at his language, but now wasn't the time to get into it.

"It's a Shay, the last Model A ever produced."

"It looks like it belongs in a museum."

"There were less than 5,000 of them made, so perhaps you're right. I bought it to drive. It's my toy. Get in."

Caspian climbed into the roadster. I put the top down.

"Put on your seatbelt. I'm a terrible driver."

Caspian looked at me quickly, trying to figure out if I was telling the truth or not, but he put on his seatbelt. I started up and Shay and headed for the west side of town. Bloomington wasn't large and I lived in the center of the north side, so just about everything was a fifteen minute drive or less.

Caspian's stiff hair didn't stir in the breeze and I momentarily wondered if he used glue to get it to stay in place. Caspian almost looked like he might be enjoying himself. I had yet to see him smile, but then he didn't have much to smile about. I wished I could erase all his pain, but I knew the best I could do was just be there for him.

Heads turned as we drove by. I was accustomed to the attention. Not very many Model A roadsters were still on the streets. I was frequently asked for permission to photograph my car. Sometimes, I was asked to sell it. Photographs were fine, but I had no intention of parting with it. It had taken far too long to locate a Shay with an automatic transmission. I was hopeless with a manual.

I backed into a parking spot with ease at the Texas Roadhouse and got out. Caspian and I headed inside. We were immediately assaulted by the strains of country music.

"You're right, the music is lousy," Caspian said. "I hope you're also right about the food."

"Trust me," I said.

Caspian looked as if he was ready to do anything but.

A hostess grabbed some rolls and led us to a booth. I picked up the menus and handed one to Caspian. The restaurant was somewhat crowded, but it was too early to be packed. I came to the Texas Roadhouse about once a month. I tended to prefer non-chain restaurants like the Scholar's Inn Bakehouse or The Irish Lion, but I loved the Caesar salad and chicken critters at the Roadhouse.

Our waiter took our drink orders and then departed. He was a good-looking college-age guy. Attractive young men were everywhere in Bloomington. It was one of the benefits of living there.

"I'm ordering the chicken critters," I said.

"The what?"

"Chicken critters. They're chicken strips. The name alone is worth ordering them."

"You aren't getting steak?"

"No, but you order anything you want."

"Anything?"

"Anything except alcohol, you are under age."

"Like I haven't drunk alcohol before!"

I let the comment pass.

Our waiter soon returned with our drinks. Now that I had a closer look at him I noticed his sexy eyes. I ordered my chicken critters, a Caesar salad, and mashed potatoes with cream gravy. Caspian ordered a ribeye with fries and more fries.

We ate yeast rolls while we waited on our food.

"So..." I said, unsure of what to say. "We need to do some shopping. I'm sure there are quite a few things you need. We'll pick up what we can today and go from there."

"Okay." Caspian was not helping to move the conversation along.

"So, what do you think about your room?"

"It's like this music. It fucking sucks."

"It is rather austere."

"It's what?"

"Plain. It was a guestroom that was almost never used. You can give it some personality with your own stuff."

11

"I don't have stuff, remember? All my stuff was destroyed along with..."

Caspian didn't finish his sentence, but I could hear "my parents" at the end.

"We will get you stuff—posters and whatever else you want."

"Why is there old stuff everywhere in your house?"

"I like old stuff. I like things with a history, things with memories attached."

"Not my style."

"Well, your room is your room. You can fix it up however you want. If you don't like the furniture, we'll get you something different."

"Are you rich?"

"No. I have enough money, but I'm not rich."

Caspian didn't know it, but he *was* rich, for a fifteen-year-old at least. His parents didn't have much put back, but their life insurance policy would provide a substantial sum and then there was the insurance on their home. I'd already arranged with my lawyer for it to be placed in account for Caspian's use when he grew older. Until then, I intended for him to know nothing about it. I feared he'd want to spend it all on electronic gadgets.

Thankfully, our food arrived. I was glad to have something to do other than talk. I wasn't quite sure what to say to my nephew and his demeanor clearly showed he was merely tolerating me. I wished we had some common ground, but all we shared were memories of his father and I sensed it was much too soon to talk about him.

The chicken critters were delicious. I loved them with honey mustard sauce. It was too bad Texas Roadhouse didn't sell their sauce because I hadn't been able to find any elsewhere that even came close to the taste. I'd tried.

I looked at the boy sitting across from me. There were times in the past I'd wished for a son. I guess the old warning of "Be careful what you wish for" was true. For all practical purposes, Caspian was now my son. At least he was my legal responsibility. He wasn't at all what I'd pictured when I'd thought of having a son. I'd thought of someone more like...

Tyler. I'd even begun to think of Tyler as my son, but now everything was changing.

What was I going to do with a teenage Goth? Stereotypes were always dangerous, but so far he'd lived up to my image of a Goth. How could I even find common ground with him?

I didn't feel especially close to Caspian, but I did care about him. He was my nephew and, even though I doubted he'd ever admit it, he needed me.

Caspian had been dropped into my life without warning. I was frightened I wasn't up to the task of parenting and I felt a little disoriented, but I was also determined to do my best.

"Why are you looking at me?" Caspian asked.

"I have to look somewhere and you are sitting directly across from me."

Caspian shot me his look of disdain—an expression I'd already witnessed several times. Yes, raising a teenager was going to be an interesting experience. I could almost hear my brother laughing at me.

"There's a lot of old people in here," Caspian said.

"Old people have to eat too. It's a little early. The older crowd tends to eat early. Don't worry; Bloomington is filled with young people. It is a university town."

Our conversation died again. I asked for a box when our waiter returned to refill our Cokes. Caspian ate all of his meal. Why was it that little guys often ate so much more? I smiled when I thought of Caspian's likely reaction if he discovered I'd thought of him as a little guy.

"What?" he asked, suspiciously.

"Sometimes I just think funny things."

"You're weird."

"I'm a writer. Writers are strange."

Caspian just shook his head and gazed around as if he'd rather be anywhere as long as it wasn't with me.

I paid the check and we walked back out to the Shay.

"How about the mall next? We can pick you up some clothes and grab a few things at Target."

"Okay, whatever."

I headed for the east side of town. My Shay could only do about 40 m.p.h. without the narrow tires causing the car to shake, but in town speeds rarely exceeded 30. Caspian didn't seem to mind riding in my vintage car. In fact, I sensed he liked it although I doubted he'd acknowledge that.

We crossed over College Avenue, then North Walnut, the streets I considered to mark the mid-point between the east and west side. In a few more blocks we were driving past Indiana University. A couple of sexy, shirtless college boys were checking out my car as we drove by and I was checking out them. Caspian noticed, but didn't comment. I doubted my brother had ever told Caspian I was gay. I wondered how he'd take the news. I intended to be completely honest with him, but I didn't want to dump everything on him at once. I also didn't like to put too much emphasis on my sexual orientation. It was only a part of me, not the sum total of my being.

Caspian seemed more interested in his surroundings when we arrived on the east side. This was where Best Buy, Barnes & Noble, Borders, and various fast food restaurants were located. I turned onto South College Mall Road and then into the College Mall parking lot. I pulled the Shay into a space near Sears and we walked inside.

"How about we start at Aeropostale or Abercrombie & Fitch?" I asked.

Caspian looked at me as if I'd just suggested dumpster diving for his wardrobe.

"Old Navy?" I asked, doubtfully.

Caspian shook his head as if I was too stupid for words. Yeah, raising a teen was going to be an experience.

I gave up on making suggestions and we walked through the mall. I loved to come to the mall to people watch. I dropped in about once a week whether I needed anything or not.

Caspian looked about with interest, but showed no sign of even thinking about going into a store until we reached Hot Topic.

"At last!" he said.

Hot Topic was not a store I frequented, but I could understand the appeal for Caspian. It was filled with tee shirts, mostly in black, and all kinds of accessories I thought of as punk or Goth. I browsed around while Caspian looked through tee shirts featuring various bands I'd never heard of printed on the fronts.

Black was the predominant color in the store, but there were a few things in other colors. I found a red, sleeveless, shirt with a cool geometric design on the front and showed it to Caspian.

"What do you think?" I asked.

"You're kidding, right?"

I put the shirt back. I discovered another in bright blue with a skull and crossbones on the chest.

"This one?" I asked.

Caspian rolled his eyes and proceeded to ignore me. I went off and browsed, trying to find something to Caspian's taste that wasn't sinister looking. I discovered a black, studded, leather belt that looked like something Caspian might wear. He needed a belt. His pants nearly hung off his butt.

"How about this belt?" I asked.

"I'm not your fucking Ken doll! Okay?"

"I'm just making some suggestions."

"God. Could you just wait outside? You're embarrassing me."

"Okay. I'll tell you what. Pick out some shirts and pants and whatever you want then come get me. I'll be outside on one of the benches."

This wasn't at all the relationship I'd pictured with my hypothetical son, but it was probably realistic. Weren't most teens embarrassed by their parents? Probably just being seen with me in the mall was about as much as Caspian could tolerate. When he started school, which would be very soon, he likely wouldn't want to be seen with me for fear his friends would spot us. I guess this was the moment when I became uncool. I smiled to myself.

I was feeling overwhelmed, but Caspian was my responsibility and I intended to do the best I could with him. I was sure I'd make mistakes, but didn't all parents? At least he was fifteen and not an infant. I didn't think I could handle changing diapers and getting up at all hours of the night.

I wasn't determined to stick with it merely because I was responsible for Caspian. He was my nephew and I cared about him. I'd made the commitment to be his guardian when he was born. True, the likelihood of actually becoming his guardian was slim, but I'd thought about it long and hard before agreeing and I wasn't sorry for my choice. I didn't want Caspian to be anywhere but with me.

I checked my email on my Droid as I waited. There wasn't anything that couldn't wait, but I liked to keep on top of my communications. The sound of a goat "bbhhhaa-ing" caused those sitting near to stare at me for a moment. It was the sound I'd selected to announce the arrival of a text message. I smiled. It was from Daniel. Just having someone special in my life gave me a warm feeling in my chest.

I typed a quick response back. Well, quick for me. I spent hours typing on a keyboard every day, but I was still getting the hang of typing on a phone. I often used the voice-to-text feature when I was alone, but in public I liked some privacy.

Caspian appeared in the window of Hot Topic and motioned to me. My exile was over for the moment. He had found some half dozen shirts he liked, a couple of pairs of pants, as well as a belt much like the one I'd showed him. I led him to the counter, pulled out my American Express and soon we were back in the mall. We hit Target next and picked up necessities for Caspian like deodorant, a toothbrush, socks, his favorite shampoo and so forth. We loaded down an entire cart so after I paid I told Caspian to wait until I pulled the Shay around to the Target entrance. We couldn't take the cart into the mall and there was no way we could carry all his stuff to the car.

I quickly walked through the mall and back to the Shay. A few minutes later I pulled up in front of Target and Caspian came out with the cart. I opened up the rumble seat and we loaded it down with bags. Soon, we were on our way back to the house.

It took us a couple of trips to bring everything in. Most of it went directly to Caspian's bedroom.

"I've emptied the closet and all the drawers in here," I said, setting the last bag on Caspian's bed. "I also cleared out space in the medicine cabinet and a shelf in the cupboard in the bathroom. I'm sure we didn't get everything you need, so make a list and we'll go shopping again soon."

"Okay."

I left Caspian to himself. If I was moving into a strange house I'd want time alone to adjust. When I was fifteen, the main thing I wanted was space, so I tried to give that to Caspian. It wasn't as easy as it sounds. I had to resist the urge to check on him and make sure he was okay.

I put away a few supplies I'd picked up at Target. I was thinking about getting some writing done, but I didn't know if I could keep my mind on the task. I had a short attention span and Caspian's arrival had thrown me off balance.

"Hey."

Caspian stood in the kitchen doorway, leaning against the door frame.

"I'm gonna go and check things out," Caspian said.

"Oh! I almost forgot..." I said, walking over to a small hanging cupboard on the wall. I opened the door and pulled out a key. I handed it to Caspian.

"This is for you. It's a key to the house. I might be out when you return and you'll need it later."

"What if I decide not to come back?"

"This is your home, not a prison. You can think of it as a prison if you want, but in case it escaped you I just gave you the key to your cell."

Caspian looked at me as if I was a freak, then turned and left without another word. I released a huge sigh. Was I making the right decisions or was I screwing up Caspian's life and my own?

Tyler

Sometimes, my life goes along unchanging. Everything is pretty much the same as the day before. That's not necessarily a good or a bad thing. It's just life. Then, bam! Everything changes overnight. That happened to me only a week ago, when my dad was reunited with the lost love of his teen years. All thanks to me!

Yay!

I'd been hoping my dad would find someone special. He'd been alone for a long time. I couldn't even remember a serious boyfriend. I knew Percy was lonely too. I was already thinking of hooking them up, but then I began to catch on that they actually knew each other and had fallen in love long ago. That was like... twenty years before, and definitely before I was born. They hadn't seen each other since, but love doesn't have an expiration date. Long story short, I brought them back together and everything has gone smoothly... so far... but only a week has passed.

And now, BAM! Something new. Percy has a son! Well, not a son, but a nephew, who has come to live with him, so the kid might as well be his son. I have mixed feelings about it. I was sure Percy would make a kick-ass dad. I thought of him as a second father; that's where the mixed feelings come in. My dad and Percy were just starting to get to know each other again, but I was already thinking of us as a family, and here this kid comes along. I know I'm getting way ahead with the family bit and the kid can't help it if his parents were both killed in a fire. Still, it's like he's invading *my* turf.

Okay. I know I've got to drop the negative attitude. I'm not that kind of guy, really! I've been reminding myself that this boy, Caspian, isn't here to push into my life. His own has been destroyed. He's a survivor of a tragedy, so I've got to be compassionate and cool with him. That's kind of in my nature, which is why I surprised myself with selfish thoughts.

This is what I was thinking as I drove over to Percy's house. Percy and my dad thought it would help Caspian out a lot if I drove him to school for his first day and showed him around. I remembered what my first day at North was like as a freshman. It wasn't pretty. Caspian had it worse because it was September, so he wasn't one new freshman among scores... he was *the* new freshman. That had to totally suck.

I parked my car in front of Percy's house and walked up onto the porch. I knocked on the frosted glass of the antique door. Percy opened it a few moments later.

"Hey, Tyler," he said.

Percy was totally cool. What I liked best about him is that he never treated me like a kid. I wasn't one. I was seventeen and would turn eighteen before the month was over. It was also cool he was a writer because I wanted to write books and he'd already taught me a lot. When I first met him, I almost couldn't believe that Percy DeForest Spock had moved to Bloomington. I sure never dreamed he'd someday be dating my dad!

"I really appreciate this," Percy said.

"For you... almost anything." I grinned.

I added the *almost* because you really have to watch what you say around a writer, especially one with a sense of humor like Percy. I tried not to give him too many opportunities to give me a hard time.

"Caspian! Tyler is here!" Percy called out.

At least the kid had a cool name.

Whoa! I quickly closed by mouth because my jaw had dropped open at the sight of the little bad-ass who walked into the room. I guess I was expecting a sort of fifteen-year-old version of Percy since the kid was his nephew but they looked nothing alike. Caspian was a Goth! I didn't have anything against Goths, but it blew me away that Caspian was one. I gazed at Percy for a moment, trying to wipe the stunned expression off my face. Percy smiled at me. I think he was enjoying this! No, I knew he was.

"Hey, sup?" I said.

"Hey."

Caspian didn't look at all thrilled to meet me, although it might have been first day jitters eating at him. I couldn't tell, obviously, since I wasn't a mind reader.

"Ready?" I asked.

"Yeah. Whatever."

"You have your key?" Percy asked.

Caspian stared at Percy for a moment like he was something he was about to wipe off his shoe, then pushed past me and walked outside. He didn't say "goodbye" to Percy or even spare him a glance. He didn't say anything to me as I led him to the car. He tossed his backpack into the back seat and climbed in.

I pulled onto the street and headed for North High School. We drove in silence. I didn't know what to say to this kid. We didn't know each other and he was quite a bit younger than me. I guess he was only three years or so younger, but the age difference seemed even greater. He was also kind of scary. He didn't crack a smile and I halfway expected him to pull out a blade and start carving on the dashboard. I could not believe this was Percy's nephew! He was nothing like him!

I stole a couple of looks at Caspian during the short drive. He was wearing a worn leather jacket, black jeans, and black canvas sneakers. His black leather collar with spikes, matching wrist-bands, and a touch of black eye liner completed his bad-ass Goth look. His spiky blond hair was a contrast to all the black and yet it went with his look. Truth to be told I would have been scared to death of meeting him in a dark alley.

I parked in the student parking lot and Caspian and I walked inside.

"Let me see your schedule," I said.

Caspian pulled the crumpled paper out of his pocket and handed it to me without a word. I found his locker number on his schedule and led him to it. He dumped his black leather jacket in his locker. He was wearing a tight black tee shirt with a skull with fangs on it. I wondered what his teachers would make of him.

"Want me to show you to your first class?"

"I don't need a fucking babysitter. You've earned your Boy Scout badge by driving me to school. You can dump me now."

"Actually, I was wondering if you'd like to join my friends and me for lunch. We share the same lunch period. I'll drive you home after school."

"Maybe."

"I just thought..."

"Dude, I get it, okay? Back off!"

I held up my hands in surrender as Caspian stalked off.

"Who's the charmer?"

I turned. It was Tyreece, a member of my small circle of friends.

"Percy's nephew, if you can believe it."

"Percy's the writer-guy you talk about too much, right?"

"Shut up and yes."

"Hmm. No. I can't believe it."

"Well, I invited him to sit with us at lunch."

"Good job, Tyler. He'll probably bite someone and give them rabies."

"I doubt he'll show up. He called me a Boy Scout!"

"Well, in all fairness you do sort of look like one. Well, you might pass for an Eagle Scout"

"Shut up."

"You say that to me a lot."

"Yeah, but you never listen."

"What do you have against the Scouts, anyway? I was one, you know," Tyreece said.

"They don't sell cookies like the Girl Scouts, only that lousy popcorn. That's what I have against them."

I headed off to my first class. I enjoyed school... mostly. There are days I would have rather been elsewhere, but most of my classes were interesting and I liked hanging out with my friends. They were an entertaining and varied group, except there were no girls. It's not that any of us had anything against girls, except possibly Caleb, but that's a story in itself. No girls had wandered into our little group, or perhaps they were just smart enough to avoid us. I don't know.

Tyreece called himself the token black of our group, but he was only kidding, about the token part this is. He was the only black guy in my circle of friends. I knew others, but none so well. Tyreece was friendly and a genuinely nice guy, although he didn't put up with crap. He was quite handsome and wore short dreads. He also had an incredible body. I'd seen him without a shirt more than once. He had a six-pack and everything. He looked like he'd been carved out of ebony. The rumor was he had a ten-incher. I didn't know about that, but it was kind of joke among our friends. Sometimes, they talked about Tyreece's dick as if it was a separate entity.

Besides Tyreece and me, there was Caleb who had been a kick-ass football player up until his junior year. Everyone thought would be our quarterback this fall, but he was involved in an accident right at the end of the previous football season and his football playing days were over. Then there was Dylan, a freshman and a total flamer. I don't mean the flamer comment in any negative or prejudiced way, but it's just the best way to describe him. He's about as stereotypically gay as they come, right down to his flaming, unnaturally blond hair, and drama queer personality. Dylan is a blast! The last member of our group was Jesse, another freshman. Jesse is... well, he's Jesse. Pretty much everyone in school, and especially Jesse, thinks he is the best looking guy around, at least as far as his face is considered. He's movie-star good-looking with curly black hair and blue eyes. He isn't built like Tyreece or Caleb, but he looks like he should be on the cover of a teen magazine. I'm sure Jesse would agree. Appearance is Jesse's number one priority, followed closely by money. I'm sure he sounds like a jerk, but he has his good qualities. It's just hard to say what they are.

I moved through my morning classes with ease. I handed in a paper for English even though it wasn't due for another two weeks. I liked to get things like that out of the way so it wouldn't be hanging over my head. It had the added bonus of making my classmates hate me for it. I had a lot of ways to entertain myself.

I thought about waiting at Caspian's locker when lunch rolled around to see if he wanted to join us, but since he'd told me to back off I thought I should.

I met up with Tyreece on my way into the cafeteria and we went through the line together. We took our trays to our usual out-of-the-way table and sat down. Caleb rolled up with his tray soon after. When I say *rolled* I mean literally. Since his accident on the football field Caleb had been confined to a wheelchair. It was a horrible thing to happen to anyone, but it must have been extra-difficult for someone who was such an athlete. I didn't want to end up in a wheelchair, but if I did it wouldn't affect my writing ability. Caleb once had big plans of getting a scholarship to a major university, and maybe even going pro. Scouts had come to look at him in his junior year. One was present the night he was tackled, tossed into the air, and then caught between two linemen. His back was broken and he was told he'd never walk again, let alone run. One accident altered his entire future.

"Hey, guys!" Dylan said, setting down his tray and flipping his bleached-blond hair out of his eyes. "How are you?"

Dylan was way too enthusiastic about everything. He was excited to see us at lunch. He was excited if we had corn dogs. He was excited if it rained. He was excited if... well, you get the picture.

"How are you, Caleb?" Dylan gave Caleb a hug. Caleb shrugged him off.

"Get off me, homo."

Caleb isn't a homophobe. Dylan is just too touchy-feely for him and sometime makes unwanted advances. He's had his ass kicked for it a few times, not by Caleb, but it doesn't seem to faze him. Dylan is friendly with just about everyone. There are rumors that he has discreet sexual relationships with several straight boys, although I never did understand how a guy could be straight if he had a sexual relationship with another guy. I mean, even if the "straight" guy is just receiving head is he really straight? I guess it doesn't matter. I figure what everyone gets up to in their private life is their business unless they're sacrificing babies or burning down homes or something. I did wonder about the Dylan rumors. There were a few bad-asses who actually looked out for him. They had to be getting something out of it. Maybe he paid them to be his bodyguards or maybe the rumors were true.

"Ohh, corn dogs! Yes!" Dylan said.

See? I told you.

"I'm kind of wondering about the corn dog and mashed potato combination," I said.

"You mean the virtual mashed potatoes. I don't think they're real," Caleb said.

"As long as we have corn dogs I don't care if the potatoes are real or not," Dylan said.

"You just like to keep in practice," I teased.

Dylan pretended he was giving his corn dog a blow.

"I don't need practice! I'm the best!"

"Dude, most guys do not brag about their blow-job expertise," Caleb said.

"Most guys don't have any blow-job expertise and I'm not most guys!"

"You can't argue with either of those points," I said.

I spotted Caspian coming out of the line with his tray. I motioned for him to join us. He hesitated, and then headed in our direction. He gave Dylan a wide berth as he neared and sat between Caleb and me.

"Guys, this is Caspian. It's his first day at North."

"My condolences. I'm Caleb."

"I'm Dylan! You'll absolutely love it here!"

Caspian looked at me for a moment as if to ask; "Is he for real?" He looked back at Dylan with a distasteful expression on his face. He was lucky the table was between them or Dylan would no doubt have given him a big hug.

"I'm Tyreece."

"Hey," Caspian said in a tone completely devoid of enthusiasm.

"I love your outfit. It just screams dominance," Dylan said.

"Down, Dylan," Tyreece said.

"The eye-liner really works for you and I *love* your collar."

Caspian lurched forward, grabbed Dylan by both sides of his head and smashed his face into the table. Okay, not really. That was just the momentary daydream that played out in my head but the expression on Caspian's face indicated my dream might come true at any moment.

Jesse, the final member of our group, arrived with his lunch, quite likely saving Dylan's life, or at least his face. Caspian stared at Jesse for a few moments as if under some kind of spell. Jesse had that kind of effect on people. He was the best looking guy in school, probably in the entire state. Caspian quickly came to himself, but not before Jesse noticed him gawking. Jesse grinned. There was nothing Jesse liked more than being admired.

Jesse scrutinized Caspian for several moments, then stood up and walked around the table.

"Stand up," he told Caspian.

"Why?"

"Just stand up."

Caspian eyed Jesse suspiciously, but did so. Jesse gripped one of his shoulders and slowly turned him around.

"What the fuck, man? Get off me!"

"You have a great look," Jesse said, ignoring Caspian's outburst. "You should wear tighter jeans and a chain draped over the left front pocket."

Jesse took one of Caspian's hands. Caspian jerked it back and looked at Jesse as if he was a freak.

"You need a silver ring, something unadorned, but highly polished."

Caspian looked at me with a question in his eyes as Jesse returned to his seat.

"You're lucky," I said. "Most of us receive citations for fashion violations."

"Most of you deserve them," Jesse said. "Like the sweat pants and house shoes *you* were wearing."

"I didn't want to change just to walk out and get the mail. I didn't go to the mall dressed like that. Who's going to see me running out to pick up the mail?" I asked.

"I saw you," Jesse said with a grin.

"Yeah, but you have some kind of weird sixth sense when it comes to fashion violations."

"With great power comes great responsibility," Jesse said.

"Thank you, Spiderman."

Caspian was eying Jesse as if he was thinking of punching him out. I had to control my compulsion to laugh.

"I think Caspian looks awesome," Dylan said. "I especially love the dog collar."

"It's a collar. It's not a *dog* collar," Caspian said.

"It's so hot," Dylan said.

Caspian reached across the table, grabbed Jesse and Dylan, and smashed their heads together.

"Anyway," I said, hoping to keep my daydream from coming true, "this is the crew."

"Great crew, Tyler," Caspian said. Now there was sarcasm.

I'd agreed almost without thinking when Percy asked me to drive Caspian to school. I thought Caspian and I might become friends, but I never dreamed he'd be so belligerent. We didn't have anything in common. Caspian tolerated my presence and that was about it. So far, I didn't like him all that much. He didn't seem to like any of my friends.

Caspian didn't join in the conversation, even though Tyreece tried to draw him out. Mostly, Caspian eyed Dylan as if he was afraid Dylan was going to try to grope him, which was a possibility. It was kind of awkward talking around Caspian, but there wasn't much else we could do.

"Later," Caspian said the moment he finished his lunch. With that he was gone. I sensed he couldn't bear to sit with us for a moment more.

"What a hostility festival," Caleb said the moment Caspian was out of ear-shot.

"I was just thinking asshole," Tyreece said.

"Oh! My! God! He is soooooooo hot!" Dylan said.

"You'd better back off or that dude *will* kick your ass," Tyreece said.

"Mmm, it would be worth it," Dylan said.

"Maybe he'll warm up?" Jesse said uncertainly. "At least he knows how to put a good look together. The bad boy thing works for him."

"And for me," Dylan said. "Mmm."

"Calm yourself, Dylan," I said.

Jesse picked up a men's fashion magazine and began reading. He was a fashion expert. He was also the only high school boy I knew who owned clothes made by Armani.

"Where did you get that guy?" Caleb said.

"He's Percy's nephew."

The guys knew all about Percy. I'd been so excited about meeting Percy and doing odd jobs for him that I'd probably talked about him too much. Then, when I began to suspect he was my Dad's long, lost love, I'd shared my suspicions with my friends. They were highly skeptical at first, but the pieces kept falling into place and I was right! Most recently, I'd shared my happiness over Dad and Percy beginning to date. My friends were totally cool with my Dad being gay and that meant a lot to me. Not everyone was so cool about it.

My friends meant a lot to me as well, which is why Caspian was a double disappointment. I'd initially been excited to meet him, but not only was he nothing like Percy he obviously didn't like my friends.

"Percy is gay, right?" Jesse asked, putting down his magazine and looking confused. "He is dating your dad."

"Uh, yeah. Why would he be dating my dad if he wasn't gay?"

"What does that have to do with anything?" Caleb asked.

"How can Percy have a nephew if he's gay?" Jesse asked.

Caleb just shook his head in frustration.

"Gay guys can have nephews," Dylan said, rolling his eyes. "They can even have kids."

"I was just asking. It's a little confusing," Jesse said.

Jesse occasionally asked a really stupid question. It wasn't that he lacked intelligence; he just didn't bother to think about things too much. Jesse wasn't big on putting out effort, unless it had something to do with physical appearance. He also didn't pay much attention to what was going on around him. If it didn't involve fashion or looks, Jesse's attention span was about fifteen seconds.

"Guys, I'm sorry about Caspian. He is kind of a jerk, but..."

"Kind of?" Tyreece said.

"Well, we just met. He's not all that nice, but he has been through a lot."

I didn't elaborate. I figured Caspian's life was his business, even if I didn't like him much.

"You think he might be gay?" Dylan asked.

"I just met him this morning, Dylan. It didn't come up," I said.

"What would you care?" Tyreece asked. "Gay. Bi. Straight. When have you ever hesitated to go after a guy, Dylan?"

"Remember Brice Parker last year?" Caleb asked. "The dude had a girlfriend and you were still after him."

"You are so lucky he didn't kick your ass," Tyreece said.

"Hey, he was hot!" Dylan said, as if that explained everything. "How do you know about Brice anyway? I was in the 8th grade last year and you guys were already in high school."

"You told us," Caleb said. "Do you pay attention to anything other than boys?"

"I haven't thought about Brice for a while…"

"Do not go there," Tyreece warned.

Dylan gave us his wide-eyed innocent look, which none of us bought. Dylan was probably the least innocent among us. If he did even half of what was rumored… Whoa!

***

I sought out Caspian at the end of the day, more out of a sense of duty than any desire on my part.

"Caspian, want a ride home?"

"Yeah, I guess. I hate buses and I don't even know which one to ride."

I waited until he gathered his stuff and shoved it in his backpack. We headed for the parking lot.

"Is Jesse a fag?" Caspian asked as we walked along. "Dylan obviously is, but I think Jesse is too."

"The word is "gay," Caspian, and no, Jesse isn't gay."

"Come on! No straight dude dresses that nice."

"Jesse is a freshman, so I haven't known him long, but he's had two girlfriends since school started, both seniors and both rich."

"Maybe he's just hiding."

"No. Dylan told me that Jesse is straight."

"And he knows this how?"

"It's none of your business, but I'll tell you anyway since I know Dylan doesn't care. He did his best to seduce Jesse and didn't get anywhere with him. Jesse is definitely straight. If a guy is even just a little curious, Dylan will have him."

"If he tries that shit with me I will fuck him up."

"Just tell him to back off. You don't have to beat him up."

We climbed in the car and slowly made our way through the traffic leaving the parking lot. Caspian remained silent until we were heading toward Percy's place.

"Why do you hang out with that freak show?" Caspian asked. "Seriously... a cripple, a flaming faggot, and a guy who acts like a fag even if he isn't one. Tyreece is the only one who seems like he might be normal and I'm not even sure about him."

Take a look in the mirror before you call anyone a freak.

"They are my friends."

"Your friends suck!"

"You've spent twenty minutes with them, if that. You don't know them."

"I know enough. Fuck, that little faggot was practically crawling over the table to molest me."

"Why do you have to be such an asshole?" I asked.

"Fuck you! How have I been an asshole?"

"Seriously? My friends were trying to be nice to you, but you were a dick and now you're talking shit about them when you don't even know them. I didn't have to give you a ride today and I certainly didn't have to invite you to sit with us. You could at least be decent about it.

"Listen, I know you're having a rough time and you've been through some shit recently that would mess anyone up, but you could at least make an effort not to be rude to those..."

"I'm not messed up!"

"I just meant that you've been through some horrible stuff lately and that it's got to be hard to deal with it. Percy told me what happened."

"And you told all your friends, right? They'll tell everyone and the whole school will be talking about me. Thanks a lot!"

"No. I didn't tell my friends. I told them you'd had a rough time recently because they wondered what was up your ass. I didn't give them any details. It's your decision if you want people to know."

"Why did Percy tell you?"

"He told me to explain the sudden appearance of his fifteen-year-old nephew. It's not like you've come for a short visit."

"Listen, dude. You seem okay. You were cool inviting me to sit with your friends at lunch. You're not... you're not the kind of guy I usually hang out with and your friends definitely aren't, but I didn't mean to be an asshole. It's just how I am. I don't put up with shit from anyone and I don't pretend I like someone if I don't. I'm not into the whole bull-shit, make-nice thing. I did your little faggot friend a favor by not punching him in the face."

"Dylan can come on strong. He doesn't know when to quit. He is a nice guy, though."

"Nice guys can suck my ass."

"Did anyone ever tell you you're charming?"

"No."

"I didn't think so."

"Fuck you."

"Dude, seriously. Get a sense of humor."

"I'm not into putting up with shit, okay?"

"It was just a joke."

"It's never *just* a joke. There is always something behind comments like that. It's an attack."

"I'm not attacking you, Caspian."

"Whatever."

I wanted to tell off Caspian, but if Dad and Percy kept dating it wasn't beyond the realm of possibility that we might all be living under the same roof someday. I bit my tongue and let Caspian's attitude slide.

I pulled up in front of Percy's house. Caspian got out and slammed the door without so much as a "goodbye" or "thank you."

"Charming," I said as I drove away.

Percy

I knocked on Caspian's door. No answer. I tried again, and then opened the door. His room was empty. I hadn't heard him leave the house. I needed to have a talk with him about letting me know when he was going out.

I left him a note on the kitchen table, telling him I was going out for supper. I thought about reminding him of what was in the refrigerator in case he came in hungry, but it's not like he didn't already know.

I grabbed the keys to the Shay and headed out. I was picking up Daniel and then we were eating at The Snow Lion, a Tibetan restaurant run by the nephew of the Dalai Lama.

I pulled up in front of Daniel's house and sounded the distinctive ahooga horn of the Shay. There was no mistaking the horn of my Model A with that of any other car in town. Daniel walked out looking so very handsome in cargo pants and a purple polo. He knew I loved purple. He climbed in, leaned over, and gave me a quick kiss on the lips.

"I almost can't believe we're back together after all these years," I said. "I keep expecting to wake up."

"If you do maybe I'll be beside you."

"Keep hold of that thought."

Daniel and I hadn't slept together since we were teens. That wasn't as odd as it seems because until a few days before I hadn't seen Daniel since we were both eighteen. Neither of us wanted to rush back into a relationship. A lifetime had passed since we'd been lovers, Tyler's lifetime anyway. We needed to get to know each other all over again.

I'd already given sleeping with Daniel some thought. Up until recently I'd had my own place where we could get together. Now, each of our homes included a teen boy. I wasn't entirely comfortable with having sex with Daniel while Tyler was in the house. I had no idea how Caspian would react, not that he'd necessarily know what was going on. Sooner or later he'd figure it out. Just when I might need my privacy again it was gone. I was getting a bit ahead of myself. Things were going well with Daniel, but we weren't quite to the sleeping together stage. At least waiting was easier than it had been previously. I was no longer a teenage boy ravished by hormones and an intense need for sex. Sometimes, though, I didn't feel all that far removed from my younger self.

I parked on Grant Street only a couple of blocks from the Snow Lion and we walked to the restaurant.

The interior was not what one would expect of a Tibetan restaurant. When I'd first entered, many years before, I'd anticipated a lot of carved wood and an almost antique feel. Of course, my expectations weren't based on any knowledge of Tibet, but that's what my writer's mind had pictured. Instead, the interior didn't have any particular style at all. It was a mishmash of booths, tables, and oddball chairs. Some of the furnishings would have been at home in a greasy-spoon-type diner and some could have come out of someone's kitchen or even a Burger Dude. The mirrors made the dark interior somewhat confusing. I couldn't claim to like the ambiance, but I didn't dislike it. It was just there. The Snow Lion was the kind of place one definitely came for the food and that was usually if not consistently good.

We were shown to a quiet booth where we browsed the menus, then ordered.

"So, how were your first days as a parent?" Daniel asked.

"I am so not ready for this."

"Not like being a camp counselor, huh?"

Both Daniel and I had been counselors at Camp Neeswaugee the year we met.

"No. I was able to enroll him in school with little trouble, but that's the only thing that's gone smoothly."

"Tyler told me he wasn't at all what he was expecting."

"I think that's his diplomatic way of saying he was shocked, not unlike me when I opened the door to find a fifteen-year-old Goth glaring at me."

"I must admit I would love to have a picture of your expression at just that moment."

"You always were just a little evil."

"You always loved that."

"True. Caspian is nothing like I expected. I've often regretted not having a son, but... Caspian is not what I had in mind. I was thinking more along the lines of a boy like Tyler, even before I met your son."

"Be careful what you wish for."

"No kidding. I'm in it neck deep and I fear a wave is coming."

"Who wouldn't? I was overwhelmed when I became Tyler's sole parent and he was only two. Sure, you don't have to deal with diapers and potty-training, but I think anyone would be exasperated in your situation. You had no time to adjust to the idea. It was just "Congratulations—it's a boy—a fifteen-year old boy.""

"He's a fifteen-year-old boy who has perfected the teen rebellion stage. He can't stand being around me. He's embarrassed to be seen with me. I can barely get him to communicate on a good day."

"I experienced some of that myself."

"Tyler was like that? I can't believe it."

"Well, it was mild with Tyler but there was a time when the thought of being seen with me would have killed him." Daniel laughed. "Tyler has always been an exceptionally good kid, but you know how teens are. Remember when we were teens? Didn't you think your parents were just the stupidest people in the world?"

"It is amazing how much they learned once I hit my twenties."

"Exactly. Caspian is just being a teen."

"Yeah, he's just being a teen Goth who wears a collar and looks like he should be holding up a liquor store. He does have a record."

"Really?"

"My brother never mentioned it, but then we didn't communicate that well. Caspian stole and wrecked a car when he was thirteen. He escaped with only minor injuries, which is one reason I knew nothing about it. He's been arrested for shoplifting and he's been suspended from school more than once for fighting. I didn't know about any of this until after my brother died. I seriously thought about hiding all the knives in the house and sleeping with my door locked the first night."

"That is intense," Daniel said. "Tyler and Caspian didn't get on particularly well today. Caspian didn't care much for Tyler's friends. He called them a freak show and had something insulting to say about most of them."

"I'm sorry. I shouldn't have asked Tyler to drive him to school and show him around. I was just concerned about Caspian's first day being difficult. He's been through so much."

"It's fine. Tyler didn't mind, although if you're expecting them to become best buddies I don't think it's going to happen. Tyler came home rather pissed off and for him that's unusual."

"I owe Tyler big."

"It's not all selfless on his part. Tyler is still hoping you and I will get serious. He mentioned that we might all be living together someday so he wants to try to get along with Caspian."

"I must admit I've also had a few day dreams about us living together. I know that's getting ahead, but hey, I'm writer. I spend a lot of time fantasizing."

"It's not such a wild fantasy," Daniel said.

I smiled and took his hand across the table for a moment.

"Now I have to include Caspian in that fantasy and I must admit the fantasy isn't as dreamy as it was." I sighed. "I just don't know where things are going with him. I want to be a good parent, but I'm just not ready."

"No one is ever ready."

Our food arrived. We'd both ordered a Tibetan style of stir fry. It wasn't bad, but I was happy eating anywhere with Daniel.

Things had changed since we'd been together before. Wow, had they changed. I laughed.

"What?"

"I was just thinking that when we were Tyler's age we would have never dreamed that someday we'd both have teenage sons."

"Yeah, the whole gay thing does make children unlikely, especially biological children."

"I bet you're not one bit sorry, are you?"

"Not in the least. Tyler is such a big part of my life I can't imagine life without him."

"At this point I don't know if I'm sorry or not. I care about Caspian, but I don't know if I can handle him. I feel a little like I did the first night after my boys arrived at Camp Neeswaugee. I just want to go home. Only this time, I'm already there."

"And yet you're excited and maybe even happy to have Caspian in your life?"

"Yeah. Something was missing, besides a boyfriend. Perhaps it's instinct to want to have a child. I don't know. Sometimes, I'd go walking around town and see dads with their sons and feel... left out. I missed the son I never had, if that makes any sense. I think that's one reason Tyler quickly came to mean so much to me. He is like a son."

"He thinks of you as a second father."

"Yeah, he's told me that. I can't begin to express how much it means to me."

"And now you have your own," Daniel said a little too cheerfully.

"You're enjoying my predicament a little too much."

"Like you said, I'm a little bit evil."

"At least Caspian's first day at school went fairly well," I said. "I asked him about it and received a one word answer—fine. He could have been ranting that he hated it instead."

"Now is a good time to put your ability to look on the bright side to good use."

"Now more than ever. The bottom line is that Caspian is my nephew. I can't quite say I love him, but I do care about him. I'm determined to do the best job of raising him I can. I think I'm in for a rough ride, but I am going to ride it out. Despite the difficulties, I am glad he's here. I wish my brother and his wife were still alive and Caspian was still with his parents, but that's not possible. They're gone and he's alone except for me, my parents, and a few more distant relatives."

"Would your parents have taken him if you didn't?" Daniel asked.

"I'm sure they would have, but they are way too old to be dealing with a teen, especially one with a record."

"I think Caspian is very lucky to have you."

"Tell him that."

"He'll realize it someday."

I smiled. Daniel always knew how to make me feel better about any situation.

I gazed at Daniel now and then as we ate in silence. My love for him had quickly rekindled or perhaps it had just always been there. I'd never forgotten about him in all the long years we'd been apart. When we'd first parted, I was wounded by his apparent rejection, but time had dulled the pain and only the love remained. I wished I knew back then what I did now. Had I known it was Daniel's parents and not Daniel that was keeping us apart I would have returned to Bloomington for him. I couldn't change what had been, so I intended to make the best of what we had now and *that* was promising.

"Tyler said he will be happy to drive Caspian to school and back," Daniel said, breaking the silence after a few minutes.

"Did he really use the word "happy"?"

"I think it was more along the lines of "willing," but he did mean it."

"Maybe he can be a good influence. Tell Tyler I'm giving him money for gas, and most of all give him my thanks. I'll tell him in person when I see him next, but I want him to know I truly appreciate this and I won't be in the least upset if he decides to kick Caspian to the curb. I'm sure even Tyler's patience has limits."

"I think Tyler considers Caspian a project. After all, he may be Caspian's big brother someday."

I grinned at Daniel. I loved the sound of that.

I drove Daniel home, and then returned home myself. There was no sign of Caspian. I made myself a pot of London Cuppa tea and sat down at the kitchen table, trying to figure out where to go from here.

After about twenty minutes I heard the front door open and close. Soon after, Caspian entered the kitchen.

"Hey, I couldn't find you when I went out to eat. Hungry?" I asked.

"Yeah, I'll find something. I'm used to taking care of myself."

At least he was speaking to me in full sentences. Caspian began to dig through the freezer and came up with some microwave pizza.

"Have a seat," I said when Caspian had popped his pizza into the microwave.

My nephew eyed me warily, but sat down.

"We haven't had a chance to talk. How was school today?"

"I told you, fine."

"Fine doesn't tell me much. It's too general."

"So what? You don't really care. It's like when people ask "How's it going?" It's just something they say without thinking."

"I do care."

"Okay, then it fucking sucked!"

"What sucked about it?"

"God, there is no end with you! Do you have to know *everything*?"

"No, but if something isn't working out for you, I'd like to know so I'll at least have a chance to help."

Caspian rolled his eyes. The microwave beeped and he grabbed his pizza and sat down again.

"I don't have all the answers and it's been a long time since I was fifteen, but I might be able to give you advice if you tell me when you have problems."

"Why don't we just cut the bull-shit," Caspian said.

"What bull-shit?"

"You pretending you fucking care about my day or me!"

"I'm not pretending."

"Listen, you've been cool taking me out to eat and buying me stuff, but I know you don't want me here. Your life looks pretty fucking pathetic to me, but I know you don't want a kid. You don't fucking care about me. You just got stuck with me."

"How the hell do you know what I want?" I asked. "This is the longest and only real conversation we've had since you moved in."

"I'm only here because you signed a paper long ago that makes you responsible for me. I probably wasn't even born then."

"You were a few months old when I agreed to be your guardian."

"Yeah, and I bet you never thought you'd have to do it."

"I thought it unlikely, but I also wanted to be there for you if you needed me."

"You didn't even know me then!"

"That doesn't matter. I know you now, or at least I'd like to get to know you. You're my nephew and I care about you."

"Bull shit!"

"Why can't you believe that I care about you? You are my brother's only son. I know your parents cared about you very…"

"Don't talk to me about my parents! Don't fucking talk to me about them!" Caspian slammed his fist on the table.

This was it. My nephew was going to pull a knife and stab me. I'd never seen such a look of fury on a young face before.

"Okay, we won't talk about them. Let's talk about you and us. Whether you believe it or not, I want you here and I do care about you. I don't have a son of my own and for a quite a while I've wanted one."

"I'm not your son."

"I know that, but I am your guardian and that means I act as a parent. I barely know you right now, but I want to get to know you. I want us to become closer."

"If you get to know me, then you *really* won't like me. The more you learn, the sorrier you'll be that you ever signed up to look after me."

"Okay, let's test your theory. Shock me."

"I've been busted for shop-lifting five times. I stole a car and wrecked it. I've been kicked out of school for fighting more times than I can count. I was arrested for trying to hold up a convenience store."

"I know all that. Do you really think the lawyer didn't fill me in on your history when we went over the guardianship papers?"

"You're bluffing."

"You were busted trying to hold up the convenience store because you had the bad timing to attempt it while an undercover cop was standing behind you, waiting to pay for his newspaper. You were released into the custody of your parents because you were only thirteen and the only weapon you had on you was a green water pistol."

Caspian crossed his arms and glared at me.

"So, what else have you got?"

"Shut up," Caspian said. He stood, grabbed a piece of pizza, went to his room and slammed the door.

I didn't feel that our first conversation had gone that badly, all things considered. I think Caspian expected he would shock me with his criminal record and other evidence of delinquency. Instead, he'd been taken aback by the fact that I already knew. Of course, I didn't let him know I'd considered sleeping with my bedroom door locked the first night. I was glad I didn't let his physical appearance sway me into rash actions. I had a better feel for my nephew now. He was certainly capable of violence but I had no worry about being murdered in my sleep... probably.

My biggest fear was that Caspian would run away. I didn't even want to think about him alone on the streets. I knew he was intelligent, even advanced for his age when he bothered to apply himself. I just hoped he was bright enough to understand that he was far better with me than he would be on his own, no matter how much he hated it here.

Caspian didn't come out of his room all evening. I considered knocking on his door and asking if he wanted to go shopping for bedroom furniture more to his taste, but then I thought I'd best give him his space. He still hadn't left his room when I went to bed, but I could hear him stirring inside so at least he hadn't sneaked out the bedroom windows.

The next morning passed without incident. Caspian didn't give me any trouble when I awakened him for school. An alarm clock was yet another item he needed. He helped himself to some cereal and even said "bye" as he headed out the door.

After Caspian departed, I made a pot of Yorkshire tea and sat down at my laptop to get some work done. Some didn't consider writing work, but if I didn't write there would be no new books. While I'd written several already, the royalties on each steadily dwindled after the initial surge of interest. I had to keep producing new material to keep the money coming in and I was going to need a lot more money now that I had the expenses of a fifteen-year-old boy to consider. Besides, I liked to write. It was something I would do whether I was getting paid or not.

I lost myself in my world of fictional characters all morning, but my mind kept being drawn back to Caspian. I had little doubt there were rough times ahead, but all in all, things were looking up. That made me both hopeful and anxious. I was hopeful that we were at least taking the first steps toward a less combative relationship. I was fearful that I was falsely getting my hopes up and that all hell was about to break loose. I could but wait and see and in the meantime do the best job of raising Caspian that I could.

In the afternoon I turned my attention to my book of Christmas tales. While September might seem an odd time to work on Christmas stories it was actually getting late in the season. Luckily, the last story was finished and I was now preparing the book for publication. There was little time to spare if I wanted it to be available in November. If I had not begun to publish my own works it would already be far too late to get the book out for the holiday season.

Try as I might not to do so, my thoughts strayed to Caspian as I worked. How was Caspian doing at school? Was he making any friends? Was he getting into trouble? There were endless possibilities to plague the mind. Was this what being a parent was like? Did all parents randomly worry about their kids at odd hours of the day and night? My biggest question was simple, but the answer elusive: Did parenting ever get any easier?

Tyler

"Here he comes. Dylan, I'm warning you for the last time, back off. Caspian isn't interested and if you keep coming onto him he will kick your ass," I said.

"What?" Dylan asked, innocently. "How have I been coming onto him?"

"Oh, please," Jesse said. "I know a come on when I see one. Girls come onto me *all* the time. If you came onto him any stronger you'd be lunging across the table and grabbing his dick."

"Dude, you do have a tendency to come on way too strong," Tyreece said.

Dylan put his hand to his chest and opened his mouth in shocked innocence.

"Dylan," I said in a warning tone. "Cross Caspian off your list. You're not getting anywhere with him. All you're going to do is piss him off and we don't need any violence at our table."

That's all that could be said; Caspian sat down directly across from me and as far away from Dylan as possible.

"Hey, Caspian," Dylan said in an over-friendly tone. I shot him a warning glare, but he ignored me.

Caspian just scowled at him for a moment, then turned his attention to his burger.

"So, how do you hate school so far?" Tyreece said.

"I hate it pretty well," Caspian said, almost, but not quite smiling. Out of all of us, he came closest to liking Tyreece.

"There is a lot to hate," Tyreece said.

"And a lot of people to hate," Caleb added as Ashley Caldemyer walked by.

Caspian didn't miss the look and gazed at Caleb with a question in his eyes.

"The ice princess is obsessed with popularity," Jesse explained. "She used to date Caleb, but she dumped him right after his accident."

"Thanks so much, Jesse," Caleb said. "Like you aren't obsessed with popularity."

"I don't have to be obsessed with it. I am popular."

"He's obsessed about physical appearance," I said with a grin.

"Just because I take care with my appearance doesn't make me obsessed."

"Dude, you're gayer than I am and you aren't even gay," Dylan said. "How long did you spend on your hair this morning?"

"An hour, maybe a little more."

"That's obsessed," I said. "I spent less than five minutes on mine."

"We can all see that," Jesse said. He had a smug grin on his face. I stuck out my tongue at him.

"So, you used to be hot stuff, huh?" Caspian asked Caleb, ignoring the rest of us.

"Used to be. I would probably have been the quarterback this year, but now I get to be the team manager. Whoopee shit."

"You're still hot stuff," Dylan said, devouring Caleb with his eyes.

"Yeah, right. I had a six-pack last year. Now I'm getting fat. Try keeping in shape when you're stuck in a fucking wheel chair."

The conversation was quickly taking a downward turn.

"Look in the mirror," Dylan said. "I'd pay to see you without a shirt."

Caspian stared at Dylan with a disgusted look on his face, but Caleb smiled.

"Thanks, Dylan."

"Hey, you've still got it and everyone knows Ashley is a stupid bitch for dumping you. If she's that shallow, you don't need her," Dylan said.

"That is the general consensus on Ashley," I said.

Caleb smiled, but I could tell he was still upset. I couldn't begin to understand what he was going through. All I could do was be his friend.

Dylan and Caleb were mischievously smiling at each other. For a moment I wondered… but no, Caleb wasn't gay. Dylan did claim to have seduced a number of straight boys and I had little doubt he was telling the truth. Still, I couldn't picture him with Caleb.

"Mmm, he's soooo hot," Dylan said.

I turned my head to see who had captured Dylan's interest. Justin Schroeder. No surprise there. Dylan was forever lusting after Justin.

"He's so built and so beautiful. Have you ever seen him in his wrestling singlet?" Dylan said.

I grinned. Dylan was now and forever boy-crazy.

"Dude, can you knock that shit off? I'm trying to eat," Caspian said.

"What? He's hot!" Dylan said.

"Seriously. I can't believe you're sitting here saying this shit out loud. Keep it to yourself. No one wants to listen to your perverted homo comments."

"Are you kidding? I'm the most entertaining part of lunch!"

It was hard to insult Dylan. He simply refused to take delivery of rudeness.

"Dude, you're sick. I don't even like being around you."

"What have you got against gays?" Caleb asked.

"It's just… sick… two guys together. I don't like being around that shit."

Dylan rolled his eyes and shot Caspian a "whatever" look.

"Um… you do know your uncle is gay, right?" I asked.

"What?"

"Percy. He's gay."

"He's not gay," Caspian said. "He's weird with all of his antique furniture and those millions of Star Trek novels, but no one in my family is a homo."

"You seriously don't know?" I asked.

"Dude…"

"Come on... the Abercrombie & Fitch catalogs, his obsessive neatness, the bronze statue of a nude discus-thrower..."

"That doesn't mean anything. Lots of preppy freaks wear A&F shit. Percy is not gay."

"Caspian, your uncle is dating my dad," I said.

Caspian just sat there and stared at me for a moment.

"Why are you making this up?" Caspian asked.

"I'm not making it up. Why would I make it up? My dad is gay and so is your uncle. They're dating."

"Fags can't have kids."

I was beginning to get angry. I took a deep breath before answering.

"Gay guys can have kids. Don't be stupid."

"I'm not stupid! Are you seriously telling me your dad is a faggot?"

"Don't call him that!"

"Why? Are you embarrassed because your dad is a fag? You don't like that he's a *faggot*. Are you one too, Tyler? Do you take it up the ass from your daddy?"

I growled and flew at Caspian in a rage. Tyreece grabbed me about the midsection and held me back. I struggled, trying to get my hands on that little bastard, but Tyreece was strong.

"Don't say that about my dad, you stupid little fuck! You don't know shit! Get off me!"

I kept struggling, but couldn't break free.

Everyone in the cafeteria was staring at us, especially at me, but I barely noticed. All I cared about was beating the shit out of that little bastard.

"You're all fucking freaks," Caspian said, standing up. "Except you, Tyreece. I don't know why you sit with this sideshow. I'm out of here."

Tyreece held onto me until Caspian had walked to the far side of the cafeteria. When he finally released me, he was tensed and ready to spring into action if need be. I returned to my seat still glaring at Caspian's back.

"Calm down, Tyler. Don't let him get to you," Caleb said.

My breath came so hard and fast I was practically panting. My heart pounded. I was so mad I wanted to rip Caspian's head off and piss down his neck, but I willed myself to calm.

"Whoa! I've never seen you that pissed off before," Tyreece said.

"I don't like anyone talking shit about my dad," I said. "You heard what he said! My dad would never…"

"Let it go. What that little creep says doesn't matter," Caleb said.

Caleb was right. It's just that I loved my dad and I was sick of people looking down on him because he was gay. I looked around the table.

"Thanks for holding me back," I said to Tyreece. "You probably saved me from suspension."

"Any time," Tyreece said, and smiled.

"I thought we didn't need any violence at our table," Dylan said, making a goofy face at me.

I couldn't help it. I smiled, and then laughed.

"Shut up, Dylan."

"You gonna make me, tough stuff? Are you? Huh?" Dylan asked.

"You'd enjoy it too much."

"Mmm. Oh yeah, rough me up, sexy."

"That's what I love about sitting at this table," Jesse said. "It's so entertaining. Well, that and sitting with you guys makes me look that much more attractive."

Caleb threw a wadded-up napkin at Jesse.

"I think I need a little walk," I said, standing up with my tray.

"You aren't going to hunt down Caspian, are you?" Tyreece asked.

"As much as I'll probably be fantasizing about ways to kill him, no. I'd only get myself into trouble and I don't think Percy would appreciate me beating up his nephew."

I didn't say so, but now that I was thinking clearly I wasn't sure it was Caspian who would get beat up. He was a bad ass and

I wasn't exactly a fighter. It didn't matter. Violence wasn't the solution. I walked away with my tray, still fuming over the things Caspian had said. Why did people have to be like that?

I put my tray away and walked over to where Caspian was sitting. He turned at the sound of my approach. I wrapped my hands around his throat and began to squeeze. His eyes bulged and he struggled as...

"Hey, wait up," Tyreece said, destroying my daydream.

I didn't realize he'd followed me until I'd dumped my tray and set it on the stack, but Tyreece was close behind me.

"You okay?" Tyreece asked as he walked along beside me.

"Yeah. Well, no. I shouldn't have let Caspian get to me like that, but he's not the first guy to give me shit about my dad."

"He was way out of line, especially that, uh, incest comment."

"That's what some people really think."

"What?"

"That because my dad is gay he molests me."

"Maybe really stupid people..."

"Yeah, but still... my dad is the greatest. Like... I want to be a writer. Most parents wouldn't support that. They'd be talking about how there is no future, no financial security in it, but my dad's attitude is go for it, be the best writer you can. He's like that with everything and I can talk to him about anything. He's... well he's my friend, as well as my dad."

"I've only been around him a few times, but he was really cool," Tyreece said.

"Yeah and it pisses me off because some people look down on him because he's gay. What's the big fucking deal?"

"There will always be ignorant, prejudiced people out there, Tyler."

"Yeah, but why do gays have to be the big target? I mean, you don't know about prejudice until you have a dad who is gay."

Tyreece raised an eyebrow and cocked his head.

"*I* don't know about prejudice? My skin isn't this beautiful chocolate brown because I'm addicted to tanning."

"Sorry. I wasn't thinking. I don't think of you as black. I mean... I know you're black, but I think of you as Tyreece."

"That's because you're not ignorant or prejudiced. Listen, Tyler, this is kind of personal, but... are you gay?"

"Do you think I'm gay because my dad is gay?"

"No, it's just that you've never dated a girl."

"I've never dated a guy either."

"True."

"I've never seen you check out a guy or a girl. Neither have Caleb, Jesse, or Dylan. You're a mystery."

"Maybe I like being a mystery. So you guys have discussed my sexual orientation..."

"Well, Dylan brought it up."

"Big surprise there."

"I hope that boy doesn't catch some disease, especially HIV," Tyreece said.

"You think he's as sexual active as he says? I do."

"I'm pretty sure of it. Guys keep quiet about messing with guys, but I've heard things..."

"Like?"

"Like Dylan supports some members of the football in more ways that just cheering for them at games."

"We should really turn North into a reality show," I said.

"Yeah, anyway, no one can figure you out."

"Does it matter if I'm gay or straight?"

"No."

I left it at that. I didn't answer his question. I'm not even sure why. I just didn't feel like answering. Tyreece didn't press me.

"Tyreece, thanks, for keeping me from punching Caspian and for talking to me."

"Feeling better?"

"I've calmed down and yeah, I do feel better. Stupid shits like Caspian can say what they want about my dad. I know the truth and everyone who knows him loves him. What anyone else thinks or says doesn't matter."

"Exactly. I know there are plenty of people who look at me and just think "Nigger" but I don't let that get to me because those people just don't matter. I know what I am..."

"Stunning, awesome, incredibly handsome, built, charming, and intelligent?"

"Exactly! You know me so well."

I wrapped my arm around Tyreece's shoulders and we walked down the hall. I felt lucky to have such good friends.

I spotted Caspian a couple of times later in the day. Thankfully, we didn't share any classes. I wished he was just some kid who didn't matter and not Percy's nephew. I couldn't help but see him now and then because I wasn't going to stop spending time with Percy because of Caspian. I guessed I'd just have to deal with him. If he shot off his mouth about my dad again I'd tell him to shut up.

I didn't drive Caspian home. He didn't show up asking for a ride and I didn't offer. If he had asked I would have let him ride with me *if* he apologized. I didn't think an apology likely.

I went home and spotted my dad next door in Mrs. Condor's yard, fixing the gate of her white picket fence. Mrs. Condor was eighty-something and had lost her husband about five years ago. Dad did a lot of handyman stuff for her and I sometimes helped out by raking leaves. Mrs. Condor knew my dad was gay. She didn't care. Why should anyone else? Faggot. It was such an ugly word. Nigger. There was another one. If my dad was a faggot and Tyreece was a nigger, then the world would be a much better place if it was filled with faggots and niggers.

I walked over and gave my dad a hug. I didn't care what anyone said about him. I was the luckiest son in the entire world.

Percy

"Why didn't you tell me you're a faggot?" Caspian shouted as he entered the kitchen.

"Nice to see you, too," I said, trying not to react in anger.

"Answer the fucking question!"

"I didn't think it mattered."

"Didn't think it mattered? Bull-shit! You didn't tell me because you want to take advantage of me!"

"You've been here several days, Caspian. When have I tried to take advantage of you?"

"You tried to touch me!"

"I hardly think gripping your shoulder can be considered a sexual advance."

"You're just waiting your chance."

"If you're waiting for me to make a move then you've got a long wait coming. Yes, I am gay, but I'm not interested in boys and I'm certainly not interested in my own nephew. Perhaps I should have told you before, but there are thousands of things I haven't told you about myself yet. You've told me almost nothing about yourself. My sexual orientation isn't something I hide."

"You should."

"No. I shouldn't. I don't hide it and I don't announce it unless it becomes pertinent. You're an intelligent boy. I really thought you would have picked up on it by now. I've even told you more than once that I was going out with Daniel."

"Yeah, but... I thought he was some buddy and you were going out to a bar or something."

"He's my boyfriend."

"So, it's all true then? You are a fag and you're doing it with Tyler's dad?"

"I don't like the word "fag", Caspian and I'm dating Daniel. I'm not *doing it with him*."

"You're fucking sick."

"And why is that?"

51

"You... I don't have to say why!"

"You don't have a very strong argument."

"Well, I'm not fucking staying here with you anymore! I don't want to get ass raped in the night!"

I shook my head. This was just what I needed—an irate, homophobic nephew.

"How many times have I entered your room without permission, Caspian?"

"You haven't, but that doesn't mean anything. Now I know why you agreed to be my guardian. You like teen boys don't you?"

"I like them, but not in the way you're suggesting. I would never do anything to hurt a boy, or anyone else for that matter, and I certainly wouldn't hurt you."

"So you say. I bet you just couldn't wait for me to arrive so you'd have a fifteen-year-old right in your house to molest whenever you want."

I was glad I was calm by nature and not prone to angry outbursts. I reminded myself that Caspian was unleashing a verbal barrage without thinking.

"Caspian, I know you're frightened..."

"I'm not scared! I'm not scared of you or anything!"

"Calm down a little and we can discuss this rationally. Want something to drink?" I asked, going to the refrigerator and pulling out two Coke Zeros.

"Yeah, I bet you want me to drink something so you can slip a date-rape drug into it and do me while I'm asleep."

"It's in a can, Caspian." I resisted the almost overpowering urge to add, "Don't be stupid."

He opened it and took a sip. I did the same before speaking again.

"I would be scared if I was living in an unfamiliar place, with someone I barely know. I'd be scared if I was starting in at a new school, if my parents were..."

"Don't talk to me about my parents!"

"Okay. I'm just saying that I would be scared in your situation. Anyone would."

"Whatever. What does this have to do with you being a faggot?"

I sat back for a moment and took a breath to calm myself.

"I'm not going to hurt you, Caspian."

"Yeah, right."

"Have I hurt you?"

"No, but you just haven't had the chance to get me yet."

"Caspian, I've had plenty of chances and nothing has happened because nothing is going to happen. You're safe here."

"I bet you'd love me to believe that, *fag*."

"Whether you believe it or not, you're safe here. I haven't harmed you and I'm not going to harm you. Lock you bedroom door if you want."

"Like you don't have a key."

"Caspian, your bedroom door locks only from the inside. There is no key."

He didn't have a response to that.

"If you try to molest me I'm calling the cops."

"Good. That's exactly what you should do."

Caspian gave me a confused glance.

"I've got a switch-blade in my room. I'm not afraid to use it."

"Just don't take it to school. Are you hungry? Want to go out to eat?"

"I'm not getting in the car with you, faggot."

"Okay, ground-rule. I don't like the terms fag or faggot. I don't want to hear you call me either of those again. I don't call you names. I'm giving you a place to live and I'm taking care of you."

"So what? I'm supposed to be your boy toy? You buy me stuff and I do it with you?"

"How do you even know the term boy toy?"

"I'm not a kid."

"Caspian, you're my nephew, not my boy toy. Get it through your head. You don't owe me for living with me, but I'm not putting up with you calling me those names. Would you put up with me calling you names?"

"No."

"So?"

"Okay," Caspian said. "God, don't have a heart attack on me."

"Why don't I have a pizza delivered?"

"Yeah, okay. Whatever."

"What do you like on it?"

"Pepperoni."

"Pepperoni it is then. I'll order."

"Fine."

Caspian got up and left the kitchen. I heard him close his bedroom door, but couldn't tell if he locked it or not. I released a huge breath I didn't know I'd been holding. Dealing with this kid was going to kill me. I just knew it.

I pulled up the Domino's site on my laptop and ordered two medium pizzas, one pepperoni, one pepperoni and pineapple. While I waited I made myself a pot of tea and sat down to browse a *Country Living* magazine. I needed something to put myself in a better frame of mind. Dealing with my nephew had stressed me out. I just hoped I'd handled things well.

Had I been too calm? Had I put up with too much verbal abuse? I sensed that getting angry and yelling would only make the situation worse, but was I going too far in the opposite direction? Was I coming off as weak? Parenting got harder every day.

There was a knock at the door a few minutes later. It was too soon for the pizza delivery. I opened the door to find Tyler. I smiled.

"Hey, come in. I just ordered a couple of pizzas. I'll split mine with you. Would you like some tea?"

"Um, sure," Tyler said, breaking into a grin.

I lead him into the kitchen and poured a cup of Famous Edinburgh tea into a blue willow cup.

"Wow, you are always drinking tea. You're a tea-aholic. Where's Caspian?"

"He's sulking in his room, unless he's climbed out the window. I should probably have bars installed."

"I came to apologize," Tyler said.

"For what?"

"I told Caspian you were gay."

"That's not a secret, Tyler."

"Yeah, well, he was going off on Dylan and gays in general so I reminded him that you're gay. I thought he knew. Then... well, he was a total ass. I lost my temper and we got into it."

"There is no need to apologize. Caspian could make the Dali Lama lose it."

Tyler laughed.

"We just finished a... discussion a few minutes ago. I wanted to strangle him."

"Hmm, I wanted to strangle him too," Tyler said. "I fantasized about wrapping my fingers around his neck and squeezing while his face turned purple and his eyes bulged."

"Nice details."

"I *am* a writer," Tyler said.

"I managed not to strangle him or lose my temper, but it wasn't easy. He was shouting at me, calling me a faggot, and accusing me of planning to molest him."

"What is *wrong* with him?" Tyler asked.

"He's going through so much right now, Tyler. He won't admit it, but I know he's scared. He's lost everything and has been dropped into this totally unfamiliar place. I'm thinking I should get him some professional help, but I can just imagine how that suggestion would be received."

"He actually accused you of bringing him here so you can molest him?"

"Yes, among his more colorful terms was "ass rape." That boy tries my patience."

"Oh, damn, Percy. I feel like this is my fault."

"It's not your fault. Caspian was a bomb just waiting to go off. He has all these emotions raging inside him and it has got to come out. If he hadn't blown up over me being gay it would have been something else. His arguments didn't even make sense. I pointed out that he's been here for some time and that I've never harmed him. When he said I was just waiting my chance I told him I'd already had plenty of chances."

Tyler laughed.

"I was worried you'd be angry with me."

"Don't worry about that. I'm not."

"Caspian didn't ride home with me and to be honest I was glad."

"Well, thank you for transporting him and showing him around. I imagine he wasn't grateful, but I am. He can just ride the bus."

"Yeah, he... well, he's a brat."

"True."

"But you still like him, don't you?" Tyler asked.

"Actually, I do. I just don't know if I can take care of him. I'm doing my best but..."

Tyler reached across the table and took my hand.

"Percy, you've become a second dad to me. If something ever happened to my dad, which I hope it never does, well... I couldn't think of anyone I'd want to be with more. I'd need you so bad. I'm sure Caspian needs you and although he doesn't know it, there isn't anyone who will try harder than you, or care about him more."

"Thanks, Tyler."

"So hang in there with the little shit. I think you're doing fine."

I laughed.

We were interrupted by the pizza delivery. I went to the door and returned with my order.

"Caspian! The pizza is here!" I called out.

I pulled out Coke Zeros, blue willow plates, and cloth napkins. Tyler and I went to work on the pepperoni and pineapple. Caspian came into the kitchen a couple of minutes later and froze when he spotted Tyler.

"Would you like to join us?" I asked.

"No, thanks," Caspian said.

Caspian grabbed the other pizza box and a Coke from the refrigerator and headed back to his room without so much as another word.

"Charming room-mate you have," Tyler said.

"At least he said 'no, thanks' instead of hurling obscenities."

"True, but I might be dead if looks could kill," Tyler said, then grinned.

"I'm sorry he's being a jerk."

"It's not your fault, Percy. I do think you should keep him on a leash, but I guess that isn't practical."

"Don't mention that around him, he'll twist it and accuse me of kinky sexual desires."

"Yeah, I'm sure you're just full of them."

Tyler grinned again. Why couldn't Caspian be more like him?

"How are you and Dad getting along?"

"Hasn't your dad told you?"

"Yes, but I want to hear your opinion."

"We're getting on *very* well. We've both changed, but we've also remained much the same. I enjoy just being with him."

"The feeling is mutual."

"I could pretty much tell that just from looking in his eyes but thanks for the confirmation."

"I knew you two would hit it off, *again*."

"It's kind of like the last twenty years never happened, as least as far as Daniel and I am concerned."

"So when are you moving in?" Tyler teased.

"We'll be taking things slowly. Your dad and I both have our own lives. Besides, do you *really* want to live with Caspian?"

"Couldn't you send him to boarding school?"

"Don't tempt me."

We both laughed and I'm sure the sound of our laughter reached into Caspian's bedroom. I wished he'd come out and join us.

"Thanks, Tyler," I said. "I was getting stressed out. I don't usually let things get to me, but this..."

"It will be okay. He can't possibly be as bad as he seems."

"Does he have any friends? Have you seen him hanging out with anyone?" I asked.

"I don't see him much. He is a lowly little freshman, after all. We share a lunch period, but that's it. I haven't noticed him with anyone in particular. I've spotted him talking to others a few times, but I don't think he's hanging out with anyone."

"Things might be easier if he made some friends. I guess I'm too impatient. He just started school."

"Yeah. I tried, but..."

"I'm very grateful."

"Well, it didn't work out."

"I'm still grateful. You gave him an opportunity to make friends."

"He does kind of like Tyreece. He pronounced the rest of us a side show. My crime is having a gay dad."

"It's interesting living with a young homophobe. It's an experience I could easily live without."

We began talking about writing, an interest we both shared. Tyler was working on his first novel and I continued to give him pointers and advice. I'd published several, as well as a few non-fiction works.

"Did I tell you I'm doing some promotional stuff for my Christmas book?"

"No," Tyler said.

"Most, if not all, the profits are going to the Monroe County Humane Society. I love animals so I thought it was something I could do to help. The book will be in a few local stores and I'll do a reading or two. There will be a little press coverage, but not much. I don't usually like to do appearances right in Bloomington, but what I won't do for me I will do for cats and dogs."

"As much as you love animals I've always wondered why you don't have a pet."

"You're my pet, Tyler."

"Funny, but I wouldn't let Caspian hear you say that."

"True. He probably already suspects we're more than friends. I am a dangerous homosexual, after all."

Tyler laughed.

"I don't have any pets because I'm sometimes gone for a few days. If I had pets I'd have to board them. I'm sure the pet boarding facilities in Bloomington are fine, but I'd feel guilty."

"Dad and I could take care of a dog or a cat for you if you wanted to go somewhere. Or I could while you *and* Dad go somewhere."

"You can stop matchmaking, Tyler. I'm already dating your dad."

Tyler grinned.

"I'm just saying..."

"Thanks, but there are other things to consider. With pets you never know what you're getting. Some are easy to care for, some not so easy."

"Have you had problems in the past?"

"Oh yeah, I had a little Yorkie named Taylor. He had some serious behavioral problems and there was no way to correct them."

"Like?"

"When any visitor was ready to leave, they couldn't make a move for their coat, jingle keys, or give any indication they were departing or Taylor would go nuts. He'd even bite."

"Really?"

"Frequent visitors knew to tell me they were ready to leave, without using words Taylor recognized. I'd put his leash on and hold him while they escaped."

Tyler laughed.

"That was just one of his oddities. He had several. I loved him, though. He was the best and worst dog I ever had. I miss him."

"What happened to him?"

"He lived to be twelve and then he developed inoperable cancer."

"I'm sorry."

"Losing him just about destroyed me; that's another reason I avoid having pets. I probably will someday, but I'm not ready. I won't go in pet stores. When I drop off donations at the humane society I won't go anywhere except the front desk. I know if I see a dog or cat I'll want to take him home."

Tyler and I sat and talked, mostly about writing, for at least another hour. It might have been longer. I often lost track of time when I was with Tyler. He would have made a good boyfriend for me when I was his age. I almost laughed at the thought. Tyler's father was my boyfriend when I was Tyler's age. Daniel didn't have an interest in writing, but otherwise they were very much alike.

Caspian emerged from his room to glare at Tyler and look at me with revulsion. I grinned when I saw Tyler scratch the side of his head with his middle finger. If Caspian thought he was going to intimidate Tyler he was mistaken. Tyler was easy-going, calm, and kind, but also confident, strong, and not easy to rattle. Caspian looked like he wanted to say something nasty, but kept his mouth shut.

I gave Tyler a hug at the door when he departed. In many ways, he was a son to me.

"Is Tyler your boy toy?" Caspian asked as I walked back toward the kitchen.

"Not everything is about sex, Caspian."

"Nice way to evade the question. I figure he's a fa... he's gay. He sure took up for his little fairy friend, Dylan."

"Tyler is the kind of guy who will take up for anyone who is being put down."

"Well, his dad is a homo. He probably turned him."

"Caspian, have a seat."

We were back in the kitchen by then.

"Why? Are you going to try to recruit me?"

"Just sit down."

Caspian rolled his eyes, but sat down.

"I want you to understand one thing. No one can be turned or recruited into being gay."

"That's not what I've heard."

"Do you believe everything you hear?"

"I'm not stupid."

"I never thought you were. In fact, I think you're highly intelligent, far more than you let show. There are a lot of prejudiced people who hate gays. They do everything they can to demonize them. One of their tactics is to claim that sexual orientation is a choice. It's not. I'm gay. I always have been and always will be. I don't have any say in the matter. I can't start being attracted to females any more than I can make myself taller or turn my eyes blue. Sexual orientation is a genetic code."

Caspian was actually listening.

"So you didn't do anything to become gay. No one... made you gay?"

"I knew I was gay years before I had my first sexual experience. No one made me gay because that's not possible."

"Is Tyler your boy toy?" Caspian asked. "You never answered my question."

"I thought I did, but no. He is not. I care about Tyler very much. I love him."

"You love a boy?"

"Your dad loved you. Was he gay?"

Caspian stiffened at the mention of his dad and a look of pain crossed his face.

"My dad wasn't gay," he said with a growl.

"Exactly. He wasn't gay, but he loved you. Love doesn't have to be connected to sex."

"He's really not your boy toy?"

"No. He's not. I don't even know if Tyler is gay or straight."

"You don't *know*?"

"No. I'm curious, but that's his business, not mine. Also, it just doesn't matter. The way I feel about him has nothing to do with his sexual orientation."

"I don't know if I believe you or not. Maybe this is all just a trick so I'll put my guard down."

"I've never lied to you, Caspian, and I never will. Trust has to be earned. I understand that. You keep your guard up as long as you feel the need, but just remember that no one can get close to you as long as you push them away."

Caspian stood.

"I'm taking a shower. Don't even think of coming in and checking me out. I'm locking the door."

"I guess you foiled my evil plan," I said.

"Faggot," Caspian muttered under this breath as he walked away. I pretended not to hear. At least he wasn't screaming it at me.

Tyler

I took my seat for my first period Advanced Placement English Literature and Composition class. I was actually getting college credit for the course and believe me I was earning it. "Advanced" wasn't just a name. My love of reading paid off for this class. One of the requirements was to read at least eight extended works. Some of my classmates groaned about the reading, but it was a breeze for me. The only drawback is that I wasn't free to read what I wanted. I had to stick with British Literature. That was no true hardship and it guided me into books I might have otherwise missed. Perhaps that was the point.

It was interesting to compare what Mrs. Bailey taught about writing with what Percy had taught me. I often discussed what we'd learned in class with him. He quite often didn't agree with Mrs. Bailey and since he was a real publisher/author I listened to him more. It's not that I didn't respect Mrs. Bailey's knowledge or opinions; even Percy said she obviously knew her stuff, but Percy actually wrote every day. He was doing what Mrs. Bailey was teaching about.

Of course, most of the class was about British Literature or Brit Lit as we called it for short. Percy highly approved of a writer broadening his horizons. One thing he told me long ago is that one way to become a better writer is to read the works of other writers while paying attention to their style.

The class breezed by. It was probably my favorite. Since it was advanced placement those taking it were serious about the class. Sure, they groaned at the reading and report requirements, but there was no disruptive element as in some of my classes. Far too often there were kids in class who didn't want to be there and couldn't have cared less about what was being taught.

I liked my other classes, but I enjoyed those connected to writing the most. I'd been enthused about a lot of stuff during my life, but I quickly lost interest in most things. Writing was an exception, writing and skating. I knew I wasn't good enough to become a professional skater, but I thought I had a good shot at making it as a writer. Having access to Percy DeForest Spock definitely didn't harm my chances.

Lunchtime rolled around quickly, but not quickly enough for me. My stomach was grumbling which told me the half a donut I grabbed before leaving for school wasn't enough breakfast.

Everything looked especially good as I passed through the serving line. Today, we were having barbequed subs, tater tots, tossed salad, peaches, and a chocolate chip cookie.

Tyreece, Jesse, Dylan, and Caleb were already seated at our usual table when I dropped down into my seat.

"No charming companion today?" Tyreece asked with a grin.

"Yeah, thanks *so* much for bringing him to our table," Caleb said. "Perhaps next time you can bring something more appealing, like a bag of dog-shit."

"Sorry guys. He's Percy's nephew and he's new. I didn't know he was going to go bad-ass on everyone, although he seems to like you, Tyreece."

"What's not to like?"

Dylan pelted Tyreece with a napkin.

"I am sorry, but I don't think he'll be back."

"Not after you tried to kill him yesterday," Tyreece said.

"You really should have let me."

"You definitely should have let him," Caleb said.

"My vote is yes," Jesse said.

I could laugh about it now, but only the day before I did want to strangle Caspian, or beat him to death. I knew I was capable of violence, but it was scary how quickly it came to the surface. Maybe it just took the right trigger to turn anyone into a madman.

"Caspian is so hot. I wonder where he's sitting," Dylan said, looking around.

"Dude, that boy is gonna punch you in face if you go near him," Tyreece warned.

"He's just playing hard to get," Dylan said.

"More like impossible to get," Tyreece said. "Give it up. All you're getting from him is a black eye or a busted lip."

"I love my men violent."

"Try saying that after he's kicked your ass," I said. "Dylan, he does NOT like gay guys. You were here yesterday. You heard what he said. I was over at Percy's last night and you should see how Caspian gives Percy the cold shoulder. I was half-way expecting Caspian to spit on him. Stay away from Caspian, Dylan. I don't want to see you get hurt."

"Yeah, Dylan, just go blow one of the jocks," Tyreece said, grinning.

"Ohhh! Good idea! *Then* I'll look for Caspian."

"The boy will never learn," I said.

"I'm sitting right here you know," Dylan said.

"You only think you are," I said.

Dylan looked profoundly confused, so my work was done.

"You guys spend way too much time talking about sex," Jesse said. "Yeah, sex is awesome, but how long does it last? Fifteen? Twenty minutes? When you think about it, it's just not as good as having a table full of cheerleaders check you out or... shopping."

"You're the only guy I know who can sound straight and gay in the same sentence," Tyreece said.

"Oh! I bought this great purple dress shirt at the mall. I'm going to look so hot in it," Jesse said.

Tyreece shook his head.

Caleb wasn't talking much. I saw him look over to the jock table where all of his old team-mates sat. Caleb had always been cool with me, but he hadn't started sitting at my table until after his accident. I wasn't quite sure why he didn't keep sitting with the jocks. It's not like they turned on him. They were still his friends and he still worked with the team, just not as a player. Perhaps he didn't want the reminder that that part of his life was over.

I looked around the cafeteria trying to spot Caspian. I half expected to see him at the stoner table. I'd spotted him puffing on a cigarette a couple of times and pot wouldn't have surprised me. He was a bad-ass, or at least a bad-ass wannabe.

I finally spotted Caspian's blond, spiky hair among a table of girls, but said nothing to Dylan. I wasn't about to encourage him to do something that would only end in misery. I sometimes wondered about that boy.

I couldn't tell from a distance, but the girls looked like they were paying plenty of attention to Caspian. I was glad. I was still pissed at him and I didn't like him, but I also didn't wish him ill. Okay, yesterday I did. I wished him a *lot* of ill. That was yesterday. Maybe the little bastard would get laid. That would probably calm him down.

After school, I crept up behind Caspian and knocked him unconscious with a quick blow to the back of his head. I tied him up and stuffed him in the back of my car. I drove to Dylan's house, dumped Caspian's unconscious form on his doorstep, rang the doorbell, and took off.

I grinned. I momentarily thought of sharing my fantasy with Dylan, but he didn't need any encouragement and probably fantasized about Caspian plenty already.

I didn't spot Caspian the rest of the day and that was fine by me. A little of the blond punk went a long way. If only he wasn't Percy's nephew! Then, I could have considered him history.

I spotted Caleb at his locker at the end of the school day. Ashley Caldemyer walked right past him without so much as a word. I remembered when she was all over Caleb, but that was before his accident. Caleb watched her go and I could read the sadness in his eyes.

"I always thought she was a bitch," I said.

Caleb looked up at me and smiled at me for a moment, but his smile quickly faded.

"Are you okay, Caleb?"

Caleb looked off into the distance for a moment, then back at me. There were no tears in his eyes, but he almost looked as if he was about to cry.

"I'm taking you out to supper," I announced. "Refusal isn't an option. I'm kidnapping you."

Caleb only had time to grab his backpack and slam his locker door shut before I grabbed the handles of his wheel chair and pushed him down the hallway.

"I've never been kidnapped before."

"I'm sure Dylan would have kidnapped you if he'd thought of it. Don't worry; you're much safer with me."

Caleb didn't say anything more as I pushed him out to the car. I wheeled him up to the passenger side and opened the door. I wasn't quite sure what to do next. Luckily, Caleb wheeled himself in close and lifted himself out of the chair and maneuvered himself into the passenger seat with his powerful arms.

I popped open the trunk and, after some difficulty with getting it to fold up, I lifted the chair into the trunk.

"How about Denny's?" I asked.

"I didn't know abductees got a choice."

"I'm a very considerate kidnapper."

"Denny's is cool."

We drove to Denny's in silence. It was located on the corner of North Walnut and the 45/46 Bypass, right by the Days Inn, and only a short drive from school.

I pulled Caleb's wheelchair out of the trunk, unfolded it, and wheeled it around to the passenger side. I was impressed he could maneuver himself into the chair so easily using only his arms.

Caleb didn't object as I pushed him toward the entrance. Soon we were sitting together in a remote booth. Denny's was crowded on weekends, but it was more sparsely populated through the week.

We ordered our drinks and browsed the menus. When the waitress returned with Caleb's Diet Coke and my iced tea we were ready to order. I asked for a grand slam, with pancakes, bacon, scrambled eggs, and hash browns. Caleb ordered a chicken deluxe salad with ranch.

"Are you sure you don't want more than that?" I asked. "I don't often offer to buy. You should take advantage."

"I'm good," Caleb said as the waitress departed. "I've really got to watch what I eat. I'm getting fat."

"You're not getting fat."

"At this time last year, I had a six-pack. Now, it's gone," Caleb said bitterly. He'd mentioned the loss of his defined abs before. It was a sore point with him.

"Is that what's getting to you?" I asked.

"That's part of it."

"Caleb, I don't want to stick my nose in where it doesn't belong, but you seem really down today. You've been down quite a lot lately. If you want to talk about it, I'm here."

"Thanks, Tyler. It's... a lot of things. Ashley, getting fat, feeling like I'm not part of things anymore... Everyone used to look up to me. Now, I look up to everyone because I'm stuck in that fucking chair!"

"I'd say I understand, but I can't even begin to imagine what that's like for you."

"I feel so damned shallow, too. I miss being popular. I miss being a jock. I miss the attention."

"I don't think that's shallow. I think we would all like to be popular."

"Including you?"

"Yeah. I don't think about it much because I'm kind of inner-directed, but it would be pretty cool to have everyone say "hey" to me instead of looking past me like I'm not there. I don't know if I'd like being *really* popular. I think it would be too much of a good thing. I'd probably end up hiding in a dark corner, but then I'm a freak."

Caleb smiled.

"I miss my old life," he said.

"Caleb, why did you stop sitting with the other jocks after your accident?"

"Because I'm not one of them anymore. They're nice enough to me, but now I'm just a cripple instead of jock."

"Caleb..."

"It's true. I won't *ever* be able to play football again. I won't ever be able to run, or even walk." Caleb once again looked like he was about to cry, but there were no tears. "I can't be one of them anymore. I'm not a part of the team. I can't contribute anything. I can't save the day. I didn't want to sit with those guys anymore because I felt so out of place. I didn't belong there. None of them ever asked me to come back, either. They say "hi" and ask how I'm doing, but they know as well as I do that I'm no longer one of them."

"You're managing the team now, right?"

Caleb shook his head.

"I quit yesterday."

"Why?"

"It was all just a reminder of everything I've lost. Being in the locker room and on the field... it was just too much. I don't belong there anymore."

"Damn, I want to say something brilliant to make everything okay, but I don't know what to say."

Caleb smiled at me sadly.

"Being my friend helps."

I took Caleb's hand for a moment. He drew it away quickly as the waitress brought our food. We ate for a while in silence. My grand slam was delicious. I used plenty of butter and syrup on my pancakes. Mmm.

"You still have a lot going for you, Caleb," I said. "You're good looking, intelligent, and if you've noticed people still like you even though you're no longer a football star. Maybe you aren't so popular anymore, but you're still more popular than I'll ever be. There's a lot you can still do with your life. What are the chances you could make a career out of football? How many guys get to go pro?"

"Not many, but I'd planned to at least play in college. I love football. It is... *was* my life."

"Freudian slip?"

Caleb shook his head.

"You still love football. Listen, I don't know anything about sports, but I do know you don't have to give up football just because you're in a wheel chair."

"I can't play anymore, Tyler!"

"I know that, but how long could you have played anyway? With college, what, five more years? If you did manage to go pro how long could you have kept playing? Until you were in your 30's? What were you planning on doing after that?"

"I was going to look back on a brilliant career."

"For the rest of your life?"

"No. I would have coached maybe. I always thought being a football coach would be cool."

"So... why can't you do that?"

"I'm in a wheel chair," Caleb said slowly and distinctly as if I was stupid.

"So what? You can't lead a team or create plays or guide a quarterback from a wheel chair? I don't see many coaches doing a lot of running on the field. They stand on the sidelines and scream at their players. I'm pretty sure you can do that sitting down."

Caleb was silent for several moments.

"You already have experience," I said. "You would have been the quarterback this year if not for your accident. I'm not saying that to rub salt in any wounds, but to point out how good you are. Part of that was your body, but even though I sometimes doubt the intelligence of jocks, I know it takes intelligence to play football. At least, it takes intelligence if you're running a play. Your legs don't work anymore, but there's nothing wrong with your head. Well, mostly..."

I grinned. Caleb stuck his tongue out at me, but he also smiled.

"You really think I could be a coach?"

"Why not? I've seen some football coaches who were so fat they couldn't run, but that didn't stop them, at least not until they died of a heart attack. Listen, I know this has been rough on you. I don't understand what it's like. I know it would be rough on me if I couldn't walk anymore and I'm certain I could write from a wheelchair. It must be much harder for you, but there's more to you than your legs."

"Yeah, maybe I have been feeling a little sorry for myself."

"You have a right to mourn what you've lost, but at least you had the chance to be a football star. I'll never have that. Most of us will never have that."

"You could try out for the team."

"Are you kidding? The practices alone would kill me. Besides, I don't know if I'm up for all that homosexual activity. The jocks slap each other on the ass so much I wonder about what goes on in the locker room."

"Don't you mean "fantasize about," Tyler?"

I shot Caleb my best smart-ass look.

"Listen, Tyler, since we're having this heart-to-heart, serious, touchy-feely talk..."

"Yeah?"

"Are you gay?"

I just sat there for a few moments. I'd evaded this very question once before and I wasn't sure why.

"It's fine if you are. You know I'm perfectly cool with Dylan. Well, let me rephrase that. I'm perfectly cool with him being gay."

I laughed nervously.

"Come on, Tyler. Tell me. I've been sharing some of my most private thoughts with you."

"Yeah. I am. I'm gay."

Caleb smiled.

"Are you?" I asked.

"No, but I meant what I said. I'm totally cool with it. Why haven't you told anyone? Why haven't you at least told your friends? Are you afraid we would turn on you?"

"No."

"Then, why?"

"I don't really want Dylan to know because he'd be all over me."

Caleb laughed.

"That's sure the truth! I'm surprised he isn't anyway."

"He has come onto me a few times, but I've pushed his advances away. I've never told anyone because, well, it's personal, and..."

"And what?"

"I don't want people talking about my dad and me."

"Like Caspian did?"

"Yeah. I've taken a lot of shit because my dad is gay and if everyone knew I'm gay too... it would be ten times as bad, a hundred, a thousand."

"Your friends would never say or think anything like that."

"I know, but there are plenty of others who will just assume, you know? People love to talk."

"Your secret is safe with me, Tyler."

"Maybe I should tell Tyreece and Jesse, maybe even Dylan if he can keep his hands to himself."

"Would it be so bad if he didn't?" Caleb asked.

I detected something in his question, but I couldn't put my finger on it.

"Listen, Tyler... do you think it would be... I dunno... weird... perverted... if a guy who isn't into guys let another guy blow him?"

"Oh my God! You've done it with Dylan! Haven't you?"

"Quiet, will ya," Caleb said, looking around. There was no one near enough to hear.

"You have!"

"Just a few times."

"Whoa."

"Don't make fun of me, okay?"

"I wouldn't do that. I'm just... shocked."

"Before my accident, I used to get some now and then, but after... well, at first I didn't even know if... I could. You know what I mean?"

"Are you saying you couldn't get an erection?"

Caleb nodded and turned completely red.

"It's okay, Caleb," I said.

"At first, I couldn't and... well, you're a guy, you can imagine how that would make you feel."

"Yeah."

"Then, I got to where I could get a semi. I was thrilled about that, believe me, but I still couldn't get all the way hard. Dylan had offered before so... I thought I could try out the equipment, you know?"

I nodded.

"Well, I let him and, it worked. It was just like the old days. Well, almost like the old days. I kind of freaked out after Dylan left. I knew he wouldn't tell anyone. There are whispered rumors among the jocks that Dylan will give a blow-job and not talk about it. From the way some of the guys joke about it I know it's their way of talking about it without admitting anything. So, I knew he would keep quiet, but then I got worried that maybe I was gay, which was stupid because I knew I wasn't. Dylan's mouth felt good, but a mouth is a mouth. I've kind of wondered since then if it's kind of messed up. I'm not gay, but I get head from a guy."

"I don't think it's messed up. Have you tried it with a girl since your accident?"

"No. My confidence doesn't go that far. I'm sure I could handle a blow-job, but as far as more... I don't know if I'd be any good. I can't move anything below my ass. I might be able to do it, but... if I can't it would be so humiliating."

"Have you thought about experimenting with Dylan?"

"You mean... fuck him?"

"Yeah."

"I... don't think I could handle that. It's one thing to get head from a guy, but... I just don't think I could."

"I just thought it would be a way to try. Maybe you can find a girl who you really trust and who would let you try with her."

"Maybe. I've been too scared to even think about it. What if I tried, couldn't do it, and people found out?"

"I understand your fear, but if you're careful about whom you choose there wouldn't be much risk. If you couldn't perform, she'd know, but no one else would. I'm sure there are plenty of girls who want you."

"Even though I'm in a wheelchair?"

"Take it from a gay boy; you are hot, just as you are, right now."

It felt good to say I was gay out loud and to actually tell a guy I thought he was hot, even though nothing physical would ever happen between us.

"Thanks," Caleb said and actually blushed. "I don't feel so hot anymore."

"Listen, I know you said you've lost your six-pack, but you are still hot. I have a thing for built guys and... well, you look hot even with a shirt on. The way your pecs press against your shirt and your biceps strain your shirt-sleeves... nice. Your broad shoulders are sexy too. I don't want you to think I'm fantasizing about you, but you are hot."

"Do you fantasize about me, Tyler?"

I could tell Caleb was teasing me.

"No. I have checked you out the few times I've seen you without a shirt, but I'm not attracted to you. When I'm friends with another guy, I notice he's attractive, but I'm not attracted to him, if that makes any sense. Now, if you were gay and I began to develop deeper feelings for you I could start being attracted to you, but that's not going to happen."

"So you think I'm hot, but you're not hot for me?"

"Yeah. It's like your sister. If I wasn't gay, I'd want to fuck her."

"I can't believe you just said that! You're talking like a straight guy, Tyler," Caleb laughed.

"Yes, and for a reason. The point is, your sister is hot. Do you fantasize about her, Caleb?"

Caleb immediately stopped laughing.

"Dude! That's just sick! She's my sister!"

"What if she wasn't? Admit it. If she wasn't your sister and you had the chance, you'd fuck her."

"Well, yeah, but she is my sister. Can we stop talking about this?"

It was my turn to laugh.

"I'm making a point. I'm not attracted to you for reasons very similar to why you aren't attracted to your sister."

"Okay. We don't have to make a big production out of this. I never really thought you were hot for me. I think I would have noticed. You gay guys are so dramatic."

"You've known I'm gay for five minutes and now I'm a gay guy to you."

"You are Tyler to me, but you are gay."

"I was gay yesterday. The only difference is that now you know, just like I know you get head from Dylan!" I laughed.

"You're just evil."

"I guess you learned two things about me then."

"No. I already knew you were evil. I don't fall for your "nice guy" façade like everyone else."

"And they say jocks are stupid."

We finished eating and were soon once again sitting in my car.

"Thanks, Tyler. Talking to you really helped, more than I thought possible. You haven't magically made all my problems go away, but you have made me look at my life in a new way. Lately, I've been depressed. Now, I feel... hopeful."

"You're welcome," I said and grinned. "Now, give me all the details about you and Dylan."

"Dude, shut up!"

"So, you guys sneak off to the bathroom at school or..."

"I am *so* sorry I told you that!"

"Hey, I have to tease you now because I can't when anyone is around."

"That's for sure."

"Tell me one thing. Is he good?"

"He's really, *really* good. I would not tell this to anyone else, but he is so much better than any girl I've been with there's no comparison."

"It's probably all the practice he gets."

"Do you get a lot of practice, Tyler?"

"Hey, that's personal!"

"Oh, like we haven't been discussing deeply personal stuff for the last hour! We've been talking about my dick, the fact that you are gay, and that I get head from a guy. So answer the damn question."

"I've only had a little practice and I'm not telling you the details."

"Who with?"

"I said I'm not telling you details."

"Come on. How many guys?"

"Just one."

"You've only given head once?"

"I didn't say that. I said I've only given head to one guy."

"So you did it more than once."

"Yes, a few times."

"Who?"

"You don't know him."

"Who?"

"An IU boy, okay? A hot, hung, IU boy and I'm not saying another word about it."

"Whoa! So, you like older men."

"We're almost in college ourselves, Caleb."

Caleb left the topic behind and I was relieved. It was one thing to tell him I was gay. It was another to talk about sex, although I wasn't as uncomfortable talking about sex as I would have thought. Caleb and I had just become a lot closer. I had a feeling talking about personal things with him would now be a lot easier. I was glad he was in a more upbeat mood anyway. I hated to see anyone down.

Percy

"Caspian! Come in here a minute," I called from the kitchen when I heard the front door slam. My nephew was just getting home from school.

"What?" he asked. Caspian stood in the doorway, glaring at me with his arms crossed.

"I bought you something. Here."

I handed him a bag from Best Buy. He reached in and pulled out a box.

"A Droid?"

"I should have bought you a phone earlier, but I keep forgetting. This one does texting, Internet, everything. You can use it like an iPod too so you can listen to your music and ignore me. It has unlimited everything, so you can use it as much as you want."

"It's not going to work, you know."

"What's not going to work?"

"I don't care how much stuff you buy me; I'm not having sex with you."

"Caspian, how many times do I have to tell you I'm not interested in you like that?"

"Yeah, right."

"If I'm so obsessed with getting into your pants why haven't I made a move? Why haven't I offered to buy you something nice in exchange for sex?"

"You want to get me hooked on receiving gifts, then it will be "Caspian, sleep with me or you're not getting anything else and you have to give it all back.""

I sighed.

"When I give you something, it's yours to do with as you please. As for the rest, I hope you'll finally catch on that I don't have an ulterior motive."

"I know what guys like you are like."

"Caspian, has someone ever... touched you where they shouldn't?"

"Hoping for a molestation story you can get off on?"

"I'm just trying to find out why you are so distrustful of gays."

"No. No one has ever molested me and I intend to keep it that way... so stay out of my bedroom." Caspian stalked away.

Did parents ever want to strangle their own children? At the moment, the thought of wrapping my fingers around Caspian's neck and squeezing was not without appeal.

How long could I put up with his accusations and insinuations? How long could I put up with his smart-ass attitude and disrespect? Was I making a mistake by putting up with it at all? Should I put my foot down and try to be a harsh disciplinarian? I had a gut-feeling that was not the way to go with Caspian, but was being patient with him and putting up with his taunts the best way to help him work through whatever demons he possessed? I felt like I was groping blindly through a snowstorm. I couldn't be sure of anything. I wasn't sure, but I suspected I was a lousy parent.

My cell rang. I answered and smiled. It was Daniel. We spoke briefly and then disconnected. I walked to Caspian's room and knocked on the door.

"What?"

"Do you want to go out for supper with Daniel, Tyler, and me?"

"No."

"Are you sure? I'd like you to meet Daniel."

"There is no way I'm getting in a car with two homos and *him*," Caspian said.

"I hate to run off and leave you."

"Oh my God! Seriously! Don't be such a homo. Go away! I'm a big boy and I can take care of myself!"

"If you change your mind I put my number in your phone."

"Yeah, yeah, whatever."

"I won't be late. Bye."

Silence. I wondered if I wouldn't have more luck talking to the door.

I headed out, this time walking because Daniel said he'd drive and his place wasn't far from mine. I was glad he'd called. I needed something to distract me from Caspian. Of course, it would have been nice if Caspian had joined us. Then again, maybe not. I could just picture him saying something rude to Daniel. I wanted them to meet, but I didn't want to expose Daniel to abuse from a teen.

"Hey, Percy," Tyler said when he opened the door. He gazed around. "Shit-head not coming?"

"Tyler," Daniel admonished from within the house.

"Hey, I said you could invite him. If he was here I'd be civil, but since he's not..."

I grinned and entered. Daniel walked into the room, took me in his arms, and hugged me. Tyler watched us with a big grin on his face.

"Why don't we walk?" Daniel suggested.

"Yeah, you'll definitely need a walk after we've finished eating," Tyler said. "Bub's has enormous burgers. The patty of the Big Ugly Burger weighs a pound after it's cooked."

"Big Ugly Burger? What a name," I said.

"I'm not quite sure why it's called that. The burgers look quite delicious in fact. *This* boy can eat a whole one," Daniel said.

"I have my picture on the wall ten times," Tyler said.

"Your picture?" I asked.

"If you eat the entire burger, they take your photo and put it on the wall," Tyler said.

It was a pleasant afternoon for a walk. While I was sorry Caspian hadn't joined us, our outing was almost a fantasy come true. The three of us felt like a family and Tyler felt as much my son as Daniel's. I felt a sense of completeness, even if our time together was temporary.

"Have you made any progress with Caspian?" Daniel asked as we walked down Lincoln Street towards downtown.

"Not likely," Tyler said.

"Tyler," Daniel warned.

"He seems to seriously believe my only goal is to take advantage of him. His near-paranoia made me wonder if someone had taken advantage of him in the past, but he says no. I'm not sure he's being honest about it, but I have a feeling he is telling the truth."

"Maybe he was dropped on his head as a baby," Tyler suggested.

"I dropped you on your head several times and it didn't adversely affect you," Daniel said.

"Yeah right, Dad."

"Are you sure it didn't affect him?" I asked.

"Hey, no ganging up on me! You guys owe me big for bringing you together."

"I hate it when he's right, don't you?" I asked.

"The thing is, he's right most of the time," Daniel said.

"Ha! You said it out loud. Now, I have a witness."

"I don't know what you're talking about," I said.

"That's it; I'm sneaking in your house tonight and rearranging your furniture."

Tyler never had let me live down rearranging my furniture over and over again until I got it looking just like I wanted.

"You'd only have to help me move it back and we both know you don't want that."

"Please, no! Anything but that!"

"That's what I thought," I said with a fake tone of triumph.

I loved walking through the streets of Bloomington. Most of the homes were just ordinary and apartments were everywhere, but there were some older homes with interesting architecture. Overall, it was a beautiful college town with more than its share of trees. I couldn't think of anywhere I wanted to live more.

We turned right on 9th Street. We were already downtown. One thing I loved about my home was the fact I could walk to so many restaurants and shops in under half an hour. We crossed over North Walnut and then College Avenue, walking past

Smallwood Apartments and Cardinal Fitness. I looked up as we took a left on Morton Street. A large sign on the restaurant read "Bub's Burgers and Ice Cream - Home of the Big Ugly Burger."

The restaurant was a long rectangle squeezed in between Smallwood Apartments and Morton Street. Nearly the entire front was made up of large windows, allowing plenty of natural light inside. I liked Bub's even before we entered.

We stepped inside and were immediately shown to a table in a small dining room. Photos of diners who had managed to finish off their one-pound Ugly Burger mostly covered the walls. I was amazed there were so many of them. I was less amazed those most of those in the photos were college boys.

When the time came to order, both Daniel and Tyler ordered one of the huge burgers so I did as well. I ordered mine with lettuce, tomato, pickle, and onion.

"You have to finish all the toppings to get your photo on the wall," the waiter warned.

"Not a problem. There is no way I can finish so bring me a box."

Our college-aged waiter grinned and winked at me. I also ordered the sweet-potato waffle fries with marshmallow dipping sauce. I'd never heard of sweet-potato fries before.

"He was sooo flirting with you," Tyler said when our waiter had departed.

"Hmm, I guess dating a younger man could be interesting..."

"Hey!" Daniel and Tyler said together. Father and son sounded exactly alike. I smiled.

"He can only date you if he puts in his twenty years of waiting," Daniel said.

"Sounds fair," I said.

Despite being forewarned about the size of the burgers, I was not prepared for the reality of their enormous proportions. Each nearly covered a dinner plate.

"Can I get you anything else?" our waiter asked, concentrating on me.

"I think we're set," I said.

"If you need anything, I'm Ben."

"Thanks, Ben."

"Do guys always flirt with you?" Tyler asked when Ben had departed.

"Of course," I said as if it didn't need to be said.

"You'd better watch out, Percy. I think Ben might try to sneak into your take-home box," Daniel said.

"You'll have to help me carry it then."

"You can forget that. You're on your own."

Ben was a very attractive young man and if I was single the thought of taking him home would have been appealing. I had Daniel now and he was all I wanted. I smiled at him across the table. He was sexier than any college boy.

The Ugly Burger was not only huge, it was delicious. The sweet-potato fries with the marshmallow dipping sauce were tasty too. I wasn't sure about the fries when I'd ordered, but the sweet taste was a nice compliment to the burger.

We talked and laughed as we ate. Once again, I witnessed the intimacy of father and son. The love between Daniel and Tyler was obvious. They were lucky to have each other. I thought of Caspian sulking at home and wished things could be different with him. All I could do was keep trying.

I sighed.

"What's wrong?" Daniel asked.

"It's hard to stop thinking about Caspian. He's not adjusting well and I'm not sure what to do about it. Was this one as much trouble when he was fifteen?" I asked, nodding to Tyler.

Tyler put his hand on his chest while a "moi" expression crossed his face.

"He was horrible," Daniel said. "He was completely out of control."

"I find that hard to believe."

"Yeah, I've always been the perfect son."

"I find *that* hard to believe too," I said. "Keep in mind I have spent time with you, Tyler."

He stuck out his tongue at me.

"I believe Tyler took up the drums when he was fifteen," Daniel said. "That did almost drive me out of my mind until I moved his drums into the garage."

"Yeah, my brilliant career as a musician didn't go very far," Tyler said.

"I think you're writing career will," I said.

"You really think so?"

"You know I don't say things I don't mean. You also know I don't hold back with criticism."

"Yeah, like the way you blasted me for lack of detail in that piece I wrote for Brit Lit."

"Yes, I live to destroy the hopes and dreams of young writers so when I say you have a future, I mean it." I grinned.

"Thanks."

"It will take you a few years to get started. I made almost nothing in the beginning. It took a long time before I could support myself solely with writing."

"What did you do?" Tyler asked.

"In the summers, I worked at Camp Neeswaugee. I did some substitute teaching, an experience I would not wish on anyone. Mostly, I bought and sold antiques."

"Big surprise there," Tyler said.

"My parents set up at flea markets now and then so I got into that when I was young. In college, while the other guys were out drinking, I was going to auctions and selling things at flea markets and an occasional auction."

"You made money doing that?"

"Yeah, I did well. I have a good eye and since I loved antiques I had a lot of knowledge behind me. It didn't make me rich and it was a lot of work, but I enjoyed it. That's the most important thing, enjoying your work. It makes life worth living."

"So my first novel won't make me rich, huh?" Tyler asked.

"No. When you publish your first novel it will be a great disappointment."

"Gee, thanks."

"It's like that for all writers. There is the initial elation of getting published and seeing your name on the cover of a book for the first time. Then, reality sets in. Beginning writers don't have a reputation or a group of followers. Sales are inevitably disappointing, leading to self-doubt. You have to understand that the quality of your writing will have little to do with sales of your first book. No matter how good the book, it takes time for word to get around. I had to face that reality myself, but I loved writing, so I kept going. I wrote and published another book and then another. Sales picked up and a group of readers began not only to eagerly anticipate my next novel, but to spread the word about them to their friends. After I had a few books published, even my early books that hadn't sold well began to sell. It's a very slow process of building an audience, so my advice to all beginning writers is to keep writing, but don't quit your day job."

Daniel smiled at me across the table. He appreciated the realistic picture I was painting for his son.

"You really think I have what it takes to be a writer?" Tyler asked.

"You already are a writer, and yes, I do think you have what it takes. You have talent that will only improve with experience, especially if you listen to me about paying attention to the details."

"Yes, master," Tyler said with a grin. He turned to his dad. "See what I have to put up with?"

"You're extremely lucky to have Percy as a mentor."

"Shhhhh, he's sitting right here!" Tyler said.

I laughed.

I was starving and managed to finish half my burger while we talked and laughed. Daniel didn't get quite that far, but Tyler kept eating and eating until his entire burger was gone. I'm not sure I would have believed it had I not seen it with my own eyes.

Ben came and took Tyler's photo, then brought boxes for Daniel and me. I'd be having leftover burger for lunch for at least a couple of days. I didn't mind in the least. I often lived on leftovers from restaurants. I was trying to change that now that Caspian was in my life, but he wasn't up for sticking around at supper time.

We headed back, taking our time strolling down the sidewalks. I loved spending time with both Daniel and Tyler. Daniel and I walked close together, arms sometimes touching. Just being near him gave me a feeling of warmth that spread through my chest. Daniel and I stopped for a moment and kissed.

"If you two would like me to get lost for a while when we get back, I'm sure I can find something to do," Tyler said, grinning.

Daniel and I pulled apart.

"Maybe you can just go to your room for a while," I suggested.

Tyler grinned and the three of us continued walking. I took Daniel's hand in mine. I was glad we lived in a place where we could walk down the sidewalk holding hands and not have to worry overmuch about being bashed. Bloomington wasn't perfect, but it was an accepting place. I suspected that was mostly due to IU. I'd long held the opinion that the young, at least those college-age, were more advanced when it came to acceptance.

"Tyler, how are the guys at North, as far as acceptance of sexual orientation is concerned?" I asked.

"Are you asking me because you think I'm gay?" Tyler asked.

There was a slight teasing tone to Tyler's voice. I never had figured out Tyler's sexual orientation. It didn't matter to me. I liked him regardless.

"I'm asking because you're in high school and it's been a few years since I graduated from North."

"A few years? More like decades!"

"Two decades!" I said. "Let's not make me, and your dad I might add, seem older than we are."

"You guys are ancient!" Tyler laughed. "To answer your question, I think most students there are fairly accepting. I'm sure some name-calling goes on and maybe even some bashing but mostly I don't think it's all that bad. One of my friends, Dylan, is openly gay and he's what one would call a flamer. No one gives him much crap. Why the interest? Are you working on a new novel?"

"I'm always working on a new novel, but I was just thinking how Bloomington is such an accepting place and I wondered if that extended to the high schools."

"It's not so bad, not great, but you can't expect perfect. I can't speak for South, of course. I'm not concerned with the enemy." Tyler smiled, as he so often did. I couldn't picture him having an enemy.

"Caspian is the worst homophobe in the entire school," Tyler said. "I'm not saying that to put him down, but he had some nasty things to say about Dylan. I've warned Dylan to stay away from him because I think Caspian will kick Dylan's ass if he doesn't."

"I worry about Caspian. He's so intelligent, but he's filled with hostility. It's as if he hates the world. I guess I can't blame him after all that has happened," I said.

"How about you?" Daniel asked.

"Me?"

"Caspian lost his dad, but you lost your brother."

"I miss him, which is weird because I almost never saw him. We didn't keep in touch like we should have, but I always knew he was there, you know what I mean?"

Daniel nodded.

"What was truly strange was how strongly I felt his absence in the house when I first found out he'd been killed. He had never even been in my house. Even when we were younger, we never lived together with Mom and Dad for long. He was so much older that he was gone by the time I was ten. I can barely remember those years. It's hard losing him, but I've dealt with loss before. It's never easy."

When we arrived back at Daniel's place, Tyler made himself scarce and Daniel and I sat on the couch. I leaned over, pressed my lips against him, and kissed him. We drew each other into a tight embrace and made out as if we were teens again. Daniel's lips, tongue, and firm body drove me insane with lust. If Tyler hadn't been in the house... Daniel pushed me down onto the couch and climbed on top of me. Our breath came harder and faster as we made out and rubbed against one another. I burned with need for Daniel's body.

"I know we agreed to take things slow," I said, panting. "But, we have been dating a while now and..."

Daniel climbed off me, took my hand, and pulled me to my feet. He kissed me passionately and pulled me toward his bedroom. I glanced once at Tyler's door, but Tyler understood the relationship I had with his dad. He knew we loved each other. I put Tyler out of my mind and thought only of Daniel.

Daniel pulled me into his room and closed the door. He tugged at my shirt and soon it was over my head. He ran his hands and then his lips over my torso. I had to fight to calm my breath. I gave in to my desires and soon our clothing was piled at the foot of the bed and Daniel and I were rolling over each other, our hands and lips everywhere. I had not made love with Daniel for years, but it was as if no time had passed at all. It was just as passionate, just as intense.

I feared Tyler would hear our moans and groans, but most of me just didn't care. All that mattered was being with Daniel—again.

Over an hour later, we got up and dressed. I was filled with the mellow after-sex feeling. I was completely relaxed. We walked into the living room and Tyler was sitting there reading. He looked up, then made a show of checking the time on his cell.

"Now bad for old guys," he said.

"You're okay with this, right?" Daniel asked.

"Of course I'm okay with it and you don't really need my permission."

Daniel mussed Tyler's hair.

"I should be getting back," I said.

"Need a ride? Are you too exhausted to walk?" Tyler asked with a mischievous glint in his eye.

"I think I can manage," I said.

I gave Daniel a goodbye kiss and then headed out the door. I was filled with happiness and contentment.

Tyler

I looked around the table at my friends. Caleb now knew I was gay and it didn't matter to him. I wondered if I should tell the others. My reluctance had little or nothing to do with worrying about their acceptance. I couldn't imagine my sexual orientation changing the way Tyreece or Jesse thought about me. Neither of them looked down on Dylan and he was about as gay as they come. I was somewhat concerned about Dylan's reaction. His acceptance wasn't a factor, but I wondered how strongly he'd come onto me. He had tried to get into my pants before and I'd turned away his advances. Dylan went after what he wanted until he got it and if he knew I was gay I feared he'd continue his assault. I was also a little frightened of myself. A guy has needs, you know? There were things I wanted to try and Dylan would likely be up for anything. I feared the temptation would be too great. I wasn't against sex, not at all, but things could get weird if I was doing it with Dylan.

I glanced at Caleb. How did he handle the situation? Now that I knew Dylan gave him an occasional blow-job I could detect little hints in the way they behaved toward each other. Of course, before Caleb had admitted their relationship I hadn't picked up on it. It was something obvious only after one had the answer. Caleb didn't seem to find it hard to be friends with Dylan even though Dylan gave him head, so maybe I wouldn't either—if it happened. Then again, Caleb wasn't gay so a relationship between Dylan and me would be different.

I had another reason for hesitating to come out to my friends—privacy. I didn't like to talk about my private life and sex was about as private as it got. If my friends knew I was gay they'd know a whole lot more about me than they did now, especially in the realm of sexual desire, and I didn't really like anyone knowing about that.

I gazed at Dylan a moment and wondered if I could ever be interested in dating him. I immediately laughed out loud. There was no way Dylan could limit himself to one guy.

"What?" Dylan asked, looking at me.

"Um..." I couldn't tell him my real reason for laughing. I thought of something Percy had once said to me. "Sometimes, I just think funny things."

"You get just a little stranger every day," Jesse said as he nodded and winked at a passing girl.

"Is that a zit on your forehead, Jesse?" I asked.

Jesse's hand flew to his forehead, then he glared at me.

"Jerk."

I grinned.

"It's just part of my strangeness."

"Touchy."

"Do you mean, touché, Jesse?"

"I'm sorry I don't know French! The only thing I know about French is kissing."

"Are you any good?" Dylan asked.

Jesse knew to tread carefully with Dylan. If he wasn't cautious, Dylan would try to manipulate him into making out.

"I'm the best *with girls*."

"You don't know about French kissing until you've made out with a guy," Dylan said.

"Be careful, Jesse, it's a trap. You'll end up tongue-wrestling with Dylan," Tyreece said.

"You talk entirely too much, Tyreece, and what could be more enjoyable than making out with me! I am the best!"

Dylan looked around the table, but we were all too smart to take the bait.

Yeah, telling Dylan I was gay would be a mistake unless I wanted to get it on with him. I kind of did, but I'd have to be sure before I told him I was a homo. Once he found out he'd be all over me. Dylan's motto was probably "yes means yes and no means yes." I smiled.

I spotted Caspian sitting alone. I wondered if he'd managed to alienate the girls I'd seen him with at lunchtime before. My guess is that he probably tried to seduce one or more of them in some vulgar way that disgusted them. He looked forlorn and lonely. Maybe it was time to give him another chance. He was Percy's nephew after all and I thought the world of Percy.

"I'm going to go sit with Caspian a while," I said.

"For God's sake, why?" Caleb asked.

"Look at him over there. He looks like he doesn't have a friend in the world."

"Which is most likely true if he's as big of an ass with everyone else as he was with us," Jesse said.

"Maybe he acts like a jerk because he's afraid," I said.

"Then he must be fucking terrified," Caleb said.

"I'm going to see if I can make peace with him."

"Are you sure?" Tyreece asked. "The last time you sat with him you tried to kill him."

"That was last time," I said, as if it actually meant something.

"I'll go with you!" Dylan said.

"No, you won't!" Tyreece said. "If you go and put the moves on Caspian there will be violence."

"What makes you think I'd do that?"

Tyreece rolled his eyes.

"Wish me luck," I said.

"I'll be over in a minute to pull you off Caspian," Tyreece said.

"Thanks for the vote of confidence. I'm quite capable of controlling myself."

"Sure you are."

I stuck out my tongue at Tyreece. He grinned. I picked up my tray and walked toward Caspian.

"What do you want, loser?" Caspian asked as I sat down.

"I thought you might like someone to sit with you."

"Maybe I like sitting alone."

"No one likes to sit alone."

"What's wrong? You and your faggy friends have a tiff? Did they cast you out of homoland?"

"You know, most of my friends aren't gay. Dylan is the only one."

"Yeah, right!"

"What does it matter anyway?"

"People hate faggots."

"Not all people."

"Well, I hate faggots."

"Why?"

"Would you just fuck off? Damn, you're like my uncle."

"Thank you."

"It wasn't a compliment."

"It sounds like one to me."

"Then you are seriously fucked up in the head."

"You don't have to be so hostile. Maybe you could make a few friends if you weren't so combative. Ever hear of trying to get along?"

"That's for losers, like you."

"Listen, I really like your uncle. He's a second dad to me."

"You take it up the ass from him, don't you?"

"No!"

"You do."

"No, I don't. Percy is... my mentor."

"Yeah, he's your mentor in homo sex. Did he teach you to suck dick or did your dad teach you that?"

I clinched my fist. I would not let his little punk push my buttons.

"It's really uncool for you to say things about my dad like that. I wouldn't say something like that about your dad."

"Don't fucking talk about my dad!"

"See? You don't like it either."

"My dad is dead, you fucking asshole!"

"I know and I'm very sorry."

"Just leave me the fuck alone."

"It can't be any fun not having any friends."

"Stop pretending to like me!"

"I'm not pretending to like you. In fact, I don't like you, but you're Percy's nephew and we'll be seeing each other a lot so I thought we should try to be civil. If you can stop acting like such an immature little asshole we might even become friends."

"I know what you want. You want to lure me in so you can get me alone and molest me. You fucking try it and I'll cut you."

"You're like a broken CD. You just keep saying the same stupid shit over and over."

"Then do us both a favor and fuck off."

"I'm so sorry for trying to be nice to you."

"Why don't you go blow your friends, or your dad?"

I grabbed Caspian by the back of the head and pounded his face into the table over and over and over.

I ground my teeth while smiling slightly about my daydream. Oh, how I wanted to beat that little shit senseless! Without another word, I picked up my tray and returned to my friends.

"From the look on you face, I'm guessing that didn't go well," Caleb said.

"I want to kill him, slowly and painfully," I said calmly, hoping I didn't sound like a psychopath.

"So you two are becoming closer," Tyreece said. "Last time you would have strangled him if I hadn't stopped you. This time you only *thought* about killing him."

"Argh! I want to try and get along with that little bastard but he won't even meet me half way! All he does is insult me."

"I bet he's incredible in bed," Dylan said. "I want him to shove me down, rip down my pants, and..."

"No details, please," Jesse said. "My hetero ears can't take it."

"No one's ears can take it," Tyreece said, grinning.

I smiled too. I still wanted to beat the crap out of Caspian, but dwelling on it would only make my day unpleasant. At least I'd made the effort.

"That's it, man, shake it off," Caleb said. "I admire you for trying, even though I think it was a stupid idea."

"Thanks, I think."

"You should have let me come along. I could put a smile on his face," Dylan said.

"Dude, that punk is not interested in your lips on his dick," Jesse said.

"If he knew how good I am, he would be," Dylan said. "I think I'll go talk to him."

Dylan started to stand up, but Jesse grabbed his shoulder and jerked him back down.

"You're not committing suicide on my watch," Jesse said.

"My hero!"

Dylan grabbed Jesse and hugged him hard, no doubt to get a good feel of Jesse's body. Jesse pushed him off.

"Dude, you wrinkled my shirt!"

"Oh, no! It's a fashion emergency. Jesse's shirt is wrinkled! Someone get Calvin Klein on the phone!" Caleb yelled.

"It's the big, messed up hair catastrophe all over again," Tyreece said.

"You know, I only sit with you guys because you're all so unattractive you made me look *even* hotter," Jesse said.

"I say we put peanut butter in his hair," I suggested.

Tyreece picked up his peanut butter and jelly sandwich and looked at it thoughtfully, then at Jesse.

"You wouldn't."

Tyreece grinned and moved toward Jesse, who jumped up with a squeal.

"Yeah, you're right. I wouldn't."

"I've grown to hate you all," Jesse said, but grinned. He walked off to dump his tray.

"See you later, Jesse!" Caleb called out.

I eyed Brice Parker and Justin Schroeder as they walked by. Brice was a sexy soccer player with a hot defined body, curly blond hair, and the hottest ass. It was no wonder Dylan had been so hot after him the previous year. Justin was a wrestler and it showed. His defined muscles bulged out in all the right places...

I walked around the table to Justin, ripped his shirt off, and ran my hands over his powerful chest as I leaned in to kiss him.

I looked around quickly. Caleb was grinning at me. He'd caught me checking out Brice and Justin, but no one else had noticed. I risked one final glance. I loved Justin's straight black hair and hard body. Both he and Brice looked good coming and going.

We were near the end of our lunch period, so I got up and took my tray to dump it. Caleb followed along. Once we dumped our trays he grinned at me.

"You definitely need to get some," he said.

"Not so loud."

Caleb motioned with his finger for me to come closer. I leaned down.

"No one knows we're talking about guys, but you need a boyfriend or at least a good, hard fuck," he whispered.

I could feel my face turning red and Caleb laughed.

"Come on, it's not like you're a virgin."

"I am in some ways," I said.

"Oh! More information! Give me details."

"Give you details on what I haven't done? You already know what I have done, so you also know what I haven't."

"You're not keeping any secrets from me, are you?" Caleb asked.

"I don't have secrets to keep. You're the one with a secret."

"Yeah and that's why I'm always so relaxed. When I need some relief I just... do a friend a favor."

I grinned and shook my head. I was quite sure Dylan did view it as a favor. Part of me wished I had such easy access to sexual relief. Of course, I could have the same easy access, but... I didn't know if I wanted to go there. I liked Dylan and it might seem weird if I let him do *that*. I knew he'd be up for it. He'd offered before, but still..."

"I don't even know who I'd ask. I think I'd want more of a relationship than a hookup."

"Hmm, that does pose a problem. Hookups are easier, especially with our mutual friend around."

"I'll be completely honest. A hookup does sound *really* good, especially if it was with someone like..."

"The pair you were checking out earlier? Perhaps you shouldn't start with a three-way."

"I didn't mean both of them at once! I just meant..."

"I know. I'm just jerking your chain, but don't be so quick to dismiss the idea of a three-way."

"Have you ever had one?"

"Twice."

"Really?"

"I promised never to tell so I can't name names, but I spent part of a night with two of our cheerleaders last year. Then, I shared a girl with Cory Caldemyer when the team stayed overnight in a motel for an away game."

"Wow. You're not making this up just to see how gullible I am, are you?"

"No. Perhaps I'm bragging, but I'm not making it up. I guess you could say I'm reliving my glory days."

"You're glory days are still ahead of you, Caleb. Someday, you'll be the high school football coach with the most wins ever."

Caleb smiled.

"Thanks, Tyler."

"I'm just telling you like it is."

"So am I. You need to get laid, boy. Give your hand a rest."

I jerked my head toward Caleb and was immediately sorry. I felt so stupid. For a moment, I wondered how he knew what I did in the privacy of my bedroom, but a second too late I realized he knew because that's what all guys did. Caleb laughed his ass off.

"I'm glad you find me so amusing."

"You're no Dylan, or Jesse for that matter, but you do have some entertainment value."

"Shut up."

"See you later, Tyler."

"See ya."

I gave Caleb's suggestion some thought. I did need to get laid or at least begin dating someone so getting laid would be a possibility in the not-too-distant future. I was nearly eighteen and had only had a very few sexual experiences and all of them involving the same partner. He never blew me and I'd been left feeling guilty and kind of used, even though I went back for more. It wasn't the ideal introduction to sex. It just sort of happened. By the standards of most my encounter didn't even count as sex. It was merely messing around. Each time lasted only about five minutes so if I wasn't a virgin I was as close as one could get without actually being one.

Why was I suddenly thinking so much about sex? Sure, I'd thought about it in the past, but I felt like it was the main topic running around inside my head. Part of me wanted to do it just so I could quit thinking about it all the time, but that didn't seem right. Besides, I had a feeling that doing it just once wouldn't satisfy my lust. If Dylan was any indication, sex was something one needed again and again and again. I didn't know if I wanted to open up that door.

My train of thought was derailed as someone shouldered me hard, knocking me into the wall.

"What the..."

"Oh! So sorry," Caspian said, then went on his way.

Sorry my ass. That kid was a complete and total jerk. I'd gone out of my way to help him, to be understanding, and to try to befriend him, but no more. I was done, finished. I didn't care if he was Percy's nephew, he was a rude little jerk and it was his own fault he didn't have any friends.

I went straight home after school and hit my homework. I didn't think it was safe to be around others at the moment. I might jump on some unsuspecting boy and Dylan might get pissed if I invaded his territory. Even if I just did a hookup I didn't want it to be a spontaneous encounter like my first. I wanted to get to know the guy before we did something. What I really wanted was a relationship, but how likely was that?

I ripped through my homework, resisted the urge to go on a walk, and worked on my story for a while. My novel was coming along nicely and I had Percy to thank for that. He didn't do any of my work for me, but his encouragement meant a lot. His advice was just as valuable. One thing he told me had been especially helpful—I didn't have to get it right the first time. I'd wasted a lot of time obsessing over whether certain scenes and sub-plots were working out. Percy told me not to worry about it. He hacked out his first draft, getting down the main story and what details he could without worrying about anything else. The secret to writing was in the rewriting he said and I was convinced he was right. Percy had given me the freedom to forge ahead and not worry about the mess I left behind. All that could be fixed later.

I typed at my laptop for more than an hour, finishing a chapter I'd started a few days before. I decided to reward myself with a walk. The evening was too beautiful to stay inside. I might not be a jock, but I did enjoy the outdoors. I thought of grabbing my skateboard, but decided my first thought was best. I wanted to walk and think.

I wandered around the streets of Bloomington with no particular destination in mind. I thought mostly about finding a boyfriend. I was in desperate need of sex, but rushing into something seemed like a very bad idea. If I found a boy I liked I could ease into it. We could take it slow like Dad and Percy were doing. I smiled when I thought of the sounds coming from Dad's bedroom the last time Percy was over. It was kind of weird thinking about my dad having sex, not that I thought about the details, but it was sign that their relationship was coming along nicely. I needed a relationship like that. I needed someone I could get to know and then... maybe start with making out and then go from there. I hadn't even kissed another boy! How pathetic was that? I was a senior in high school. Most guys had done it all by then, but I'd done almost nothing.

I ended up in front of Percy's house. Perhaps I'd unconsciously walked there. No matter. Since I was there I figured I might as well stop in. I was just coming up the walk when the front door opened and an enraged Caspian emerged, spouting profanities that made me blush. He shouldered me as he passed, calling me a faggot before he ran down the street.

"Bad time?" I asked Percy who had stepped to the door.

"No. Come in. It would be nice to talk to someone who isn't screaming at me."

"What's up his ass this time?"

"I mentioned his parents. I guess it was a mistake, but he hasn't dealt with their death. He absolutely will not talk about them. He gets angry if they are even mentioned."

"Yeah. That I know."

I could tell Percy was majorly stressed out, which was unusual for Percy. He made us some Scottish Tattoo tea and we sat at the kitchen table as we had so often before.

"I wanted to go out with your dad tonight, but I decided another attempt to reach Caspian was more important. I needn't have bothered. Every attempt I make at communication ends up with him screaming at me."

"Yeah. I heard what he was screaming."

"I can't get him to open up and I can't get him to trust me."

"It looks like he'd trust you by now."

"You'd think so, but no."

I walked around the table and gripped Percy's shoulders.

"Damn, your muscles are tight."

I began rubbing the muscles of his shoulders and neck.

"Living with a teenage boy will do that to you."

"I wouldn't know, but I guess my dad does."

"I'm sure your worst is better than Caspian's best, but enough about him. How is your novel coming along?"

"Great!" I said.

I began to tell Percy what I'd been writing while I continued to massage his shoulders. I could just imagine what Caspian would say if he came in and saw me touching Percy. I'm sure the words "boy toy" would instantly come to his lips. I told Percy about the scene I'd just written and listened to his suggestions. The tension left his muscles and I resumed my seat and sipped tea while we talked. What was wrong with Caspian? Percy could be the greatest parent ever if the stupid kid just gave him a chance.

Percy

"Come with us, you might like it."

"Yeah, and someone from school might see me with two homos."

"Autumn is coming on fast. The farmer's market won't be open many more Saturdays."

"And this concerns me for what reason?"

"Caspian, please. I want you to see what Bloomington has to offer. People travel for miles to come to the market."

"They travel for miles to look at some corn?"

"It's much more than that. Please come."

Caspian rolled his eyes.

"If I go, can I spend the rest of my Saturday in peace, without you trying to pull me into some stupid cultural crap?"

"Yes."

"Okay, then. Let's get it over with." Caspian paused. "Wait a minute, is Tyler coming too?"

"No. Daniel said he's already out with friends."

"Good. I don't like him"

I resisted the urge to defend Tyler. I reminded myself that Caspian didn't much like anyone. I wished he'd make at least one friend. At this point, I didn't much care who, just so he let someone in. I hated to see my nephew in pain. He was hiding it, even denying it to himself, but I knew he was suffering. I wanted to help him, but I couldn't until he was willing to let me.

I put the top down on the Shay and Caspian and I climbed inside. Caspian couldn't quite hide the pleasure he experienced by riding in the roadster. He almost smiled.

"You guys aren't going to hold hands or any shit like that, are you?" Caspian asked.

"We won't embarrass you."

"Yeah, right. Just don't do anything gay."

"It may surprise you, but gays go shopping just like everyone else. We do most things just like everyone else."

"Stop trying to recruit me."

"Caspian, we discussed this before. It's not a club you can join."

Caspian crossed his arms over his chest and glared at me. He was no doubt trying to be intimidating, but when I looked at him all I saw was a boy who desperately needed a hug.

I pulled the Shay up in front of Daniel's house and sounded the ahooga horn. I climbed out and opened up the rumble seat. Caspian climbed in the back without protest. No doubt he didn't want to ride in the crowded confines of the front seat with Daniel and me. The three of us would have been squeezed in like sardines in a can. I love my roadster, but it wasn't roomy.

Daniel came out of the house, carrying a reusable cloth bag from the Monroe County Public Library. He gave me a quick hug. I glanced at Caspian. He had a disgusted look on his face, but didn't comment.

"Hi, Caspian. I'm Daniel. Percy has told me a lot about you."

Daniel reached out his hand. I was surprised when Caspian shook it.

Daniel climbed in beside me.

"It's so beautiful out today! There's just a hint of fall in the air. I love it!" Daniel said.

I couldn't help but grin. Daniel always made me happy.

I leisurely drove us downtown. The farmer's market was only a few blocks away. We could have walked, but I had a habit of buying more than I could comfortably carry. Besides, I loved driving the roadster and I'd have to garage it for the winter all too soon.

As always, the roadster drew a lot of attention. Most people seemed to love old cars. The college boys were more into muscle cars, but even they admired the vintage appearance of a Model A.

I found a parking spot not too far from the farmer's market, which was lucky. We climbed out and walked to the market, which was located on Morton Street, just across and down the street from Bub's Burgers and Ice Cream where I'd watched Tyler demolish a one-pound burger. I wished Caspian had joined us that evening. I hoped I could take him there soon. There was so much to enjoy in Bloomington, and in life, if he would just open up to the possibilities. It would ease the pain of his grief.

"Whoa! *That's* the farmer's market? I was expecting a few stupid stands with tomatoes and corn," Caspian said.

"Oh no, this farmer's market offers just about everything that is in season."

The farmer's market spread out before us. There were three large pavilions with tables filled with vegetables and fruits on both sides. There were more vendors behind and to the sides of the pavilions. I'd say there were at least 75 different sellers offering squash, pumpkins, tomatoes, corn, green beans, zinnas, mums, herbs of all descriptions, peaches, apples, and just about any kind of Indiana produce one could name. There were even farm fresh eggs, cheese, and hot and cold beverages for sale.

I'd expected Caspian to stuff in his earphones and completely ignore his surroundings, but he actually seemed interested. Daniel looked at me and smiled.

The three of us walked slowly along, which was the only way to walk as the market was quite crowded with shoppers of all ages. Everyone from college kids to the elderly came to the market. There was even a small band performing at one end and a rather talented young guitar player strumming away near a booth filled with early-fall pumpkins and squashes.

I stopped to purchase a dozen eggs. I always bought my eggs at the farmer's market during the months it was open and tried to avoid buying them at all the rest of the year. Most egg farms kept chickens cooped in far too-crowded cages. The chickens that laid the eggs sold at the farmer's market were free to run around a barn yard. The eggs here were far more expensive, but I didn't have to feel guilty about being an accessory to cruelty.

We stopped at booth after booth, purchasing apples, peaches, pumpkins, and plums. I went more for fruit and vegetables that could be eaten raw as I wasn't big on cooking. Daniel was the cook. I bought a small rosemary plant, mostly to decorate my kitchen, but also for the unique fragrance and for use on those rare occasions I cooked chicken breast. Yes, I know someone who goes on about not purchasing eggs sold in stores shouldn't be an accessory to chicken-murder, but I couldn't quite bring myself to go vegetarian. Most of us live lives of contradiction and hypocrisy.

I bought a small bouquet of zinnias. I knew they wouldn't last long, but I love flowers. I saw Caspian roll his eyes at my purchase, but he was behaving quite well. I noticed him watching Daniel and me as we browsed and made our purchases. He seemed rather thoughtful.

"All this food is making me hungry," Caspian said.

"There are booths in the back that sell baked goods, sandwiches, and drinks," I said, pulling out my wallet. I handed Caspian a twenty. "Here, knock yourself out. Call or text me if you can't find us a little later."

"Thanks."

Caspian took off.

"He's unusually polite today," I said.

"I think you've just been making up all those stories about him," Daniel teased.

"If only I was."

"Maybe there is hope for him yet. He doesn't seem like a bad kid."

"Isn't that what they always say about serial-killers? There's always a neighbor commenting on how nice the killer was and how they just can't believe he kept human hearts in his freezer."

"True."

"I agree with you. Caspian is a good kid, or at least there's a good kid hidden somewhere inside him. If only I can coax him out."

"You will."

"Both you and Tyler have greater faith in me than I do."

"I remember you as a camp counselor. You truly cared about your kids. I even heard other counselors comment how you were the perfect counselor. You never went out drinking like the others. You were always there for your kids. You put them first. You've been there for Tyler, too. I'm busier than I'd like to be and not always around when he needs me. You've helped him more than you know. If anyone can help Caspian, you can."

"I hope you're right."

"I'm always right."

"Uh, huh."

We must have stayed at the farmer's market for an hour. I texted Caspian and he met us near the entrance. He even helped Daniel carry his purchases back to the roadster. When we departed, Caspian had to share the rumble-seat with several bags of produce. He didn't seem to mind. He ate a peach he'd purchased and gazed around at his surroundings as the wind ran through his spiky hair.

I helped Daniel carry his purchases inside. While we were out of sight we hugged, then kissed. I couldn't wait to be alone with him again. I gave him one last peck on the lips and returned to the car. Caspian had moved into the front seat.

"What do you think of Daniel?"

"He doesn't seem like a homo."

"Most of us don't. We're just like everyone else, Caspian. We're all different. The only common difference is that we like guys."

"Maybe so, but that's a huge fucking difference!"

Caspian's bad attitude was beginning to return. At least I'd seen a glimmer of hope.

"It's a big difference to some people, not so big to others."

"You guys shouldn't be seen together too often. People will figure out you're homos."

"We don't hide what we are, Caspian. That would indicate we have something to be ashamed of and we don't."

"Yeah, you do. You're homos!"

"That doesn't matter to most people. It shouldn't matter at all."

"Your deviant life-style shouldn't matter?"

"It's not deviant, Caspian."

"The fuck it's not!"

We drove the rest of the short distance home in silence. Caspian went inside and locked himself in his room. I carried in my purchases. Daniel and I had planned to go out again a little later, but now I was having second thoughts. I wasn't sure I should leave Caspian alone. By the time I'd put away my purchases, I decided I'd better say home. I called Daniel and gave him the bad news. He was disappointed, but understanding. We would be seeing each other the next evening anyway. Tomorrow was September 24$^{st.}$ It was Tyler's 18th birthday.

***

I walked toward Daniel's house holding a large box wrapped in purple paper. When I asked Caspian if he would like to come with me to Tyler's birthday party he merely stared at me as if I'd gone insane.

I walked around the rear of the house where Daniel was grilling burgers on a gas grill. A small table held gifts and a larger one was surrounded by chairs. I placed Tyler's present on the table and gave Daniel a hug.

"Hey, sexy. I guess Caspian didn't want to come?"

"No, but then that shouldn't come as a surprise."

"Unfortunately, no. Tyler is not his favorite person."

"You guys are sooooo sexy together," said a slim blond boy. "Of course, you're both plenty sexy alone, too."

"Back off my dad and his boyfriend, Dylan. They are both taken," Tyler said.

"Some couples like to spice things up with a third," Dylan said.

Tyler grabbed Dylan by the ear and pulled him away.

"Oww!"

"I cannot believe you just said that to my dad and Percy!" Tyler hissed.

I couldn't help but laugh.

"That is Dylan, one of Tyler's friends," Daniel said.

"I take it he's gay."

"Yes, and before you ask I'm sure he was quite serious about being our third."

"Now I'm glad Caspian didn't come. I can just imagine what he would have had to say about this. Dylan can't be more than fifteen."

"He is fifteen."

"Well, I guess we still have it," I said, laughing.

Tyler pulled me away from Daniel after a couple of minutes and introduced me to his friends; Caleb, Tyreece, Jesse, and Dylan. Dylan held onto my hand after shaking it far longer than was necessary and openly checked me out, but at least he didn't proposition me again. Tyler also introduced me to Brittany, the only girl at the party. Once the introductions were made, I rejoined Daniel.

"Tyler has a nice group of friends," I said. "Caspian described them to me as sideshow freaks."

"It's a shame he can't get along with them. They would do him good," Daniel said.

"True, but let's not talk about Caspian."

"Agreed."

Daniel finished the burgers and we all sat down to eat. There were cold soft drinks from an icy galvanized tub, potato chips, and cucumber and onion salad. Daniel and I sat side-by-side. Tyler beamed at us, obviously proud to show us off to his friends. He was a truly remarkable boy. His friends were accepting. I didn't see a trace of disapproval. Caleb, the rather handsome and well-built boy in the wheel-chair grinned whenever he saw us being affectionate.

We all talked and laughed. Daniel and I forgot we weren't teens anymore. I felt like I was back in high school.

"Cake and ice cream or presents next?" Daniel asked.

"Presents!" Tyler yelled.

"Open mine first," Caleb said.

Caleb retrieved a small package, wrapped in blue and silver stripped paper from the table and handed it to Tyler. He sat there grinning as he watched Tyler rip through the paper. When

Tyler saw what it was he turned completely red and his mouth dropped open. His friends howled with laughter and Daniel and I couldn't help but laugh too. Caleb had given Tyler a box of condoms.

"I hate you," Tyler said, but Caleb was too busy laughing to pay him any attention.

Tyler's other friends weren't so cruel and gave him CDs or gift cards for mp3s. I handed Tyler the present I'd purchased for him and he eagerly ripped through the paper.

"An Xbox 350 Kinect! Thanks, Percy!"

Tyler gave me a hug. I was glad he liked his present. I didn't know much about game systems but the sales clerk at Best Buy told me the Xbox 350 Kinect was the current big thing.

Daniel presented his present last. Tyler unwrapped it and grinned.

"A laptop! This is great! My old computer is... decrepit."

"I thought you could use it for writing and college. Percy advised me to have the newest version of Word installed on it."

"Thanks, Dad!"

Tyler gave Daniel a big hug.

We moved onto cake and ice cream next. The cake was decorated with blue icing and read "Happy 18th Birthday Tyler" in large letters. Daniel put his arm around my shoulders and we watched as Tyler blew out the candles. At just that moment he felt like "our" son.

Everyone sat around talking and eating. Daniel, Tyler, and I sat at one end of the table.

"Who is the girl?" Daniel asked. "She isn't one of your usual friends, is she?"

"I invited Brittany so she could meet Caleb. They know each other from school, but Caleb had been a little down and I was hoping..."

"Playing matchmaker?" I asked.

"Yeah. Caleb's girlfriend, Ashley, dumped him after his accident and he hasn't dated since. He needs someone to show him he's still got it."

"It looks like your friend Dylan thinks he's still got it," I said, watching the young blond flirt with Caleb.

"Oh, God! I'll be right back. Dylan needs to be put on a leash but it would excite him too much."

Tyler hurried over and pulled Dylan away from Caleb so he could talk alone with Brittany. Daniel and I watched the pair for a while. They were talking and Brittany seemed smitten with Caleb.

Tyler returned after a few moments.

"Tyreece is going to keep an eye on Dylan for me. He said it was an extra birthday present. Dylan does need a keeper. I'm really sorry about what he said earlier."

"About Daniel and me needing a third?" I asked.

"Yeah."

"Actually, we've been discussing that. Would it make you uncomfortable if we invited your friend over some evening?" I asked with a straight face. "If it's a problem we could get together with Dylan at my place when Caspian is out. Dylan is one of your friends..."

Tyler's eyes widened and his mouth gaped open slightly. He looked at his dad then back at me. Daniel kept his expression neutral.

"If it's going to be too weird for you just say so," I said.

"Uh, uh... you know Dylan is fifteen, right?"

"He's a little young, but he's old enough to make his own decisions and he's obviously interested so..."

Tyler was at a loss for words for several moments. I couldn't keep the act up any longer. Despite my best efforts I cracked a smile.

"You jerk!" Tyler said.

I began laughing out loud. Daniel laughed more quietly. Tyler punched me in the shoulder.

"I thought you were serious! I couldn't believe you were serious, but... and on my birthday too!" Tyler turned to Daniel. "He's a bad influence on you, Dad."

"Hey, I didn't say anything."

"Yeah, you just played along. You guys are evil."

"What are you guys laughing about?" Jesse asked as he joined us.

"The old guys think they're funny," Tyler said. He pulled Jesse away and whispering into his ear.

"Old guys?" Daniel asked, looking at me. "When did we get to be the old guys?"

"I think somewhere in our mid-20s. I'm not sure."

Daniel leaned over and kissed me on the lips.

The party went on for another couple of hours and then began to break up. Caleb left with Brittany, so maybe Tyler's matchmaking had a chance at success. I didn't get the opportunity to speak with Caleb much, but he seemed like a very nice young man. Jesse and Tyreece left soon after Caleb. Tyler and Dylan joined us "old" guys.

"Dylan wants to go shopping. Do you mind if we go?" Tyler asked.

"Of course not," Daniel said.

"It was a great 18th birthday party, Dad. Thanks!"

Tyler hugged Daniel and then he hugged me.

"You two take off. I'll rope Percy into helping me clean up."

"It was very nice to meet you, Dylan," I said.

"It was nicer meeting you," Dylan said.

Tyler rolled his eyes and pulled his friend away.

"You've definitely got an admirer," Daniel said when Tyler and Dylan had departed.

"Where was Dylan when I was fifteen?" I asked.

"He wasn't born yet, Percy."

"Thanks for reminding me."

"What are boyfriends for?"

Daniel leaned in and kissed me. I smiled. I loved him more every day.

Tyler

I strolled around the IU Campus. It was Saturday morning and I knew the warm, sunny days of fall would soon be just a memory. The leaves were turning to their fall colors and the slightest hint of a chill was in the morning air. I loved autumn, but I was not eager for fall to edge into winter.

I was walking on the main pathway between the Memorial Union and Dunn Meadow. On my left was a small stream, stately old trees, and just beyond that the old stone buildings of IU. On my right was the green grass of Dunn Meadow. On hot days it was filled with shirtless college boys, sunning and playing Frisbee and football. That's one of the reasons I liked to walk here. The trees, grass, and stream were nearly as much of an attraction for me. I loved the little bits of nature that Indiana University had so wisely preserved.

My eyes narrowed as I spotted my least favorite person coming down the path in the opposite direction. With all of Bloomington to walk in why did *he* have to come here? It wasn't enough that he went to my school, made fun of my friends, and was intruding upon my relationship with Percy, now he was invading my space. Caspian was always in the way.

Caspian hadn't noticed me yet. Perhaps there was still time to avoid him. I could cut to the left and take the bridge over the stream, but no, I wasn't going to let him drive me away. He'd taken enough from me.

Caspian looked up and spotted me. It was too late even if I wanted to slip away. He frowned. He wasn't any happier to see me than I was to see him. He hesitated, then came on. He smirked at me when he drew close.

"Walking downtown to work your street-corner?"

"Are you incapable of being civil?" I asked.

"Hey, I have an idea. Why don't you just fuck off? Faggot."

I growled in anger and frustration.

"What's wrong, pussy boy? Do I make you angry?"

I clinched my fists. I wanted to punch him in the face. I opened my mouth, and then shut it again. I would not sink to his level.

"You have something to say to me? Do ya, queer? Or are you too afraid?"

Caspian smirked at me again. Oh, how I hated him.

"You fucking pussy."

"Just shut up, Caspian!"

"You going to make me? Ha!"

"Shut. The. Fuck. UP!" I yelled. "Why did you have to come here? You're ruining everything!"

"I'm ruining everything? Why? Because you want your dad and Percy to live together and establish some kind of happy homo home?"

I was angrier than I'd ever been in my life and all the more so because I was near tears.

"Everything was working out fine before you came along and now you're fucking everything up!"

"Awe, you *do* want your dad and Percy to live together, don't you? You want two dads. I'm *so* sorry that isn't working out for you." Caspian's voice dripped with sarcasm.

"Two dads would be a hell of a lot better than none!"

I was sorry the moment I said it. I was so angry I wasn't thinking. Even Caspian didn't deserve that. I could see the wave of pain and anger displayed on his face. Before I could even begin to say I was sorry he was on me. He slugged me in the face and then the stomach.

I snapped. I wasn't a violent person, but I'd wanted to beat the crap out of Caspian ever since he said that nasty shit about my dad in the cafeteria. I punched him right in the face and then the chest. We were all over each other then, beating the crap out of each other.

I'd never been in a real fight before and getting hit hurt. My anger and frustration allowed me to push the pain aside and focus on punching that little bastard over and over. He was a tough little shit. No matter how I pummeled him, he just kept coming at me. He jabbed me hard in the stomach and I doubled over in pain. He clocked me in the face and I went down. The next thing I knew he was sitting on my stomach with his fist pulled back, his muscled tensed, ready to punch me in the face again.

I looked up at him, blinking back tears, trying not to flinch. I wasn't going to beg for mercy, if that's what he wanted. He could just go ahead and hit me. Despite what he said I wasn't a pussy.

Caspian drew his fist back further. I struggled to get up, but he had me pinned. He glared at me with hatred and I could see tears welling in his eyes. A sob escaped from his throat and his lower lip trembled. He grabbed me by both sides of the head, shoved his lips against mine, and kissed me.

I was so stunned I didn't react. In a moment, Caspian was off me and running as fast as he could up the path. I just lay there, wondering what the hell had just happened. We were fighting. I'd clearly lost, and then... Caspian kissed me. The little homophobe kissed me *right on the lips*!

I sat up slowly.

"Oww!"

Being in a fight hurt. Now that it was over I felt bruised and... well, like I'd just had the crap beat out of me, which I had. I smiled for a moment with the knowledge that I'd given almost as good as I'd taken. My smile faded. It wasn't right to feel good about hurting someone, but still... At the moment, the ethics of fighting weren't nearly as big a consideration as what had happened after. Caspian kissed me. I wouldn't have been surprised if he kept pummeling me, or spit on me, or called me names, or demanded that I beg for mercy, but... he *kissed* me. I was totally confused.

I pulled out my cell and texted Caleb.

"U busy? Need to talk."

I waited. In only moments I received a text back.

"Not busy, about what?"

"Something serious. Can we talk in person?"

"Yes. Where?"

"Bakehouse?"

"K. B there asap."

"Thanks."

The Scholar's Inn Bakehouse was only a few blocks away, on the square. I stood up, stumbled a bit, then limped on down the path. I was beginning to wonder if I shouldn't have asked Caleb to meet me at Soma, or somewhere else closer than the Bakehouse, but the Scholar's Inn was the first place that came to mind. I could make it. It was mainly my face, chest, and stomach that hurt the worst. I wished for a couple of aspirin.

My stroll wasn't as pleasant as it had been, but then no one had kicked my ass before the first part of my walk. My head was still spinning. Caspian had kissed me! I was... shocked, bewildered, and confused. I felt like... like I was a computer and someone had entered some data totally incompatible with my system and now sparks were flying and my processor was overloading. I tried not to think about it. Maybe Caleb could help me make sense of it.

Caleb beat me to the Bakehouse. He waved at me from a booth and I limped toward him.

"What the hell happened to you?" he asked.

I rubbed the side of my face.

"Oh, crap. Do you have any aspirin?"

"Um... actually..."

Caleb dug into a pocket on the side of his wheelchair, which was sitting beside the booth and pulled out a bottle of Tylenol.

"Just a sec," I said.

I went up to the beverage area and got myself a cup of water. I returned to the booth, downed two Tylenol, and sipped some water.

"Thanks," I said, "and thanks for coming. I *really* need to talk."

"You sure you don't need a ride to a doctor's office? You look like crap."

"I feel like crap, it's a matched set, but no. I don't think anything's broken, it just hurts like hell."

"So, what happened?"

"I got into a fight with Caspian."

"Why am I not surprised?"

I told Caleb how the fight went down, giving him all the details while wondering how he'd react to my big news.

"Wow, man. I'm sorry. It does sound like you did pretty well."

"Well enough for someone who has never been in a serious fight before, I guess. When did I become violent? I've always been against violence, but lately... first I wanted to strangle Caspian and now this."

"I'd say you became violent when you met Caspian. I think that boy could piss off Jesus." Caleb laughed for a moment. "I don't think you're to blame for this fight, though. Caspian did attack you."

"Well, I don't know about that. I provoked him. I should never have said what I did. It was out of my mouth before I knew I'd said it. Once he hit me, I lost it. I was all over him. I wanted to make him pay for all the shit he's said to me. I wanted to hurt him and I enjoyed hurting him. Maybe I'm not such a good person after all."

"You're human. You're one of the nicest people I know. Caspian pushed you too far. You shouldn't have said what you did about not having a dad, but he's been piling on the crap almost since he arrived, and he did hit you."

"He also kicked my ass. How embarrassing; beat up by a freshman."

"Well, at least it wasn't at school. There were no witnesses. Caspian is a freshman, but he's also a tough little bastard. He's kind of built and he's mean as shit, so I think most guys would have trouble with him. Don't be down on yourself."

"Thanks, Caleb. Actually, the fight is only part of what I needed to talk to you about. It's not even the main thing. Um, have you ordered?"

"No."

"What would you like? I'm buying to pay you back for the ride you're going to give me after we're finished talking."

"You don't have to do that."

"I know. I want to, so what would you like?"

I was stalling and I wasn't sure why. Maybe it was because what happened almost didn't seem real. I know I didn't just imagine it. It wasn't one of my daydreams. It just didn't fit with my sense of reality.

I walked up to the counter and ordered Caleb's bacon, tomato, and brie Euro with a Coke and my three-cheese scramble that came with the Bakehouse's gourmet toast. I also ordered myself some iced tea. I took our drinks back to the table and once more sat down across from Caleb.

"So, what else did you want to talk to me about? I can't imagine anything bigger than the fight."

"Oh, it's bigger, much bigger."

"So tell me."

"Caspian kissed me."

"*What?*"

"He kissed me."

"That doesn't make any sense, Tyler. Maybe Caspian hit you in the head harder than you realized."

"It happened! I was totally shocked and I still am, but he kissed me, on the lips, with tongue!"

"When did this happen?"

"At the very end of the fight. He had me on my back, pinned. He drew his fist back and I thought he was going to punch me in the face as hard as could, but then he darted in and kissed me. It happened fast, but he kissed me hard."

"You're serious?"

"Yes, I'm serious!"

"Calm down. I believe you. I just... it's hard to believe."

"Yeah! I'm just... I don't know what to think. He's been a total bastard, and homophobic too, and now... it doesn't make *any* sense."

"Maybe it does."

"How could it possibly make sense?"

"Well, in grade school, and even in middle school, I teased girls I really liked. I didn't know how to act around them, so I teased them."

"Caspian hasn't been teasing me. He's been verbally abusive and today he attacked me."

"Yeah, but maybe it's the same thing. Think about it. Caspian is lonely. He doesn't have any friends. He's in a completely new school and town. He's gay and, for whatever reason, hates himself for it. That makes him angry and afraid. He covers up his fear and his lust by being a bully and going off on fags, if you'll excuse the term this once."

"He doesn't even know I'm gay and we don't know that he's gay either."

"He thinks you're gay. Remember the stuff he said about your dad and about you and Percy? I'm not saying he thinks that stuff is true, but in his mind it's evidence you're gay. You're also very friendly with Dylan, who is openly and obviously gay. Maybe in his mind he thinks you can't be accepting unless you are gay too. It doesn't really matter why he thinks it, only that he's thinks you are gay. He hates you, because he sees in you what he hates in himself. At the same time, he's drawn to you and he wants you. He wouldn't have kissed you if he didn't want you so he's got to be gay or at least bi. His desire for you only makes him hate you more. So, he attacked you and then kissed you. It's two sides of the same thing. It's the only thing that does make sense."

"Maybe he's just a psychopath."

"If he was, he would have just kept on beating you and you'd be lying unconscious or dead on Dunn Meadow right now."

"So what now?" I asked.

"You tell me."

I sat there in thought for a while.

"You think he actually likes me? I mean, *likes* me?"

"Yeah, I think he likes you and he can't handle it."

"That's messed up."

"Look at the world we live in, Tyler. Not everyone has an accepting dad like you. Hell, your dad isn't just accepting, he is gay. Look at the way all those religious nuts talk about gays. Look at all the nasty things those family groups say."

"Yeah, but that's all total bullshit."

"You know that, but does Caspian?"

I shrugged my shoulders.

"He's been taught to hate himself. He sees part of himself in you and he hates you for it at the same time he's drawn to you, physically and emotionally. He abuses you because he can't love you."

"I don't know if I can handle being around someone who is that messed up."

"Maybe you shouldn't. He did just kick your ass."

"True." I was lost in thought for a few moments. "He always looks so lonely. He's been through *so* much. That's why I kept trying with him, before I finally got so fed up I walked away, but..."

"Just stop. I can see where this is going. I know you too well. He's like a puppy you've found wandering the streets. You can't help but take him home."

"I am not taking him home."

"Yeah, but you are going to take him on. Maybe you don't even know it yet, but you are."

"I know it. I'm such an idiot, but I can't help it and... I kind of like him."

"Oh man, you homos are hopeless."

I laughed.

"Oww," I said.

"Tyler?"

I looked up. A cute waiter was calling my name. I held up my hand and he brought our orders to the table.

"So, you kind of like Caspian? I thought you hated him," Caleb said and then took a bite of his Euro. "Maybe Caspian isn't the only one who's messed up."

I looked up from the toast I was buttering. Caleb grinned.

"Well, that stuff he said about my dad that day at lunch... that really hit a sore spot. That wasn't the first time I'd heard crap like that. Caspian has been a major jerk and I've nearly grown to hate him, but that kiss changed everything."

"Are all homos so easy? One kiss and they're yours?"

"I didn't say I was his. I'm not in love with him. I've just fallen out of hate with him. I knew Caspian had issues, but I never suspected for a moment that one of them was being gay. It doesn't make what he's said and done okay, but I think I'm beginning to understand him."

"And you kind of like him."

"Well... he is kind of hot, if you can look past his personality. The thing is, I don't know how much of his personality is created by self-hatred. Even if he can get over that he might still be a jerk."

"He might never get it over it."

"That's where I come in."

"See, I knew you'd want to take this lost puppy home."

"Caleb, you are right about me. I've had it easy. My dad couldn't be more accepting and now I have Percy, too. I know it's not like that for a lot of guys."

"Yeah, yeah, let's just cut to the end. Despite the fact that Caspian just kicked your ass, you're taking him on as your new project."

"Yes, and stop saying he kicked my ass. I got in some good punches. I'm not the only one with a black eye."

"Yeah, but you ended up on your back with Caspian sitting on your chest."

"Okay, so he won, but we kicked each other's ass. Give me some credit for my first fight, okay?"

"Maybe you should become a professional. You could be a boxer or enter one of those tough guy competitions," Caleb said.

"Just shove your Euro in your mouth and shut up," I said.

Caleb laughed.

We ate in silence for a while. My three-cheese omelet was great, as was my toast. I loved the strawberry jam at the Bakehouse. Everything was delicious.

"You know, you might have thought of me before you decided to help Caspian deal with his homo issues," Caleb said.

"You?" I asked.

"Yeah. I know I'm going to get dragged into this. I bet all of us are. You'll probably expect us to be nice to the little shit and everything."

"I'm so sorry to inconvenience you," I said.

"I just want you to be aware of the sacrifices I make for you."

I rolled my eyes and then looked across the table at Caleb.

"Thanks for coming today when I called. The fight shook me up and I desperately needed to talk about Caspian and especially the kiss. You've *really* helped."

"Yes, it's tough being beautiful and brilliant," Caleb said.

"Yes, Jesse."

"Hey!"

I laughed.

"Do consider one thing, Tyler. You may not be able to help Caspian. He may not want your help. He lost control when he kissed you. The next time you see him the façade may be right back in place. He may even attack you again."

I nodded.

"I have to try, Caleb. He's gay, so that makes him one of my... my tribe."

"We're not sure he's gay, Tyler."

"We're pretty sure, aren't we? He did kiss me. His tongue was in my mouth."

"I will admit that is good evidence."

"He's also Percy's nephew. He's probably giving Percy so much shit for the same reason he's been such a dick to me, even more so because he knows Percy is gay. Even if I didn't care about Caspian at all, I'd still want to help him, to help Percy."

"You *really* like Percy, don't you?"

I shot Caleb a warning glance.

"I don't mean like *that*. I don't mean you want to have sex with him. I mean that he means a lot to you."

"Yeah, he does."

"You're lucky, Tyler. You've got two dads who care about you."

"Yeah, I do. So... let's talk about you for a while. Have you been spending any time with Brittany lately?"

"You invited her to your birthday party to meet me, didn't you?" Caleb accused.

"Well... I noticed her checking you out at school and we got to talking and..."

"You thought you'd butt into my personal life and set me up for a blind date."

"More or less, but mainly I just provided the opportunity for the two of you to talk. So..."

"Well... we've been talking more."

"And?"

"We are going out, tonight actually."

"Great!"

"It makes me really nervous, though."

"Caleb, she likes you. Just be yourself."

"Yeah, but... what if she wants to mess around?"

"So mess around."

"What if she wants to *really* mess around?"

"I don't think Brittany is that easy, Caleb. I don't know her well, but that's the feeling I get."

"Yeah, but what if? You're probably right. We probably won't go beyond making out, if that, but what if we go out again and again and..."

"Then you'll get some."

Caleb speared me with his eyes.

"Listen. I think Brittany is a really nice girl. If things get intimate between the two of you I think she'll understand if there are... difficulties. Worst case scenario, you can't perform, right? It will be embarrassing, but no one is going to know."

"I'll know and so will Brittany."

"She won't tell anyone, Caleb."

"How do you know that?"

"I don't, but when the time comes you'll know if you can trust her or not. Just don't act like the average straight boy and move too fast. Take the time to get to know her. Have some make-out sessions. You need some female companionship, Caleb, and it's not all about sex."

"I'm just scared, Tyler."

"Which is why you need to do this. You have to face this fear, Caleb. You have to stare it down and defeat it."

"What if it wins?"

"It won't. You used to face 300-pound linemen. You can do this."

Caleb smiled for a moment, but only for a moment.

"What if I really can't perform?"

"Then you'll know for sure and we'll find a way to deal with it. You know I'm here for you."

"Thanks, Tyler."

We spent the rest of our time eating and talking about less weighty topics. The Tylenol was kicking in and my pain lessened. My mind kept going back to Caspian, of course, but I tried to lose myself in just talking to Caleb. The fight and the kiss had shaken me up and I needed to calm and center myself. Spending time with Caleb helped me to do that.

Caleb drove me home after our early lunch. Dad was reading a magazine when I walked it. He jumped up the moment he saw me.

"I'm okay. Nothing's broken. Don't freak out on me."

Dad gingerly examined my face.

"Are you sure you're okay? Maybe I should take you to the emergency room."

"Do I look *that* bad?" I asked.

I quickly made my way to the nearest mirror and peered at my reflection.

"Wow."

Caspian had truly done a job on my face. There was a large bruised area around my left eye and another on my right cheek. My lip wasn't busted, but it was bruised. I was sure my chest and stomach had a few bruises too. I grinned. I actually looked tough.

"It's not as bad as it looks," I said, turning back to Dad.

"What happened?"

"I got into a fight... with Caspian."

"Caspian?"

"Yeah."

"I'm calling Percy."

"No! Sit!" I said, pointing to the couch. "Don't go all crazed parent on me. Everything is okay. I think I know why Caspian has been giving Percy so much crap for being gay."

"You learned this by fighting him? What brought the fight on? I know the two of you don't get along, but..."

"Dad, the actual cause doesn't matter. The underlying cause does. Caspian kissed me."

"The two of you fought and he kissed you?"

"Yeah. We fought and I was doing pretty well. It was my first fight and Caspian is tough. I got some good punches in, but then he got me on my back. I thought he was going to slug me in the face, but instead he darted in and kissed me hard on the lips. He kissed me, and then he jumped up, and ran off."

Dad looked thoughtful for a few moments.

"Caspian is gay, Dad. I was talking to Caleb and he thinks Caspian hates himself for being gay, so that makes him hate me, and Percy, and Dylan, and a lot of others."

"Are you sure you're okay, son?"

"Yeah, Dad. I'm okay. The fight and the kiss shook me up, but I'm okay. I'm tough."

"Oh, I know you're tough. I just don't like to see you get hurt."

"Just think about how cool I'm going to look at school on Monday. I'll look so bad ass."

Dad smiled.

"Listen, um, I plan to talk to Caspian about all this. I think I can help him," I said.

"Be careful, Tyler. A boy like him can be dangerous."

"I know, but he's in a lot of pain. He's lost everything and he hates himself. I can't imagine losing you and I can't imagine going through life hating myself. I can't give him his parents back, but maybe I can help him realize it's okay to be gay."

"I'm proud of you."

"For getting in a fight?" I grinned.

"Well, I'm proud of you for defending yourself, but I meant I'm proud of you for wanting to help Caspian. I'm proud of your compassion."

"Thanks, Dad."

Dad gave me a hug. I hadn't realized it, but I needed a hug just then. Caleb was right and I knew it. I was very, very lucky.

Percy

The front door slammed. Caspian came running into the house, crying. I expected him to run to his room and lock the door, but instead he ran to me, buried his face in my chest, and sobbed. I wrapped my arms around him and held him tight. I was so shocked I didn't know what to say, so I just held him. We must have stood there just like that for five minutes and then Caspian pushed me away.

"What happened?" I asked.

Caspian had a black eye and bruises on his face. His clothes were grass-stained and rumpled.

"I got into a fight with Tyler."

"Tyler? Are you okay? Is he okay?"

"Yeah, you're little... yeah, he's okay. I'm... okay."

"What happened?"

"It doesn't matter. It's over."

"Caspian..."

"I said it's over, okay?"

"Do you need some Tylenol or maybe I should take you to see a doctor."

"I can take care of myself."

"Caspian..."

I put my hand on his shoulder.

"Get off me!"

He was acting like himself again. That, more than anything else, told me he was okay. Caspian closed himself in the bathroom without so much as another word. I sank down on the couch. For just a few moments Caspian had let down his guard. He'd let me hold him while he cried. I noticed too that he hadn't called Tyler my boy toy. He almost said it, but then something stopped him. My mind was filled with questions. I was quite sure I'd get no answers from Caspian, but I might from Tyler.

I sat and thought before I acted. I knew Tyler and Caspian did not get along. I wondered what had brought things to a head.

I had a feeling there was something going on I didn't quite understand, too. I didn't know what it was, but something was out of place. Caspian was behaving out of character and it wasn't just the crying or letting me hold him. I considering calling Tyler, but what was I going to do? Invite him over to talk with Caspian within earshot. Instead, I waited.

Caspian came out of the bathroom and gazed at me for a moment.

"What just happened... you holding me and stuff... it never happened," he said, then went into his room and closed the door.

That was more like Caspian, but the lack of any accusation of sexual impropriety wasn't. Yeah, something was up.

I was itching to talk to Tyler, but I had to make sure Caspian was okay. He looked fairly beaten up, but not seriously injured. I was more concerned about his emotional state, but when wasn't I? The kid was going to turn my hair gray for sure.

I busied myself about the house, tidying up as I sometimes did on weekends. I remembered as I did so that Tyler was scheduled to come over, mow the lawn, and do some yard work for me. That made up my mind for me. I wouldn't call. I'd wait for him to show up, unless he didn't. Then, I'd call.

Caspian emerged from his room well past lunchtime. I hadn't eaten, mainly because I was far too busy trying to figure out what was going one.

"Are you hungry? Want me to take you someplace to eat?"

"I'll find something in the refrigerator."

"Are you sure? I can take you to Hardees or Arby's or wherever you want."

Caspian looked like he was preparing to unleash a verbal assault, but it never came.

"No, thanks"

Yeah, something was up. I was accustomed to being yelled at, insulted, or ignored. This was not the Caspian I knew.

Tyler arrived a couple of hours later, but didn't come in. I wasn't even aware he was around until I heard the mower running. Caspian took off soon after, most likely because he had no desire to see Tyler. I was glad for the opportunity to talk to Tyler alone.

I waited until Tyler finished mowing and then stepped out into the back yard. I was greeted with the scent of freshly mowed grass. The roses waved in a gentle breeze and their scent, too, was on the air.

"Come in, I'll get you something to drink."

Tyler didn't say anything, but looked at me a bit fearfully. He came in the back door only a few moments later. He was shirtless and sweaty. What I noticed most was the bruises that covered his chest and abdomen. He also had a black eye and a bruised cheek.

I poured him a large glass of ice tea and handed it to him.

"Thanks."

Tyler drank half of it down as sweat trickled down his chest.

"So, you and Caspian had a fight," I said, motioning to the chairs around the kitchen table. We both sat down.

"Listen, I'm sorry," Tyler said.

"For?"

"I kind of started it. Caspian threw the first punch, but I said something I really shouldn't have said. I wasn't thinking. I was just so angry."

"I have little doubt Caspian provoked you. I know you both well enough to know where to put the blame. I've wanted to strangle him myself a few times and I've seriously considered listing him on eBay."

Tyler grinned.

"Are you okay, Tyler?"

"Yeah, but something happened I want to talk to you about. At the very end of the fight... Caspian kissed me... hard... with some tongue. Then, he jumped up and bolted."

I was stunned into silence for a few moments.

"Wow," I said at last. It's all I could say. I was in a state of disbelief and yet I knew Tyler would not lie to me.

"Yeah. Wow. It was a far bigger shock than him punching me in the face. I think he's... well, I'm sure he's gay."

"Tyler, I've never asked you this before because it doesn't matter to me, but are you gay?"

Tyler nodded.

"Yeah. I am. I'm not sure why I've never told you. I guess it's like you said. I didn't think it mattered."

"It doesn't, but knowing helps me understand how you feel about my nephew kissing you. At least I know you aren't a straight boy disgusted by it."

"I... uh... kind of liked it. I kind of like Caspian... like that, I mean. I know that doesn't make sense because Caspian and I have been more enemies than friends. It kind of blindsided me, but when he kissed me... it... changed things."

"I'm more than a little surprised by that and by all of this. I knew something beyond the fight was going on. When Caspian came home he wasn't himself. He was so upset. He seemed so frightened and alone. I wanted to get him to open up about it, but he closed down on me again before I had the chance to talk to him."

"I'm sure he wasn't frightened of me. I didn't do too badly, but I have to admit he won the fight."

"I think he's frightened of a lot of things, but he's trying to hide it. He's trying to hold it all in and emotions can't be held in like that. The pressure just builds and builds until all the suppressed anger and fear and other emotions come bursting out."

"I talked to one of my friends, Caleb, about Caspian right after the fight. He thinks Caspian hates himself because he's gay and he hates me because he sees himself in me. I think that's why he gives you so much crap, too."

"You could be right or there could be a lot more involved. That may be clouding Caspian's relationship with me, but it's only one of our problems. I think he's so afraid that I don't want him around and that I'll make him leave that he won't let himself get close to me. I don't know what's going on in his head. I feel so inadequate trying to deal with him, but we weren't discussing me."

I smiled. I tended to get off topic and my problems with Caspian were never far from my mind.

"Do you think Caspian likes me or was I just a convenient outlet for suppressed sexual desire?" Tyler asked.

"Only he can answer that for sure, but maybe it's a little bit of both. I'm sorry this happened, Tyler. You did not deserve to be attacked. I'm not quite sure what to do about it. I'll talk to Daniel."

"I don't want you to do anything about it. The way I see it, this is between Caspian and me."

"I don't know, Tyler. He assaulted you."

"That's right. He assaulted *me* and I'm asking you to let me handle it."

"What does your dad have to say about this?"

"We didn't discuss it, but I'm sure Dad will let me handle it my way. He trusts me."

"I trust you too. I just don't want to see you get hurt."

"Are you worried Caspian will attack me again?"

"Yes. There is no predicting when he will explode again."

"You make him sound like a volcano."

"Caspian is very much like an active volcano. He just erupted. He's let off some of the pressure building inside him so now may be the best time to talk to him. The pressures will immediately start to build again and he will erupt once more if they aren't released. Just be careful, Tyler. I love you like a son."

Tyler smiled.

"You've never said that to me before."

"It's how I feel. It's how I've felt for quite a while now. I feel like you are my son."

"I feel like you're my dad. I have two dads."

Tyler got up and hugged me. I hugged him back. After a few moments, we stepped apart.

"You're really sweaty," I said.

"Sorry."

"It's okay." I smiled.

"Listen, do you mind if I leave the rest of the yard work for another day? I think I want to go home, get cleaned up, and then try to talk to Caspian."

"As long as you come back and finish sometime. You don't want me to have to do it, do you?"

"Oh, no. We can't have that!"

"Certainly not."

"Can you pay me for what I've done? I might need some cash."

I pulled out my wallet and handed Tyler a couple of twenties.

"I think this makes us even, for now."

"I think you're overpaying me again, but thanks!"

"Now get your sweaty body out of here and go get cleaned up."

Tyler hugged me again, this time I think just for meanness. At least that's the impression I got from his mischievous grin. He departed and I carried the empty glasses into the kitchen and put them in the dishwasher.

Today had certainly been eventful. Caspian had actually hugged me and cried, if only for a few short minutes. He'd fought with Tyler and kissed him. Tyler had admitted he *liked* Caspian. All of it, with the exception of Caspian getting in a fight, completely blindsided me. I'd make a lousy psychic, that was for sure.

Was this the first glimmer of hope that things might someday be okay or was it the first step down into a hellish abyss? Only time would tell.

Tyler

I walked home with my shirt hanging in my belt-loop. It wasn't particularly hot, but I was still sweaty. I lifted my arm and sniffed my pit. Phew! Maybe I shouldn't have hugged Percy before I left. Then again... An evil grin appeared on my face.

I'd talked to Caleb, Dad, and Percy about Caspian. Now, it was time for me to make the decisions. At this time yesterday I would never have dreamed I'd be thinking of what I was thinking now. I'd gone from debating whether or not I'd bother to slow down if Caspian stepped in front of my moving car to wanting to help him. I especially would never have dreamed I'd be thinking these thoughts so soon after a fight with Caspian. Caleb was right about me. His words still echoed in my mind: "He's like a puppy you've found wandering the streets. You can't help but take him home." I was sure Caspian wouldn't appreciate the analogy, but it was true. I couldn't just walk away from Caspian. He needed someone and whether as a friend or something more, than someone was me.

When I made it home I walked into the bathroom, stripped, and stepped into the shower. The cool water was refreshing on my hot skin. My mind wandered to Caspian's kiss. It had been brief, but passionate, as if years of pent up lust had burst forth for only a moment. Even through the pain, it had aroused me. My penis was beginning to stir between my legs. Maybe I did need to get laid. If one five second kiss could turn me on so much I definitely needed some.

I put that thought out of my mind. When I talked to Caspian it would be about sexual orientation, but not about sex and definitely not about his sexual interest in me, or vice-versa. I had to avoid those topics completely. Besides, the goal was to help Caspian deal with what was troubling him. Anything else had to come later, if ever.

I washed, then rinsed off, and climbed out of the shower. I dried off, wrapped the towel around my waist, and then walked to my room. I opened my closet and thought about what to wear. As I looked through my clothes I realized I was putting way too much thought into what I'd wear to talk with Caspian. Then again, I often spent too much time picking out clothes. Maybe it was a gay trait or maybe Jesse was rubbing off on me.

I settled on a purple polo shirt and cargo shorts. I looked good in that outfit without looking like I was trying to appear too sexy. I decided against wearing my gold chain and put on just a little cologne. This wasn't a date. I almost laughed at myself. I'd never been on a date. How pathetic.

I pulled off my towel, pulled on some purple Areopostale boxer-briefs and then dressed in the clothes I'd selected. I looked in the mirror. I didn't look half-bad, except for the bruises and black eye. I worked with my hair for a couple of minutes, but didn't allow myself to linger. I did not want to become another Jesse.

Chances were I wouldn't be able to find Caspian, but it was worth a shot. I sure couldn't talk to him at school. I had to find a way to talk with him away from everyone else. I tried to think of where he might be, but I realized that I knew very little about him. If I was searching for Jesse, I'd start at College Mall because he loved to shop and be seen. If I was looking for Dylan I'd go wherever there were boys since Dylan was boy-crazy. Caspian dressed like a Goth, but that didn't tell me much. I didn't know if he was into Goth-culture or just like to dress that way. I didn't think he was into sports, so there was probably little use in checking out the ball courts over by Briscoe dorm. It was getting too cool for swimming, so he probably wouldn't be hanging out at the IU outdoor pool on 17th and Fee Lane, also near Briscoe. I knew very little about Caspian when I thought about it, but then he hadn't allowed me to get to know him. He didn't let anyone get close.

I checked out Miller-Showers Park, located between North Walnut and College Avenues just above 17th Street. It was close to Percy's house and I thought Caspian might go there to walk and think. The park was basically a long, narrow walking track with a stream and grassy area in the middle. At the southern end was a man-made waterfall and pond that drained into yet another pond and then another before flowing into the stream. It was a pleasant place to walk. I passed a cute college boy walking a Yorkie, an older lady walking a Shih Tzu, two middle-age couples walking, and two sexy college boys running together. There was no sign of Caspian anywhere.

I headed for Percy's house, hoping that Caspian had returned. If he wasn't there maybe I could get his cell number from Percy. I should have probably thought of that before.

Calling or texting would have been a much easier way to find Caspian than wandering around hoping for a chance encounter. Then again, I'd be a lot easier to ignore over the phone. I had no idea what kind of reception I'd get when I tried to talk to Caspian.

I walked to Percy's house and knocked on the frosted glass of the antique front door.

"Hey, Tyler. Come in," Percy said. "Hmm, you smell better than you did an hour ago."

"Funny, but also true. Is Caspian home?"

"Yeah, he's in his room. He came back not five minutes ago."

"What kind of mood is he in?"

"I have no idea. I didn't see him. I only heard him come in. He didn't slam any doors, so that's a good sign."

"I guess I'll try my luck."

I walked toward Caspian's door and Percy headed for the kitchen. I felt a little safer with Percy in the house. It's not that I thought Caspian would jump me, exactly, but who knew what that kid might do? I knocked on his door.

"What?" Caspian asked, rudely.

"It's Tyler. Can I come in?"

There was no answer, but a few moments later the door opened. Caspian had a prominent shiner and a couple more bruises on his face. He looked every bit as bad as me.

"Can I come in?" I repeated.

Caspian stepped back. I entered and he closed the door behind me. Caspian's bedroom didn't look like him. It looked like Percy. There was an antique bed and dresser and antique pictures on the walls.

"This doesn't look like your style," I said, looking around.

"It's not. Percy said he'd buy me new furniture, but... whatever."

"Listen, we need to talk..."

"So talk," Caspian said.

"You're gay, aren't you?" I said.

133

I realized cutting right to the heart of things might be a huge mistake, but since I had no idea what to say I started there. Caspian didn't answer. He just looked away from me.

"It's okay if you are," I said, putting my hand on his shoulder.

"Don't touch me!" Caspian jerked away from me and sat down on his bed.

"Okay. I won't."

"Kissing you was a mistake, okay? It just happened. I'm not a fag."

"Wow, I never thought you'd be a coward."

"What did you say to me?" Caspian asked, jumping up, his fists clinched.

"I thought you'd have the balls to admit what you are. Guys don't kiss other guys without reason. It didn't just happen. If you slip and fall down, it just happens. If you're walking and texting and walk into a tree, it just happens. If you're holding another guy down and then you kiss him, it didn't just happen. Maybe you didn't mean for it to happen, but at least part of you wanted to do it."

"I don't want to be that!" Caspian shouted.

"I didn't especially want to be gay either. I don't remember ever thinking, "Hey, I'd love to be a homo," but I am one."

"I knew you were one. You're not obvious like that Dylan kid, but I knew you were a homo almost from the first day."

"It's okay to be gay, Caspian. Look at your uncle. He's totally cool and he's gay."

"Cool my ass."

"Why do you work so hard to dislike him? Percy is a great guy. He's been cool to me since the day I met him. He has helped me in so many ways and he's been there when I needed him."

"Are you his boy toy?"

Caspian's eyes bored into me. His gaze was angry, accusing, and resentful.

"No, Caspian. It's not like that between us."

"I think you're lying to me."

"Why would I lie to you about it, Caspian? It's not like you wouldn't find out. If I was Percy's boy toy you'd catch us at it sooner or later so there would be no point in lying about it."

"You think he's hot, though, don't you?"

"Well, yeah, but I think lots of guys are hot. Percy is dating my dad. Percy is attractive, but I don't think about him like that."

"Ever?"

"Almost never."

"I bet he's hot for you."

"He finds me attractive. I'm not stupid. He's never made a move on me, though, and I know he won't. It's not like that between us. It wouldn't be like that even if he wasn't dating my dad. Two gay guys can have a relationship that doesn't involve sex."

"You're *really* not his boy toy?"

"What did I just say? No. I am not Percy's boy toy."

"He wants me."

"What makes you think that?"

"I can just tell."

"That's not like Percy. Has he tried anything with you, *ever*?"

"No, but... he's just waiting his chance."

"That is just fucking stupid, Caspian."

"Don't call me stupid, asshole!"

"I didn't say you were stupid, I said you were acting stupid. Everyone acts stupid sometimes. Percy isn't "waiting his chance." He's not into you like that. Do you really think he'd wait this long to try something if he was after you? I know Percy well enough to know he would *never* do something like that. He'd never take advantage of anyone. He loves you, Caspian."

"He doesn't love me! No one loves me!"

"He cares about you at least. I know he cares about you. He worries about you too much not to care about you. He's always talking to Dad about how worried he is about you and how he wants to help you but doesn't know how. He's talked to me about you too. He cares about you, Caspian, whether you want to believe it or not. He's not the only one who cares either. I'm sure your parents loved you."

"Don't talk to me about my parents!"

"Okay, I'm sorry and I'm sorry for what I said in Dunn Meadow about you not having a dad. I was angry and I spoke without thinking. I'm sorry I said it and I'm sorry I hurt you."

Caspian got quiet. I didn't know what to say so silence lingered in the room. Neither of us said anything for a good five minutes. I could tell Caspian wanted to say something, but couldn't make himself.

"How do you..." Caspian began at last, but then halted. He paused for a moment. "How do you keep from hating yourself?"

"Hating myself because I'm gay?"

"Yes."

"I don't hate myself for being gay. Why should I?"

"How can you even ask that?"

"Because there is no reason I should hate myself for being gay."

"Everybody hates faggots and it's wrong."

"Some narrow-minded, ignorant people hate gays. No matter who or what you are, someone out there will hate you for it. It's not wrong."

"The Bible says it is."

"Bull shit."

"It does!"

"No, it doesn't and even if it did it also says anyone who works on a Sunday should be stoned to death. Do you see that happening? It says eating shellfish is an abomination, but you don't see anyone picketing Red Lobster, do you? It also says it is forbidden to get your hair cut, but I don't see anyone being executed for stopping by Great Clips."

"It doesn't say that stuff."

"Oh yes it does! Look it up. It's all in there and plenty more."

"Well, all those groups are always saying how the country will be destroyed if gays are allowed to marry."

"Caspian, I want to ask you something, but please don't blow up because it involves your parents."

Caspian began to protest, but I cut him off.

"You don't have to talk about them. I just want to know something. Were your parents upset because you're gay? Did they tell you it's wrong?"

Caspian's lip trembled for a moment. He stared hard into the distance and blinked quickly to keep his tears at bay.

"They didn't know, but they would have hated me for it."

"Why?"

Caspian looked at me as if I'd just asked the stupidest question ever.

"There has to be a reason you think that."

"I don't have to tell you anything."

"No, you don't, but aren't you tired of holding everything in? Aren't you tired of not being able to talk to anyone about what's bothering you? I've been watching you, Caspian. You don't have any friends. I'm not saying that to hurt you, but it's true. I'll be honest. Until earlier today I really didn't give a damn whether you had friends or not. I know you don't communicate with Percy and you don't have anyone else. You don't have to tell me anything, but don't you think you'd feel better if you did?"

"Why do you care? Huh? Why would you care?"

"I'll be blunt. You've been a jerk and an asshole from day one. You insulted my friends, you insulted me, and you said things about my dad that made me so mad I wanted to kill you. For a while the only reason I would have cared if you were hit by a truck is that it would have hurt Percy. If you weren't Percy's nephew I'd have written you off the first day. Despite the way you've been a jerk, I do care because I know you're in pain. You wouldn't be such an asshole if something wasn't eating you up inside. I care because I don't want to see you hurting and I don't want to see Percy hurting because he's so worried about you. That and... I kind of like you, just a little."

Caspian gazed at me. He didn't say anything for a few moments.

"My parents would have hated me because they would have been ashamed to have a gay son."

"Did they tell you that?"

"Of course not."

"Did they look down on Percy because he's gay?"

"No, Dad was always telling people about his little brother, the famous writer."

"Then why would you think they would hate you, Caspian?"

"I don't have to tell you that the worst thing you can be called is a faggot. There are those family groups that are always saying how bad it is. There are all those people donating money to fight gay marriage. Everybody hates fags. How could my parents not have hated me had they known?"

"Wow, you really are stupid," I said, my voice dripping with scorn.

Caspian glared at me.

"You know, even though I thought you were a jerk, the one thing I liked about you is that you did what you wanted no matter what anyone else thought. You didn't worry about being popular. You didn't worry about whether or not you pissed anyone off. Percy said you were highly intelligent and I believed him. I figured you had to be smart to be that sure of yourself, but you really think your parents would have hated you just because some stupid fucks say nasty things about gays? Can't you think for yourself, Caspian? Can't you see that people make up all this nasty shit about gays just so they can justify their own bigotry? Seriously, do you *really* think the Republicans are concerned about gay marriage? Can you really not see they're using all those stupid fucks just so they can grab power? I can go on, Caspian. Can't you see any of this?"

Caspian's face was red and his expression sullen, but he didn't speak.

"That's all you've got?" I asked. "That's the only reason you think your parents would have hated you if they'd known? If they went off on gays, then you'd have something. If they'd said they would rather for you to be dead than gay, then you'd have a reason to think what you do. If they had talked trash about Percy or merely hidden the fact they were related then you'd have some evidence. You've got nothing, Caspian. Your argument about your parents not loving you if they would have known you are gay doesn't have anything to back it up. It's just like your reasons for insisting that Percy plans to molest you. None of it makes any sense."

Caspian just sat there. He didn't say anything. The silence became oppressive.

"Shouldn't you be jumping up and kicking my ass for saying all this shit to you? Shouldn't you at least be screaming obscenities at me?" I asked.

"It's my afternoon off," Caspian said quietly.

I turned my head in his direction and smiled, then laughed. Caspian laughed too. It was the first time I'd ever heard him saying something funny. His laughter lasted only a few moments. All too soon, his expression was painfully sad.

"I don't think your parents would have hated you if they'd known you were gay, Caspian. I don't know for sure, but I think they would still have loved you. I have a feeling it wouldn't have made any difference to them at all. They would still have loved you."

"Don't say that," Caspian said quietly.

"Why not?"

Caspian bit his lip for a moment before answering. I could tell he was struggling to get himself under control.

"Because... because if I think they would have hated me then it's not so hard dealing with the fact that they're gone!"

Tears streamed down Caspian's cheeks. I moved to hug him, but he pulled away.

"Don't touch me!"

"Okay. Okay. I won't."

Caspian wiped his tears away.

"Maybe I'm not gay anyway."

"Caspian..."

"I've never done anything with a guy! What happened today... I was just curious is all."

"Caspian, come on..."

"You just want me to be gay! You, Percy, Dylan... all you homos want me to be gay so you can have me!"

"You are infuriating," I said. "You spout all this stupid, stupid shit and pretend it makes sense."

"Stop calling me stupid!"

"We've already covered this, Caspian."

"Just leave me alone, okay?"

"If you ever want to talk..."

"I don't want to talk! I shouldn't have told you any of this! Now you'll go blab it to the whole school! Just leave me the fuck alone!"

So much for making progress with Caspian...

"I won't tell anyone what you've said."

"Yeah, right."

"I won't."

"Just go."

I hesitated for a moment, but Caspian had turned away from me and was staring at the wall so I quietly left. I walked into Percy's office, where he was typing away at his computer.

"Are you okay?" he asked when he noticed me. "I heard some yelling."

"I'm okay. I thought I was getting somewhere with Caspian for a few minutes there. He was opening up and actually talking to me, but then he closed down and started saying stupid shit again. He makes these pronouncements that are backed up by nothing."

"He's very good at that."

"I just want to punch him in the face sometimes."

"I believe you already did."

I smiled.

"I also believe you told me you like him."

"I do. I guess that makes *me* stupid too. I have no idea why I like him."

"It's been my experience that there doesn't need to be a reason for liking someone—for disliking them, yes, but for liking them, no. That said, there are reasons you like him, you just can't bring them to mind. You know the reasons, but you don't."

"You mean... like when I don't think I know the answer to a question on a test, but I actually do know it? I pick an answer and it's right and I wasn't just lucky?"

"Yes. The mind is a tricky thing. Sometimes, we know something even though it appears we don't. There is something behind your feelings and someday you'll figure it out."

"Good, I don't want to be like Caspian. He was giving me his reasons for something he believes and it was just load of crap. He knows it too; he just doesn't want to stop believing."

I wanted to tell Percy that Caspian was trying hard to believe his parents would have hated him if they'd known he was gay, but that seemed like an invasion of Caspian's privacy. He expected me to betray his secrets, but I wouldn't, not even to Percy.

"Thanks for trying, especially after..."

Percy indicated my bruised and battered face.

"I didn't do much."

"You said he started to open up. He's *never* done that before. That's huge, Tyler. We can't expect everything to be okay in an instant."

"He's such a dick, but I still feel so bad for him. I think he is such a dick because he's afraid."

"Maybe he'll act like less of a jerk when he feels a little more secure. I've been trying to make him feel more secure, at least here at home, but it's an uphill battle. I've tried to help him, but he doesn't want to be helped, not yet. That may be changing. I expected you to come rushing back out of his room almost as soon as you went in."

"That makes two of us. I figured he'd just start screaming at me or punching me."

141

"You're very courageous, Tyler. The fact that you were in there talking to him for several minutes is a huge sign of progress."

"Yeah, but he told me to get out in the end."

"That doesn't matter. He still talked to you and he knows you're willing to talk. This is a turning point, Tyler."

"You really think so?"

"I know so. That doesn't mean that everything is going to be fine from now on, but it's a beginning."

I smiled. Percy always could make me feel good about myself.

"I think I'm going to head out. I need to walk and think."

"Walks are very good for thinking. I hope to see you again soon, Tyler.

"Thanks, Percy."

We hugged. I wished Caspian could trust Percy the way I did. Maybe someday; Percy seemed to think there was hope and he was usually right about such things.

I walked toward the stadium, although it didn't matter where I was walking. I just needed to think. I had a lot more pieces to the puzzle that was Caspian, but I was far from having him figured out. He held some obvious contradictions in his mind. He'd admitted to me that believing his parents would have hated him if they'd known he was gay made losing them hurt a little less. I was almost certain he knew they wouldn't have hated him and yet he went on lying to himself. He denied being gay at the same time he talked about his homosexuality as if it was an accepted fact. He went off on Dylan for being gay at the same time he was probably lusting after guys. Caspian was a walking contradiction.

I was convinced that Caspian was gay. He was also attracted to me. I wasn't the hottest guy around, but I did have some attractive attributes. He needed someone to confide in or he wouldn't have opened up to me like he did. True, he did shut back down, but he'd told me deeply personal things before doing so. Like Percy said, I couldn't expect everything to instantly be okay. Caspian had been a big jerk about most things, but how much of that was just a defense against being hurt? I didn't think for a moment that Caspian was a sweet boy at heart. Even if he lowered all his defenses I think he'd still be a jerk sometimes. I didn't think he was the total asshole he appeared to be, either. The truth was somewhere in the middle.

I guess what I really needed to think about was how I felt about Caspian. I did kind of like him. I had to consider the possibility that this newfound emotion was inspired by lust and thoughts of sexual activity. The kiss we shared was as brief as it was sudden, but it did turn me on. I had to adjust myself before I could stand up. The thought of doing more was appealing. Was that why I suddenly liked Caspian when I'd despised him such a short time before? I didn't like him a lot, just a little. It was as if I had a crush on him. Was it just because he was the first guy who had shown any sexual interest in me in a long time? Dylan had shown interest and it didn't make me develop a crush on him. There were other guys I *thought* might be interested, but they didn't count. I wasn't sure about any of them and none of them had kissed me. That was for sure!

I wanted to be honest with myself. I didn't want to lie to myself the way Caspian lied to himself. Watching him live with contradictions made me wonder if I did the same without admitting it to myself. I didn't think I did, but how could I be sure? Then again, I think Caspian knew he was lying to himself. I didn't detect any lies when I searched my feelings. I wasn't even sure how I really felt about Caspian. I did want to get along with him because he was Percy's nephew, but beyond that I was uncertain. I liked him, but at the same time I found him frustrating and maddening. I kind of wanted to kiss him again, but I also wanted to run away from him screaming. I recognized and accepted both those desires. Why was life never easy? Why couldn't I just like or dislike Caspian? Why did it have to be both at the same time?

I walked on, trying to just enjoy the beautiful day. I had a feeling I could analyze my feelings for Caspian until I drove myself insane and still not come up with any answers. Maybe it was because I was trying to think of Caspian as a story that was finished when obviously his was a tale that was to be continued. I guess I just had to wait and see what happened next.

Percy

Caspian came into the kitchen late in the evening and stood in the doorway with his thumbs in his pockets.

"So, are you going to yell at me, or what?" he asked.

"For?"

"The fight."

"Tyler was here. You guys worked it out, right?"

"More or less."

"Then it's over."

"That's it?"

"I don't approve of fighting and don't believe it's the way to solve problems, but this was something between Tyler and you. If you've worked it out then it's none of my business."

I could almost swear Caspian was disappointed he wouldn't get to yell or argue.

"Well, if you think we're going to be buddies you can forget it. I still think he's a pussy."

"He did a pretty good job on your face for a pussy."

"He's older than me."

"And you're stronger than him."

"You like him better than me, don't you?"

"I don't know you well enough to answer that question. I like you both, but you haven't given me the chance to get to know you."

I was waiting for an accusation of some sexually predatory intent on my part, but it didn't come.

"Listen, the furniture in my room..."

"Sucks?"

Caspian almost smiled for a moment.

"No, but I could use a computer desk."

"And a computer," I said.

"Yeah."

"Let's go shopping," I said.

Caspian eyed me with suspicion.

"So... what am I going to have to do in exchange?"

Here it comes, I thought.

"The same thing you had to do for your cell phone. Nothing. This is your home. You don't have to pay for anything, Caspian. Now, if you'd like to take out the garbage sometime or do a little vacuuming, I wouldn't object, but you're my nephew, not my employee."

Caspian didn't answer.

"Let's go check out computers first. We'll see what Best Buy has to offer," I said.

We hopped in the roadster and took 17th Street to the Bypass. It was the quickest route to the east side, although the Bypass was extremely crowded at certain times of the day. Caspian seemed to leave his anger and suspicions behind as we rode in the Shay. The wind made it difficult to talk, so we didn't try. In less than ten minutes we'd arrived and were walking in the door at Best Buy.

A college-boy-salesman asked if he could assist us as we browsed the computers.

"I want a laptop. Which one is good for games and music?" Caspian asked.

My attention wavered as Billy, our salesman, rattled off the specs and features of a few laptops. I mainly used my computer as a word-processor, so I wasn't overly worried about speed, graphics abilities, and storage.

"Can I get this one?" Caspian asked after a few minutes.

"You can get any one you want," I said.

"Wow, you are lucky. I wish my dad was that generous," Billy said.

I tensed as I waited for Caspian's reply. I hoped he didn't explode on the salesman.

"He's my uncle," Caspian said, without anger.

"Wow, you are definitely a lucky guy then."

"We need Microsoft Office too," I said. "I'm sure it will be useful for schoolwork."

Billy grabbed up a card from the shelf we could use to activate the program already on the computer.

"Anything else?" he asked.

"A mouse, mouse pad, surge-protector, and some speakers would be good," I said.

"Yeah, laptop speakers aren't bad, but you need a subwoofer for the best sound," Billy said.

I followed along behind as Billy led Caspian around and they picked out the needed accessories.

We carried everything up to the cash register and I pulled out my American Express. We locked everything in the rumble-seat and headed the short distance to Staples. There, I stood back while Caspian picked out a computer desk and a nice executive chair. I arranged for the pieces to be assembled and delivered. I was far too smart to fall for the "assembles in only a few minutes" line.

"I'm starving. How about you?" I asked.

"Yeah."

"You like Italian?"

Caspian nodded.

"I'll take you to Bucceto's. It's in the little strip of stores on the other side of Best Buy. It's like the Olive Garden, except local and even better."

I parked the roadster once again and Caspian and I walked into Bucceto's. It was a pleasant little restaurant with a comfortable, modern ambiance and an intimate feel. I gazed at Caspian as we were led to a booth. Even with his black leather jacket and spiked collar and wrist-bands I experienced a warm-fuzzy feeling as I looked at him. He was my nephew and the closest I'd ever come to having a son, unless some day Daniel and I moved in together and I adopted Tyler. Regardless, I was feeling very paternal at the moment. I enjoyed taking Caspian out. Like Tyler, he filled up an empty space in my life. Despite all the problems, I was glad he'd come to live with me. It was a little like my first summer as a camp counselor all those years ago. The first night after my boys arrived I wanted nothing more than to leave. Soon enough, however, I wanted to stay forever.

Don't worry, Anthony, I'll take good care of him, I silently thought to my brother.

Our waiter, James, arrived and took our drink orders. We browsed the menus as we waited. When James returned with Caspian's Coke and my Coke Zero Caspian ordered the shrimp Santa Cruz, which the menu described as "sweet, spicy, smoky, and buttery, served with angel hair." I ordered fettuccine Alfredo.

James returned with salads and garlic bread just a few minutes later and we began eating. I enjoyed having a dinner companion. There was a time when I always ate alone. Now, I had Daniel, Tyler, and Caspian. I could rearrange my schedule with relative ease, but everyone else was so busy. In my dreams, all four of us ate together as a family, but I didn't know if that dream would ever come to be.

"How is school going?" I asked.

"Fine."

"Have you met anyone you like?"

"What's that supposed to mean?" Caspian asked, suspiciously.

"I mean have you met anyone you like to spend time with; have you made any friends?"

"It's none of your business and I know what this is really about."

"I'm not sure I do so enlighten me."

"Tyler told you about what happened at the end of our fight, didn't he?"

"Yes, he did. He was trying to figure things out. We talk about a lot of things."

"I bet you've been fantasizing about it."

"About *it*?"

"You know what I mean. You're just trying to make me say it."

"I'll say it then, you're accusing me of fantasizing about the kiss." Caspian turned ever so slightly red. "I'm not fantasizing about it. I have better things to do with my time. I am concerned about the two of you. I don't want to see either of you get hurt."

"Yeah, right! I bet you just loved finding out I'd kissed another boy."

"I was surprised. You've been acting like a bad-ass since the day you arrived. You had me fooled; I thought you really were a bad-ass."

"What's that supposed to mean?"

"It means I never thought you'd be a coward."

"What?" Caspian asked, his tone indignant.

"You've been hiding behind a mask this whole time. I thought you were a homophobe, but you were really just too scared to admit you're gay."

"I wasn't scared!"

"Then why did you hide it?"

"Because I didn't want you pawing me."

I didn't say a word. I just gazed at Caspian and held his eyes with my own. The silence grew oppressive.

"Okay, because it was none of your business!"

"Now that is a reasonable answer. You're right. It's none of my business. You didn't have to pretend to be just the opposite, though, Caspian. You don't have to tell me everything. I don't intend to tell you everything either. We do need to be honest with each other. I can't help you if you're not honest with me."

"I don't need your help."

"Everyone needs help sometimes, Caspian."

My nephew looked sullen. It was a look he wore often.

"If you ever need to talk... about dealing with being gay, or anything else, I'm here."

"Can we *not* talk about this?" Caspian asked, looking around to see if anyone could hear us.

"We don't have to talk about it. I just know that it can be difficult, especially when you're young."

Caspian glared at me.

"Okay, I'll shut up," I said.

Our food arrived soon. Caspian's shrimp Santa Cruz looked delicious, but I was more than content with my fettuccine Alfredo. We ate without talking. Caspian seemed to enjoy the ambiance of Bucceto's. I was amused by some of the looks the older patrons gave Caspian. He did present a frightening appearance with his Goth-look and angry visage. I had a good feel for the boy behind the collar, wristbands, and black eyeliner. He was scared, lonely, and insecure. On top of that, he was also gay. I had not suspected that, but then there was so much going on with Caspian I hadn't given his sexual orientation any thought. I did believe that some of the biggest homophobes were gay themselves and couldn't deal with it. I didn't think that Caspian's sexual orientation was the root of his problems. It was just one small part of something larger. My nephew was a complex puzzle to be sure. At least he wasn't denying he was gay.

"Ready to go back?" I asked when we'd finished. "Your furniture will be delivered in about an hour. I'm sure you'll want some time to rearrange your room first."

"Yeah."

I paid the check and we headed back out to the roadster. We drove the short distance home and then I helped Caspian carry his purchases inside.

I left Caspian to himself. I didn't know much about raising kids, but I did know they wanted and needed their space. I was lucky Caspian was willing to eat out with me. I made myself some hot apricot tea and lost myself in a Star Trek novel. I grinned for a moment, thinking of how both Daniel and Tyler liked to tease me about what they called my "Star Trek obsession." They exaggerated... mostly.

"Hey, um, can you help me for a sec?"

I looked up from my book. I'd been on the Enterprise for half a chapter and hadn't even heard Caspian approach. I put a marker in my book and followed him to his room.

"I need to move this. I want to put my computer desk here."

I grabbed one end of the Victorian dresser and helped Caspian move it a few feet out of the way.

"I like the way you've arranged the room," I said. "Anything else?"

"No. Thanks."

"You're welcome."

Maybe it wasn't much, but even the slight courtesy of saying "thanks" marked progress for Caspian. Any improvement in our relationship was welcome.

My reading was interrupted again when Staples delivered Caspian's desk and chair. I risked a peek in Caspian's room when the van had departed. He was busy setting up his new computer. He seemed content, so I left him alone. I smiled. Despite everything, I liked having Caspian in the house. Maybe I could handle this parenting thing after all.

Tyler

"Whoa, what happened to you?" Dylan asked as he spotted me in the hallway before first period.

"Caspian and I had a little fight."

"It looks like he kicked your ass."

"Hey, his face looks just as bad as mine!"

"I'm just messing with you, dude. You look tough now. Wanna make out?"

"Down boy."

Dylan curled his fingers and put his hands in front of his chest to imitate paws and panted with his tongue hanging out.

"I guess we know what you were in your last life," I said.

"Hey!"

"Relax. I love dogs."

"Wanna do it doggy-style?"

"Go away, Dylan. I heard Brice Parker showers in the gym before school. Go check it out."

Dylan jerked his head up. He was so suddenly alert I nearly laughed out loud. He took off like a shot. Dylan was going to be very difficult to handle when he found out I was gay. I didn't want him to know for that very reason. It was funny in a way. The guy I most wanted to hide my sexual orientation from was gay himself.

I doubted Caspian would spread the word about me. He couldn't very well without outing himself. I wasn't too worried about people finding out. I didn't think I'd be harassed much, probably no more than I already was for having a gay dad, and only a very few gave me any crap for it. It would give those few extra ammunition. Those that accused me of sleeping with my dad would see my gayness as proof. That was what worried me. Why did there have to be so many idiots in the world?

Mostly, I didn't want my classmates to know I was gay because I didn't like others getting into my business. I liked to keep a low profile and fly below the radar. Some of my classmates would do just about anything to be the topic of the rumor mill, but I just wanted to live my life without everyone scrutinizing every little detail.

Unfortunately, my weekend fight put me at the top of the day's headlines. I first realized it when I started getting a lot of looks in the hallways. I figured it was because of my black-eye and bruised face, but Tyreece stopped me between second and third periods.

"I heard you tangled with the punk. I knew you couldn't control yourself without me around," Tyreece said.

"Hey, he attacked me."

"Sure he did."

I glared at Tyreece for a moment.

"I'm just kidding, man. Wow, Tyler Keegan in a fight. This does not happen every day."

"I'm glad you're excited about it."

"So, did you enjoy punching him in the face?"

"I'm ashamed to admit it, but yeah, although I wasn't thinking about it much at the time."

"Ha, ha! I knew it! I have to go, but I'll see you at lunch, slugger."

I wondered what Tyreece would have thought if he knew the whole story. I didn't plan on telling him and I sure wasn't telling Dylan. If Dylan knew he'd become a real pain in the ass. He'd be all over Caspian, too, and Caspian would kick his butt for sure. I'd already told Caleb and he was the only classmate that I intended to have that bit of information. The rest would have to content themselves with the fight alone.

I expected Caspian to glare at me when our paths crossed, but the look he gave me was more questioning, as if he was trying to figure me out. That look made me wonder what was going on his head. It also made me wonder what was going on in mine. I'd been excited to meet Percy's nephew. Then, I'd been disappointed that he was a little jerk. Soon, I'd grown to despise him. Finally, after a fist-fight of all things, I'd come to kind of like him and even have a small crush on him. How messed up was that?

The shock of my life came at lunch-time. Well, the shock of my life was Caspian kissing me, with tongue, at the end of our fight, but what happened in the cafeteria ran a close second. I had just sat down with my corn dog, applesauce, salad, and chocolate-chip cookie when Caspian walked up and sat down right across from me.

"Hey," he said, as if he'd been sitting there all along and had never called my friends a freak show.

"Hi," I said, uncertainly.

"You're back!" Dylan said and hugged Caspian.

Caspian had dared to sit next to Dylan and was now paying the price.

"Touch me again and I will kill you," Caspian said.

Now *that* sounded more like the Caspian I knew.

Caleb was watching the whole scene with great interest. I shot him a warning glance, but I knew he'd keep his mouth shut about the kiss.

"So, do we get a round two?" Tyrone asked with a mischievous grin.

"I think one round was enough for me. What about you, Tyler?" Caspian asked.

"Huh? Oh, yeah. One was definitely enough."

I was waiting for Caspian to make some smart-ass comment and to tell everyone how he had me down on my back, but he mentioned neither. I looked at him, confused. He smiled mischievously and it made me nervous.

Caspian didn't talk much during lunch, but he wasn't hostile. Dylan didn't dare to touch him again, but he did plenty of looking. Mostly, Caleb and Jesse carried the conversation. I was pleased to hear Caleb talking to others about his plans for someday coaching high school football. He even announced he was going back to managing the team and had talked to the coach about some on-the-job training. Caleb looked at me and grinned. I felt very good about myself just then. Caleb would have eventually figured out he didn't have to give up football because he was stuck in a wheel-chair, but I knew I'd sped up the process considerably. I wondered how he was getting along with Brittany. I planned to ask him soon.

I kept wondering about Caspian the rest of the day. What was up with him? He confused the heck out of me. Curiosity was eating me up, so I stalked him at the end of school. I walked right up to his locker and just stood there until he looked at me.

"Let's go somewhere and talk," I said.

We shouldered our backpacks and walked outside and then toward the football field.

"What's up with you?" I said. "I thought you hated my friends. You called them a freak-show."

"Well, they are kind of weird," Caspian said.

"Okay, true. So am I, but..."

"I mean... come on... Dylan? He's such a flamer he could spontaneously combust."

"So? He's being who he is and I think everyone should be himself or herself. I admire his courage."

"Courage?"

"Don't you think it takes courage for him to come to school knowing he's going to be put down?"

"Yeah, I guess, although I've never seen anyone give him much shit."

"There are a few guys who look out for Dylan—big guys."

"So the rumors I've heard are true?"

"You mean that Dylan does some favors and in return those guys watch out for him?"

"Tyler, just say it. Dylan sucks dick and the guys he blows keep him from getting beat up."

"Well, rumors get blown way out of proportion. I have little doubt that Dylan provides some services..."

"Sucks dick."

"Why do you have to be vulgar?"

"What's vulgar about it? I'm just saying exactly what he does instead of just implying it."

"Anyway, I'm sure Dylan does... blow some guys at school. Well, I know he does."

"Who?"

"That's none of your business. I only know about one for sure and I'm not telling you or anyone else about it. I think it's likely that some of the guys he blows do look out for him. I don't think it's a straight-forward arrangement. I think the guys he does protect him because they care about him in a way."

"They just don't want his mouth damaged." Caspian laughed.

"Can we talk about something else?"

"Why? Does talking about sucking dick bother you?"

We had reached the football field. I led Caspian high up into the bleachers. The football team was just beginning to show up for practice. I didn't want anyone to hear us.

"You're being very bold now for someone who was hiding behind the façade of a homophobe two days ago," I said.

"Shut up, Tyler!"

"Hey, I'm just saying exactly what you did instead of implying," I said, throwing Caspian's words back at him.

"You think Dylan is a slut?"

"Why are we talking about Dylan again? I thought you hated Dylan or was that part of your act?"

"I don't hate him. I don't like him, but I don't hate him. He's... too much. Everyone says he's a slut."

"I think that's exaggerated. He is boy crazy and he gets around..."

"Gets around? Why can't you just say what you mean?"

"I don't think I need to precisely spell it out. You know what I mean."

"So... he sucks dick, takes it up the butt..."

"Caspian! Dude, stop."

"Stop being a pussy, Tyler."

"You know, I want to get along with you, but you make it so hard because you're always an ass!"

"I say it like it is. You're being a pussy."

"You're being an asshole."

"That's better. You're saying what you mean now. Yeah, I am an asshole sometimes. It's not an act. I don't believe in beating around the bush."

I glared at him. Why did I like this guy? He pissed me off and yet I liked him, at least I thought I did.

"As I was saying before I was so rudely interrupted; I think Dylan's promiscuity is exaggerated. It almost has to be. To hear people talk you'd think he's had sex with half the guys in school, including some of the teachers. There is no way the truth could even come close. I have little doubt Dylan will go down on any boy he thinks is hot, but there can't be that many boys who will let him. Even if some straight boys are willing to get head from a guy, I bet most aren't. So, I don't think Dylan is as sexually active as everyone says."

"Okay, so he's a slut. He's had sex with a few dozen guys instead of several dozen."

"That's not what I said."

"Whatever."

"You are infuriating! Why do I even bother with you?"

"You sense my underlying charm."

"Charm my ass."

"Hmm, you do have a hot ass, but I wouldn't call it charming."

"Caspian!"

"Hey, you're the one who wants me to be honest about what I am. I think your ass is hot, so I'm telling you."

I exhaled loudly in frustration.

"Listen, if you're going to sit with the guys, you have to try to get along and not make trouble," I said.

"I made nice today, didn't I?"

"Mostly, but this was the only day you've not been an ass."

"True, but today I wasn't and today is the most important, don't you think?"

"You have to cut Dylan some slack. I know he can be aggressive, but he's basically harmless."

"I cut him slack today!"

"You threatened to kill him if he touched you again."

"Exactly. I merely threatened him. I didn't kill him or even kick his ass."

"Just lay off Dylan."

"You seem very protective of Dylan. Is he sucking your dick, Tyler?"

"Not that it's any of your business, but no."

"Why not? I bet he's offered. He's got to be good with all that practice he gets."

"He doesn't, okay?"

"Why are you such a prude, Tyler?"

"I'm not a prude!"

"You have a hot guy who will suck your dick and you don't let him. That's being a prude."

"Dude! Seriously! Stop!"

"Wow, you're really cute when you get angry."

"Then you must think I'm cute a lot because you piss me off!"

"You obviously need to get laid."

I shook my head and stared down at the field. The players were running around the track. Caleb and the coach had their heads bent over a clipboard. Caleb looked totally involved. I was glad he'd joined the team again. I smiled. When I looked back at Caspian he was sitting still, just gazing at me.

"I've been thinking about what you said before. That's what I really want to talk to you about. You're right. I don't have any friends. I did back in California and now that I'm back online I got some emails they sent. Here, no one likes me. I don't like anyone bugging me and getting into my business, but... being alone all the time gets lonely."

The change in Caspian was pronounced. Gone was the cockiness and in-your-face attitude. He had just taken his shields down. I never thought I'd live to see the day. I smiled to myself over the Star Trek reference. Percy was influencing me.

"People might like you if you gave them a chance to like you. I made an effort, but you pushed me away. You push everyone away."

"I know."

Caspian didn't speak for a few moments.

"Why do you do that?"

"I figure I'm not going to be around long, so why get to know anyone?"

"What do you mean you're not going to be around long?"

"I know it's probably hard for you to figure out how much of me is real and how much is an act, but most of what you see is me. Okay, I'm not a homophobe, at least not as big a homophobe as I pretended, but the rest is pretty much me. Most people get tired of me after a while. Percy is going to get tired of putting up with me sooner or later and when he does..."

"Listen, Percy is your uncle but I know him a lot better than you do. I'm sure he will get tired of putting up with you. He probably already is, but if you think he's going to kick you out or arrange for you to be stuck in a foster home you're wrong. He will never do that. No matter how big of a jerk you are he's going to stick with you."

"It would be nice if I could believe that."

"I'm not lying."

"I have no doubt you believe it, but that doesn't make you right."

"I am right, Caspian."

He shrugged.

"You know, I'm still not sure how much I like you, but when you're not being jerk you're not so bad," I said.

"Wow, you were honest that time. You weren't subtle. You just said it, point-blank. Maybe you're not always a pussy."

Caspian smiled slightly. He was really cute when he smiled.

"I guess I can keep from punching Dylan in the face if that's the price for sitting with you and your friends."

"It is. They might become your friends, too."

"I don't know about that. They don't like me and I'm not sure I like them, except for Tyreece. He seems pretty cool."

"He is, but they're all cool."

"Okay, Tyreece, sure. Caleb, maybe. Dylan, no. Jesse?" Caspian laughed out loud. "I have never seen a dude so obsessed with his own appearance."

"He is overly concerned about his looks. We used to call him Narcissus behind his back until he overheard us and took it as a compliment. Jesse thinks very highly of his looks, but he's a nice guy."

"And he's gay, right?"

"Wrong. I already told you he's not gay."

"Come on, no guy who dresses that neatly, has perfect hair, and is completely obsessed with the way he looks can be straight."

"Since when are you an expert on gays?"

"I am one. I admitted that. Remember?"

"I'm one too and I'm telling you Jesse isn't gay. Don't fall for the stereotypes. You're smarter than that."

"You're sure he's not gay?"

"I know for a fact he isn't."

"Tyler, just because he turned you down..."

"I've never hit on him!"

"Dude, I'm just jerking you around. You are so easy. No wait, that's Dylan."

"Dylan told me Jesse is straight."

"So he hit on him and got shot down?"

"Yes. I told you that before, remember? Jesse told Dylan he has no sexual interest in guys."

"He could be lying."

"True, but Dylan believed him. I do too. I've seen Jesse getting pretty hot and heavy with a girl before. There are a couple of girls who make no secret of having slept with him."

"Okay, so he's straight, but he's not cool."

"He's cool when you get to know him."

"Yeah, yeah. Anyway, I won't punch slut-boy, I mean Dylan, in the face and I'll make an effort to get along. Will that make you happy?"

"Just try not to be yourself."

"Funny."

Caspian sat and gazed at me. He just sat there, not saying a word. I uncomfortably shifted on the hard bleacher, trying not to look as disconcerted as I felt. It was almost as if he could read my mind, but that was ridiculous. I looked back at him, but couldn't maintain my gaze. There was something feral in his eyes. I wasn't sure how I felt about him. I shifted back and forth between kind of liking him and thinking he was just a little jerk. Sometimes, I liked him even when he was being a jerk and other times I didn't like him at all. I wanted him to just go away and yet I didn't. That was me, Tyler, the mass of indecision.

Caspian was kind of cute and he was definitely sexy. I liked his collar and spiky hair. He was dangerous and there was something hot about that. My mind went back to our kiss. He'd been so forceful when he pressed his lips against mine and slid his tongue into my mouth. The kiss was brief, but had sent a jolt right to my groin. I'd stiffened instantly, just as I had now as I sat there thinking about it with Caspian gazing at me. There was no way I could stand up at the moment.

Caspian moved in closer, still steadily looking at me. He leaned in and kissed me, slipping his tongue into my mouth. I kissed him back with hunger. This time, he didn't break the kiss but sustained it, moving his lips over mine and twirling his tongue around my own. I felt like he was trying to get inside me and I wanted him there. The front of my jeans threatened to rip from the pressure. My heart pounded and I began to breathe harder. We sat there on the bleachers and made out until I realized football practice was going on down below. I jerked away and looked down at the field. Three of the players were nudging each other one of them was pointing at us. I felt a sense of panic, then I looked toward Caleb. He was looking up at us too. He gave me a thumbs-up. I buried my face in my hands. So much for keeping a low profile.

"Are you okay?" Caspian asked.

"I don't know."

"What's wrong?"

"Dude, they *saw* us."

"Weren't you recently going off on me for pretending to be something I'm not?"

"This is different. We were making out in front of the football team!"

"So you hide being a homo?"

"I don't hide it; I just... keep it under wraps."

"You hide it."

"I don't want everyone knowing my business, okay? I like to keep a low profile."

"Bull shit. You don't want people knowing you're gay."

I glared at Caspian.

"You know I'm right. Deny it if you like but you've been hiding."

"Just shut up!" I said.

Caspian laughed. I wanted to punch him. I didn't like him calling me on my shit and I also didn't like that he was right. Maybe I was capable of lying to myself. Now that I'd just been outed I didn't like it. I realized that I didn't want anyone to know I was gay and it wasn't just because I liked to keep my private life private.

"I don't even like you!" I said.

"You sure like kissing me. I didn't feel you pushing me away. Your tongue shoving its way down my throat says you like me and what about this?"

I couldn't believe it! He groped me!

"Dude! Stop it!"

"You mouth says "stop" but your cock says "go for it.""

"I can't believe you just did that! Some of the football team is watching us!"

"So, they can get their kicks from being voyeurs. I don't care."

"I care."

163

"Yeah, because you're a pussy."

"Hey, I have an idea. Why don't you just fuck off?!"

"Wow, strong language coming from you. If you want to hang out later give me a call or come over."

Before I could stop him, Caspian darted in and quickly kissed me on the lips. He was in and out before I even had a chance to try and shove him away.

"Get away from me," I said, pointlessly since he was already stepping down the bleachers.

"Call me. We can make out in my bedroom."

"Arrrgh!" I growled in frustration. I could swear I heard Caspian laugh as he walked down the bleachers and onto the football field.

I sat and watched him as he walked past the players. The ones who had seen everything didn't say anything to him. They just watched him. After he'd passed, they looked up at me. They were already whispering to their buddies. By the next morning I'd be the number one topic of the rumor mill. Great. Just great.

I was out now. It wasn't a moment I'd been dreading, but I hadn't intended to come out in high school at all. At most, I thought I'd let a few friends know. When Caleb asked me directly the first time, I'd evaded the question so I was more reluctant to admit I was gay than I'd thought. That had kind of bothered me, but then again it was something deeply personal. I was glad I'd answered him the second time he'd asked me, especially now that everyone was going to know.

I wondered how my life was going to be changed by this. I didn't really think anyone was going to corner me and kick my ass. It could happen, but even now I wasn't overly concerned about it. Some guys would probably call me names. I could handle that. I wasn't so sure I could deal with the inevitable lewd comments. Why did Caspian have to kiss me in public? Why did I let him? Why didn't I shove him away?

Because you wanted him to kiss you and you wanted to kiss him back.

Great, now the little voice inside my head was calling me on my shit, too. Why did I want to kiss Caspian? He was a jerk! Yeah, he was sad and lonely and shitty things had gone down in his life, but he was still an asshole. Why did I like him at all? I didn't even like him all the time, just sometimes.

I didn't like the way Caspian got in my face about things. He didn't let me get by with half-way saying things. He was cocky, rude, and annoying. I shouldn't have kissed him back. I should have punched him in the face.

Yeah, but that wouldn't have been nearly as fun.

"Shut up!"

I looked around when I realized I'd said that out loud, but no one was close enough to hear. The football players were no longer paying attention to me, except Caleb, who glanced in my direction as I looked down toward the field.

I just sat there for a while, watching the players practice. Some of them had stripped off their shirts and their muscular bodies glistened in the sunlight. My penis stirred in my pants. I swear it had a mind of its own. I forced myself to stop staring at the built studs on the field. If they caught me gawking at them after they'd seen me making out with Caspian they might kick my ass after all.

I had to wait a few minutes before I could stand up. I sat there and through of dead pets and naked grandmothers. When the action in my pants calmed down I stood and walked down the bleachers. Some of the players looked at me and laughed, whispering to each other, but most ignored me. I hurried away from the football field. I wanted to get somewhere no one could see me.

The parking lot was mostly empty. Only the cars driven by the jocks, the drama crowd, and those who belonged to after-school clubs were still sitting there. I was glad there was no one to look at me or talk to me.

I climbed in, started up the engine, and headed for home. Dad wasn't home when I arrived, which suited me fine. I probably would talk to him about what happened and if not, I'd talk to Percy. At the moment, I didn't want to talk to anyone.

I went to my bedroom and lay back on my bed. The mattress and pillow were comfortable and helped me to relax. I wasn't upset about being outed. I always knew I'd come out someday. I was just uncomfortable that now everyone would know something very private and personal about me. For a few days at least, and probably several, everyone would be discussing the kiss. They wouldn't stop with discussing what had happened. They would speculate on what else had and was going to happen. There would be rumors about who I'd hooked up with. I was friends with Dylan, so everyone would assume we were getting it on. A lot of people would think I was like Dylan and did "favors" for jocks and other straight guys. I wasn't judging Dylan. What he did was his business. I admired him for going after what he wanted and for so often succeeding. His promiscuous life wasn't for me. I wasn't a prude as Caspian had accused, but I didn't want to do it with just anyone. I wanted something in between.

Worse, people would be talking about my dad now, and my dad and me. Dad was gay and so was I. Some would say he'd turned me gay. Many would suspect an incestuous relationship. My dad would never do that. He loved me, but he'd never make love to me.

I must have drifted off because I was jolted to alertness by the sound of a cricket chirping loudly which meant I had a text message. I looked at my alarm clock. Two hours had passed since I'd come home.

I check my message. There was a text from Caleb.

"U ok?"

"Mostly," I typed.

"Want 2 talk?"

"Yes, come over?"

"B there in 10."

I put my cell down. Part of me still didn't want to talk, but I needed to talk. I just wondered what Caleb would have to say about Caspian and me making out.

Caleb had no trouble getting to the back door. Our house had a ramp instead of steps at the back. I don't know if some previous occupant had been in a wheel-chair or if it was put in for another reason, but I was glad it was there after Caleb and I started hanging out.

I opened the door to find Caleb grinning at me.

"You really know how to come out with a bang, don't you?" he said.

"Oh, just shut up and get in here."

"You're pretty testy for someone who just got a new boyfriend."

"We aren't boyfriends."

"Okay, a butt buddy then."

"We aren't butt buddies' either! I've never... just shut up!"

"Come on, you have to let me mess with you a little. This kind of opportunity doesn't come along often, especially with you."

I pleaded for mercy with my eyes.

"Okay. Okay. I'm done. So, how are you feeling about all this?"

I got us both Cokes from the refrigerator and sat down across the kitchen table from Caleb. I shared the thoughts that had been going through my own head before I'd drifted off to sleep. Caleb listened intently.

"I have a question," Caleb said when I paused. "Why did you kiss Caspian right there in full view of the entire football team?"

"I didn't! He kissed me! He does stuff like that! He doesn't think about anything! He just does what he wants."

"You did kiss him back. I looked up right when your lips touched and you guys were going for it."

"Well, I, uh... wasn't thinking about where I was just then..."

"He must be one good kisser."

"Yeah, he's good. I don't have any experience for comparison, but yeah..."

"So, Caspian sits with you at lunch and you've been making out. I guess this means you two have made up."

"Well, I guess, but... it's complicated."

"How?"

"He's driving me crazy! Today, he was vulnerable and honest, but then he's so cocky and such a jerk! I was thinking more about punching him in the face than kissing him. Seriously, sometimes I feel like I can't stand to be near him."

"And yet you had your tongue in his mouth. That's not the usual method for telling someone to get lost or do you gay dudes have different ways?"

I shot Caleb a look that clearly said "you're an ass."

"I kind of like him and I mean *like* like him, but he's sooo infuriating! I want to kiss him, then I want to slug him."

"Sounds like you're into rough sex."

I just stared at Caleb for a few moments.

"Okay. Sorry. So you have mixed feelings. That's not so unusual. I like Dylan a lot, but sometimes I just have to tell him to shut the fuck up. My mom is really cool, but she hovers over me so much sometimes I just want to scream at her to go away. I am surprised you like Caspian, I mean after you tried to kill him and all."

"Do you think... do you think maybe I like him because he's the first guy who ever kissed me? I messed around with another guy before, but that was with someone I didn't really know. Do you think I'm so desperate to get laid that I'm latching onto Caspian because he's interested in me?"

"You tell me."

"Don't laugh, but I am getting pretty desperate. I need some!"

"Whoa! Calm down, stud. Don't hurt me. You know you could have sex with Dylan if you wanted."

"Yeah, but...that would feel kind of weird. No offense. I'd just feel odd doing it with a friend."

"So you want to get it on with an enemy? Maybe that's why you're hot for Caspian."

"Funny."

"I get what you mean about Dylan. It was a little weird for me at first, but I got over it and Dylan is obviously into it. I get the relief I need and he gets what he wants."

I sat there thinking and sipping Coke for a while.

"There's something I like about Caspian. I can't say exactly what it is. There's other stuff I like about him too. As much as it annoys me, I kind of like his cocky attitude. I like his look and have you seen his ass?"

"Um, I can't say I've paid much attention to his ass."

"He's vulnerable too, you know? He really needs someone. I have the feeling he could be really sweet and loving."

"Sweet and loving? Are we still talking about Caspian?"

"Yes, you didn't hear the tone of his voice or see the expressions on his face when we were talking. I can sense what's inside him."

"I hope you're not planning to change him into what you want him to be. That won't work."

"No. I know the parts of him I don't like aren't going to go away, but he really needs someone, even if it's just a friend."

"You are a goner. This is the whole lost puppy thing I talked about after the two you had your fist fight. He's a lost puppy and you can't help but take him home."

"I don't know, maybe, but I want to be friends at least."

"There is no way you two will be just friends, not if the lip wrestling I witnessed is any indication. I have a feeling you'll be getting laid very soon."

I shrugged.

"If you do it with Caspian, you have to tell me, just no details please."

"Ah, come on, Caleb. You got off on watching us make out. Maybe we'll invite you over to watch if we get it on."

"Eww, eww. That is something I definitely do not want to see."

I laughed.

"Thanks for coming over to talk, Caleb."

"You've been there for me, now I'm here for you. That's one of the things friends do for each other. Besides, this way I get the real story and don't have to wonder about rumors. Hmm, I could probably start some good ones since everyone knows we're friends."

"Don't you dare."

Caleb laughed evilly. I smiled. He was a good friend.

Percy

"Acting strangely, how?" Daniel asked as I poured him a cup of tea.

"He was grinning, that's not like Caspian. He scowls, glares, pouts, and shoots looks that could kill, but he rarely smiles and he never grins like he did when he came home from school. I thought some other boy had walked into the house by mistake for a moment."

"Did he say anything?"

I sat down across from Daniel at my kitchen table.

"His grin disappeared the moment he realized I was looking him. I asked him school went and he said "fine.""

"Well, that's something."

"He always says "fine." For Caspian, that's the same as "no comment." I hope he's not up to something."

"We both know *you* never got up to anything when you were a teen."

"We're not talking about me."

Daniel grinned.

"Maybe you should just be happy that he's happy."

"I am, but he keeps me shut out. He looked like he was just bursting to tell someone about whatever it was he was so happy about, but he didn't say a word to me."

"Perhaps you're too old. Maybe it's one of those things that can only be shared with someone your age. When I was fifteen I never dreamed my dad could understand me. Kids Caspian's age don't seem to be able to comprehend the idea that we used to be them."

"He still doesn't trust me. What am I doing wrong?"

"You aren't doing anything wrong, Percy. He's been thrust into a new life. He just needs time."

"I've given him time. I'm doing what I can to make things easier on him. I'm trying to take care of him without pushing into his life. At least he hasn't accused me of waiting my chance to molest him recently."

"Maybe that's a good sign. Maybe it's a sign of trust."

"Maybe he's getting tired of me knocking holes in his arguments."

Daniel walked around the table and began to massage my shoulders.

"You need to relax. Just hang in there and keep doing what you're doing. You don't have the ideal relationship with Caspian, but things could be much worse. He could be out drinking, or doing drugs, or selling drugs."

"He hasn't lived up to his record, thank God, although most of the trouble he got himself into occurred two years before my brother died."

"So stop worrying so much. You can't worry about what might be happening to him."

"That's easy for you to say. You have over a decade of experience being a father. I've only been at parenting for a few weeks. Plus, you have the world's greatest son."

"I can't argue with that, but don't tell Tyler."

I smiled, even though Daniel couldn't see it.

"Oh, that feels good."

Daniel kept massaging my shoulders until all the tension was worked out and then resumed his seat across from me.

"I wish we could go away somewhere for the weekend, just the two of us," I said.

"I like that idea. Maybe we can."

"I couldn't enjoy myself for a moment. It will be a long time before I can leave Caspian and not worry about him."

"Oh, you are a novice, but I understand. Maybe we can take the boys on a trip soon."

"I can't even get Caspian to agree to join the three of us for dinner."

"Don't give up hope."

"I won't. It's a nice fantasy, isn't it? I'd love for the four of us to go out for dinner together like a family."

"As fantasies go, I think this one has a good chance of coming true."

"Caspian and I have made a little progress and that's something. I had no idea just getting him to communicate would be so hard. I'm sorry. I'm sure you're tired of listening to me talk about Caspian."

"No, I'm not. I'd be telling you about Tyler too, but I think you spend as much time with him as I do."

"That doesn't bother you, does it?"

"Absolutely not. I can't be around as often as I'd like. It's reassuring to know that if he has a problem or if there's an emergency he can come to you. I'm not worried about Tyler going out and getting into trouble, but even so I'd rather he hang out with you than be running around town. I trust him, but I don't trust everyone else."

"I think you're just a little protective," I teased.

Daniel smiled. It was the same smile that so charmed me the summer we met, back when we were both seventeen.

"I guess Tyler's only real trouble recently has been the fight with my nephew."

"Some good has come out of even that," Daniel said. "Tyler has always been capable, but he's never been in a fight. Caspian won, but I could tell when Tyler told me about the fight that he was proud that he'd stood up for himself. He was also a little surprised he'd done so well. It's boosted his confidence."

I sighed.

"Sometimes, I don't know if I'm making any progress with Caspian at all."

"He's grown closer to you, Percy. I know he projects a tough-guy image, but you're the one who is always here for him. You're the one who held him as he cried after his fight with Tyler."

"Don't ever tell Caspian I told you about that. He would never forgive me. He only let him hold him a few minutes and then he pushed away and became belligerent again."

"Yes, but he came to you and he let you hold him. That is significant."

"I guess I just don't want to get my hopes up. I don't want to expect too much, too fast."

"I think you're doing just fine, Percy."

"I guess time will tell."

Tyler

It began as soon as I got out of my car in the student parking lot. Everyone was staring at me. Well, not really, but that's the way it felt. When anyone looked in my direction I just knew they'd heard about Caspian and me making out on the bleachers during football practice.

Once I made it inside, I felt as if I was under even greater scrutiny. Most of my classmates didn't even look at me, but several did and I was sure they *knew*.

I was a little surprised that I didn't care that they knew I was gay. This was 2009. Despite the efforts of the narrow-minded and bigoted, being gay wasn't *that* big of a deal anymore. Most people had figured out that being gay was normal. Gays were a minority, of course, but we were naturally occurring. We were part of the big plan, whatever that was. We had always been around and we always would be. Hitler had tried to wipe us out along with the Jews, but he'd failed with us just as he had with them. We were here to stay.

I shook my head. I was going off into one of my tangents again. I did that sometimes. What was I thinking? Oh, yeah. I was surprised, but I didn't care about everyone knowing I was gay. I didn't like anyone knowing I'd made out with Caspian, but it wasn't because he was a guy. I didn't like people knowing about the personal details of my life. I didn't like what they probably assumed either. Most of my classmates probably thought Caspian and I did a lot more than kiss. Again, it wasn't the fact that Caspian was a guy that bothered me. If my classmates were picturing me getting it on with a girl I would have been just as uncomfortable. Of course, since Caspian was a guy there was the added problem of harassment from bigots and boys who were insecure about their sexuality. I wasn't too worried about that. I'd done okay when I fought Caspian. I had lost, but I thought I did very well for an inexperienced fighter. Most importantly, I didn't back off. I didn't cower. If someone tried to bash this homo they were going to get hurt!

"What was it like? I want all the details! What else have you guys done? Why didn't you tell me you were gay?"

I turned my attention from the dial on my locker and looked at Dylan. The dreaded moment had come. Dylan knew I was a homo.

"I don't really want to talk about it now, Dylan."

"Come on! Give me something! Caspian is soooo hot and you made out with him! I can't believe he's gay! This is soooo cool!"

"Dylan, do not start pestering Caspian. Don't start coming onto him again."

"He's your boyfriend, right? I'd never try anything with a friend's boyfriend. Now, if we weren't friends..."

"He's not my boyfriend. I... I don't know what we are, but I'm warning you not to bother him because he will kick your ass."

"Do I get to make out with him if he does? He kicked your ass then then you guys made out."

"Hey, I did okay when we fought! He has a black-eye, too, you know!"

"Yeah, yeah. You're tough and it makes you even sexier, but I'm just saying it's a price I'm willing to pay."

"Do you *ever* listen to *anything* anyone says?" I asked.

"I listen. I'm just not good at heeding warnings or advice. I'm a risk-taker when it gets me what I want."

"You're a horny little bastard who is obsessed with seducing as many boys as possible."

"Thank you!" Dylan grinned. He took my comment as pure compliment.

"You're also incorrigible."

Dylan merely grinned again.

"We *must* talk later," Dylan said earnestly and promptly disappeared.

Great, now Dylan was going to pester me for the details of a physical relationship that didn't even exist. I wondered if he'd believe me when I told him the truth. At least he hadn't tried to seduce me, but the day was young.

As I was walking to first period, two sophomores looked at me, whispered together, and then laughed. They didn't call me names or harass me, they just laughed. I could feel my face turning red and I hurried on.

I had a problem with blushing all morning. Whenever there was a whispered conversation around me, I began to blush. Most of the conversations probably weren't even about me, but I knew at least some of them had to be about the kiss. When a boy shouldered me between second and third period and said "faggot" I was surprised I found that easier to deal with than the whispered conversations. I knew what that guy was thinking and could dismiss him without difficulty as a fool.

Tyreece was waiting by my locker just after the "faggot" incident.

"You could have told me," he said.

"Um... sorry?" I shrugged my shoulders.

"It's cool, man, but you could have told me. You know I'm cool with your dad being gay."

"I'm just not good with discussing personal details and this is something very personal."

"Like I said, it's cool. I just want you to know I'm here for you and this changes nothing, although I'm not bending over in the showers to pick up the soap if you're around."

"What?"

"It's a joke, Tyler. Lighten up."

I smiled.

Tyreece went on his way. At least he was going to be a lot easier to deal with than Dylan. I already knew Caleb was cool with the situation. Out of my small circle of friends that only left Jesse as an unknown. I didn't think he'd go homophobe on me. His only negative reaction to Dylan trying to hug him was getting upset because it wrinkled his clothes and might disturb his perfect hair. I didn't know quite how he'd react, but I wasn't worried.

The only true unpleasantness of the morning came when Andy and Erik, two football players, cornered me in a remote hallway between third and fourth period. They stepped in front of me, blocking my path with their broad shoulders and muscular bodies. They were both kind of hot, but I wasn't about to comment on that.

"So, will you be offering blow-jobs to all the guys like your homo-buddy Dylan?" Andy asked.

"Um, no."

"Why not? Isn't that what you guys do?"

"I believe you're misinformed."

"Oh, I see, so you just don't like us." Andy looked at Erik. "I think this homo is insulting us. He doesn't think we're hot enough to blow."

"You're hot!" I said, getting just a little panicky.

"This sicko thinks were hot, man, what are we going to do about that?" Erik asked.

I was quickly growing tired of their bull-shit.

"Listen, just do whatever you going to do to me, okay? Let's quit playing this stupid game. Beat me up, call me names, spit on me, whatever, just fucking do it so I can get on with my life. I'm tired of your bull-shit and think you're both stupid fucks for picking on me because I'm gay, so just fucking do it!"

"I'm impressed," said Andy. "Are you impressed, Erik?"

"Yeah, this guy has balls. Maybe you should come out for the team. Hey, I made a joke. Get it? *Come out* for the team?"

"That's really pathetic, Erik," said Andy.

"Shut up!" Erik said.

My face blanched as Erik gripped my shoulder and gave it a hard squeeze. I thought he and Andy was getting ready to kick my ass, but instead they moved around me. Andy gave me a hard smack on the ass. I walked on down the hallway, my eyes wide, and my heart pounding in my chest. One thing was for sure; life was more exciting as an openly gay boy.

There were eyes staring at me from everywhere in my classes and even more so in the hallways. I felt like a microscopic creature under the lens, only everyone in the entire school was staring into the microscope at the same time.

When I reached my locker just before lunch, I climbed inside and closed the door behind me, shutting out all the prying eyes. At last, no one could see me, but it was kind of dark. Maybe I could just live in here and watch the world through the louvers of my locker door.

"Escort you to lunch?"

I shook my head, clearing away my daydream, and turned.

"Hey, Caleb. Yes, please."

"So, how is life in the spotlight?" Caleb asked.

"I was just fantasizing about crawling into my locker and closing the door behind me."

Caleb laughed.

"The scrutiny will calm down in a few days. One of my teammates will cheat on his girlfriend, she'll dump him, and then everyone will be talking about them. I was only the talk of the school for a couple of weeks after my accident. You didn't even get carted away in an ambulance. You have a lot to learn about showmanship. I thought all you gay guys were dramatic."

"Dylan stole my share."

"So *that's* where he gets all that extra energy. I guess it's okay to openly call you a gay guy now, right?"

"Yeah, that secret is no longer a secret."

I was grateful to Caleb for escorting me to lunch. With him wheeling along beside me I didn't feel quite so much on display. Talking to Caleb also helped prevent me from indulging in the paranoia that was my obsession for the day.

"Hey, guys," Caspian said.

"Well, hello," Caleb said.

I wanted to elbow Caleb, but controlled myself. I couldn't help but look around to see if anyone was watching.

Get a grip, Tyler.

"Sup?" Caspian asked.

"Lunch! I am starving!" Caleb said. "Come on."

Caspian eyed me for a moment with a slight smile on his face. He acted as if the confrontational aspects of the day before had never happened. My heart beat a little faster at the sight of him and my uh... boxer-briefs grew a little tighter.

Caspian actually talked as the three of us went through the line. It was as if the silent, brooding Caspian was gone. He didn't act cheerful, but he wasn't so guarded. I wasn't quite sure what to make of him.

We paid for our lunches, and then carried our trays to our usual table. Caspian sat down with us as he had the day before, just as if he'd been sitting there all along and hadn't spent most of his days at North eating alone and giving everyone the cold-shoulder.

I picked up a chicken strip and looked at Caspian sitting across from me. His expression was a cross between a smile and a smirk. I was torn between wanting to smack him and wanting to kiss him. Damn, why did I feel the way I did about him? It was so much easier just thinking he was a prick.

Instead of thinking about his prick?

Shut up little voice!

Great, now I have having conversations in my head. Not only was I messed up over my feelings for Caspian, I was becoming a nut-case.

"Isn't the weather *fabulous* today," Jesse said.

I eyed Jesse suspiciously, but he ate his mashed potatoes as if his comment was innocent. I thought I could detect a little smile on his face, but I wasn't sure. I watched him for a few moments, but he moved onto his green beans without looking the least suspicious.

"So... who is your favorite character on *Glee*, Tyler?" Jesse asked, with a mischievous expression on his face. "Let me guess, Kurt?"

I tried to give Jesse my stare-of-death, but I began to smile. The stare-of-death loses all power once I smile.

"I'm undecided. I like them all."

It was the first time I'd ever talked about *Glee*. It was one of the many topics I'd shied away from for fear it would give me away.

"Mine is Sue, definitely Sue," Caspian said.

"Big surprise there," Caleb said.

Caspian flipped him off, but the gesture wasn't delivered with his usual belligerence. He acted as if he actually might like Caleb.

"*Glee* is definitely homo-tastic," Jesse said.

"Hey, guys! What's up?" Dylan said in his usual too-enthusiastic tone.

"It's called lunch, Dylan," Tyreece said as he joined us as well.

"So..." Dylan said, as he eagerly looked back and forth between Caspian and me.

Here it comes.

"I can't believe you guys are gay! This is sooooooooooooo cool!"

"They're gay, Dylan. They didn't both win the Nobel Peace Prize," Jesse said.

"You're just upset because now there is a balance of power. There are three gay guys and three straight guys here, unless one of you has something to tell us?" Dylan asked, looking around the table expectantly.

I watched Caspian for a moment, wondering how he'd react to being called gay. He didn't seem to care. I wondered if an alien had replaced him during the night.

"I'm so glad you've come out!" Dylan said, hugging Caspian and laying his head on Caspian's shoulder.

"Get off me or I will kill you right now."

Yep. The old Caspian was still in there.

"That's what's so cool about gay guys. There is always drama," Jesse said.

"So, are you guys dating or just fuck buddies or what?" Dylan asked.

Leave it to Dylan to be thoughtlessly blunt.

"I don't think they want to talk about that," Tyreece said. "It's really none of our business."

"Oh, no! They made out in public. That makes it everyone's business," Dylan said.

Caspian and I looked at each other. There was no answer for Dylan's question. If Caspian was half as confused as I was he didn't have a clue. I was so mixed up about what was going on between us I didn't know if we'd end up kissing each other again or punching each other's lights out.

"So, there really wasn't a fight, was there?" Jesse asked. "You guys are just into rough sex."

I could feel my face go crimson. Caspian wasn't affected by Jesse's jibe at all.

"Guys, could we talk about something else?" I asked.

"Oh okay, got it. It was rough sex. I understand. That's private," Jesse said.

Jesse was really getting into giving Caspian and me a hard time. He was usually so self-obsessed he didn't say much. I guess all I had to do to get him to talk more is come out. Either that, or Jesse had been replaced by an alien too.

Caspian glared at Jesse, but it was obvious he was only pretending to be angry. He was playing with him. It was a side of Caspian I'd never seen before. I was beginning to like him more, but I still had no idea where things were going between us.

"At least you guys had a gay old time during football practice," Jesse said.

I growled.

"Okay!" I said. "Caspian and I made out. There's no use in denying it. Everyone saw it. I feel like the whole freaking cafeteria is staring at us. I've felt like everyone has been staring at me all day! I'm a homo and I'm fine with being a homo."

"This public announcement was paid for by... sorry," Caleb said, looking at me apologetically.

I grinned.

"Pressure getting to you, Tyler?" Tyreece asked.

"Yes. I don't like being the center of attention."

"Then you really shouldn't have made out with another boy during football practice," Jesse said.

"It wasn't planned! It just... happened."

"So... Caspian tripped and you tried to catch him with your lips?" Jesse asked with a smirk.

"You guys are enjoying this *way* too much," I said.

"Come on, Tyler. How often do we get to give you a hard time? You never do anything stupid. You never give us any material to work with, until now," Tyreece said.

"Some friends you are!" I said.

"Great, now he's pretending to be angry," Jesse said. "Should we pretend we're falling for it and act contrite?" Jesse looked around the table.

"Yeah, let's go with contrite," Caleb said.

"I hate you guys!" I said. Of course, I smiled about five seconds later. Dammit!

"You're really not good at pretending to be angry," Jesse said.

"Screw you," I retorted.

"No. No. Dylan, Caspian, and you are gay. I'm not. Maybe we should wear little tags to remind him," Jesse said, looking around the table.

Caspian was silent during all of this, but he seemed to be enjoying it. Dylan was gazing at Caspian dreamily, but keeping his hands to himself. Caleb and Tyreece were grinning at me.

"Listen, Tyler, Caspian. We've got your backs if there is any trouble," Tyreece said.

"Yeah, anyone gives you shit I'll run them over with my chair," Caleb added.

I looked around at my friends. They had enjoyed giving me a hard time way too much, but I knew it was their way of telling me they were totally cool with me being gay.

"Thanks, guys."

It wasn't me who had spoken, but Caspian.

"You know, there was a blond guy who looked just like you sitting here a few days ago, but he was a total bastard," Caleb said. "I like you a lot better."

Did I have forgiving friends or what?

"Yeah, I've heard about him," Caspian said. "I think he was some imposter, pretending to be me."

"Well, if you guys aren't dating, then maybe..." Dylan began, gazing at me.

"Forget it, Dylan. We're friends. I don't think about you like that," I said.

"Oh, so you only hook up with guys after you've fought them? Can I blow you if I punch you in the face?"

"That would be a big NO."

"I have no problem with having sex with friends. It's just another way to be friendly," Dylan said, grinning.

"*He* should be on *Glee*," Tyreece said, pointing to Dylan.

I was grateful when the conversation turned solely to *Glee*. I was surprised that all the guys actually watched it. I had always thought admitting I watched it would make me look gay and I kind of wondered about the others. Dylan didn't care, of course, but Jesse, Caleb, and Tyreece obviously watched it every week. I thought about mentioning something about them being closet-*Glee* fans, but I didn't want to turn the conversation back to me.

Lunch ended. Caspian disappeared. Caleb and I dumped our trays together and moved toward our lockers.

"That was the weirdest lunch ever," I said.

"You brought Jesse to life. I have a feeling you'll be hearing a lot more homo comments from him," Caleb said.

"He does enjoy teasing me."

"Well, it is true that you give us very little material to use against you."

"I'll try harder to be an idiot. Have any tips for me?"

"Rowr," Caleb said, raking his hands through the air like claws. "The kitty is a bitch today."

"I'm gay. I'm allowed to be a bitch. If I'm going to be out, I might as well enjoy the fringe benefits."

Caleb laughed.

"I know this is hard for you, but you are more fun than you were before. You should have come out long ago."

"Yeah, I guess. Maybe I shouldn't be so uptight about everyone knowing my business. Percy told me that once high school ends this all becomes meaningless."

"I never thought of that, but I guess he's right. Once we graduate, we move on and North High School is no longer our world."

"I'll be sad to leave this world and yet I want to see what's out there," I said. "But, enough about me—more than enough. How are you and Brittany getting along?"

"We've gone out a few times. I think she really likes me. The chair doesn't seem to bother her and we've been messing around."

"So... is everything working properly?"

"Well, we haven't gone all the way, but so far all systems are go. I think I'll be up to performing when the time comes. I get aroused easily with Brittany. All she has to do is kiss me and I'm hard as a rock."

"Congratulations. So she gets you more excited than Dylan, huh?"

"Dylan is good, but he is a guy. He's a good substitute for the real thing, but that's all. Listen, Tyler, thanks for encouraging me to take a risk. I think I was mostly creating my own problem. The more I do with Brittany, the easier it becomes. Now I feel like that only thing that kept me from being able to perform was the fear that I couldn't."

"The only thing we have to fear is fear itself."

"Thank you, Franklin Delano Roosevelt."

I jerked my head toward Caleb.

"What? You think I'm an idiot because I'm on the football team?"

I grinned at Caleb's words *I'm on the football team.* That meant he felt like a member of the team again. I just hoped he wouldn't quit sitting at our table.

"You said it. I didn't."

"Bitch. Seriously, though, thank you. I needed someone to give me a push. I had myself too scared to pursue any girls and I'd even walked away from football. Now, I have two of my favorite things back, thanks to you."

"Girls and football—how disgustingly heterosexual. Maybe I didn't do you a favor."

Caleb laughed.

"I mean it, Tyler, thank you."

"You're welcome. It's the burden of us gay boys. We were placed on Earth to teach jocks about courage."

"You say that as a joke, but maybe you're right."

***

I spent the rest of the day on stage as "Tyler the Homo." I was uncomfortable and self-conscious, but it wasn't nearly as bad as it could have been. The harassment was limited to a few dirty looks and I think I heard a boy mutter "faggot" under his breath a time or two, but I wasn't sure if I really heard it or was just imagining things.

Caspian was waiting for me by my locker at the end of school. That made me feel self-conscious, but he was oblivious to the looks he was getting from our classmates. He had to notice, but he so completely ignored them it was as if he didn't see.

"I thought we should talk," Caspian said. "Drive me home?"

I nodded. I exchanged the books I didn't need for those I did and then zipped up my backpack. I slammed my locker shut and Caspian and I walked together toward the parking lot. We'd walked together before, back at the very beginning when I was showing him around the school, but not since the kiss in front of the football team. The feeling that everyone was watching increased exponentially.

I halted as a thought occurred to me. I was a senior and Caspian was a freshman. Nooooo. Everyone thought I was dating a freshman! That was worse than dating a guy!

"Doesn't it bother you that people are looking at us?" I asked as we walked on again.

"Should it? I figure they can look if they like."

"Yeah, but you just know what they're thinking?"

"That we're butt-buddies?"

"Yes!"

"So, what? They can think whatever they want. I do not give a shit."

"You really don't, do you?"

"Nope and your life would be easier if you didn't either."

"I'm sure you're right about that, but it's not easy to just stop caring what others think. You've only been going to North for a short time. I grew up with these people."

"So, what? I can understand caring what your friends think, but beyond that, no."

"Aren't you the same guy who was going on about everyone hating gays?"

"Yeah, but... I was ignorant, okay? You made me really think and I figured out I didn't have a clue. I just believed what I'd read and seen on TV. When I thought about it, *really* thought about it, I realized what I'd been told didn't match what I was seeing around me. Now, on to more important things; why didn't you call last night?"

"You expected me to call after you were a jerk?"

"If telling it like it is makes me a jerk, then I'm guilty as charged."

"You did more than that."

"Okay, maybe I went a little further than that and maybe I enjoyed calling you on your shit a little too much, but I'm a smart-ass. It's part of my natural charm. You did kiss me back when I kissed you and I know you were into it," Caspian said with a meaningful glance down at my crotch.

I looked around to see if anyone had noticed, but everyone was too busy hurrying to his or her cars.

"I don't even know how I feel about you. Mostly, you've been a bastard."

"Wasn't I nice today at lunch?"

"You threatened to kill Dylan, again."

"Only if he hugged me, and I didn't really mean it. I exaggerated for dramatic effect. I just didn't want him hanging on me. A few days ago I would have decked him."

"Why the change?"

"I told you, I got tired of not having any friends," Caspian said as we climbed in the car.

"Yeah, but it's like you've instantly become this whole other person."

"And, you don't trust me?"

"Why should I?"

"Maybe you shouldn't, but I am telling you the truth. If you think I'm going to revert back to what I was just a few days ago you're wrong."

I looked at Caspian for a moment after we both climbed into my car. I pulled the car out of my parking spot and navigated through the lot. The very end of school was a hectic time with everyone trying to leave all at once.

"That is what you think, isn't it?" Caspian asked.

"I don't want to let myself care about you if you're only going to hurt me." I was sorry the instant I said it. I'd revealed way too much.

"You like me. Admit it."

"I don't dislike you as much as I did."

"Come on! Why can't you just say it? Don't be a pussy!"

"Don't call me that! Okay, I kind of have a crush on you. I kind of like you, but you've been such a dick I don't know if you're worth the risk."

"Now, you're speaking the truth. So, you have a crush on me, huh?"

"I said I *kind of* have a crush."

"Which means you do. I like *you* a lot."

"You do?"

"I wouldn't have kissed you if I didn't."

"Are you sure you weren't just horny?"

"Well, I was horny, but I also like you, so... wanna park somewhere and make out?"

I was tempted more than I was willing to admit.

"Maybe we should try to get to know each other or are you only interested in hooking up with me?"

"I do want to hook up with you, but I am interested in more. What do you suggest?"

"I'll drop you off at your place, go home and back, and then we can go out to eat."

"So, we're going on a date?"

"Yes," I said, feeling bold.

Caspian smiled, but then frowned again.

"Listen. I'm not going to be the dick I have been since I arrived in Bloomington, but I'm I can't magically transform into a nice guy who never acts like a jerk. I am a jerk sometimes and I piss people off because I say what I think. It's just the way I am. I just want you to know that."

"Oh, I know that. Anyone who thinks of you as sweet and innocent is a fool. I kind of like your rough edges. As long as they aren't sharp enough to cut, I can deal."

I let Caspian out at Percy's house just a few minutes later and drove the short distance to mine. I wondered if I was making a mistake. Caspian had mostly been a little shit. His sudden change of heart was hard to believe, but he did seem sincere. He was intelligent; intelligent enough to come to the realization that pushing everyone away would only prolong his loneliness. I seriously doubted he'd put a lot of effort into play-acting just to mess with me. More than anything, I could sense the lonely, frightened boy inside Caspian. He was worth the risk. He'd also been honest. He didn't promise to be a nice guy. He only said that he wasn't going to be as big of an ass as he had been.

I went home, put on a pair of jeans and a red polo shirt, and sprayed on just a little cologne. I was more excited than I should have been. This was Caspian after all and the evening might well turn out to be a disaster. It was time to take a chance. If Caspian was going to be a dick, I'd find out soon enough.

I drove back to Percy's house and parked my car by his Shay. I walked up the front steps and knocked on the door. Percy answered.

"Caspian said the two of you are going out to eat," Percy said as if he hadn't believed his nephew.

"Yeah."

"So, you're getting along better I guess."

"A lot better."

I wondered how much I should tell Percy. I confided many things in him but I couldn't exactly tell him Caspian and I were going on a date. It was too unbelievable for one thing and "date" seemed too strong a word for it. We were just going to get to know each other. Then again, we did care about each other and we were going out to eat, so that did sound a lot like a date. Percy knew Caspian had kissed me after our fight, but I couldn't quite bring myself to tell him Caspian had kissed me again on the bleachers, or that I'd kissed him back, or that I was thinking about kissing Caspian again. I kind of expected to wake up and find it all a dream anyway. Caspian and me... it was just too unreal.

Percy looked suspicious when Caspian came out of his room. Caspian had changed into tight black jeans and a black, muscle-cut tee shirt that made him look totally hot. I was sorry to see him put on his leather jacket, but then it did help me to keep from staring. Percy looked back at me, as if noticing for the first time that I was unusually dressed up. I could almost see the gears turning in his head. I smiled slightly. I enjoyed the confused expression on his face.

"Ready?" I asked.

Caspian nodded.

"We'll see you later, Percy," I said.

"Have fun, guys." Percy was still perplexed.

Caspian and I walked out to my car and climbed in.

"Where do you want to go?" I asked.

Caspian shrugged. "You know this town way better than me."

"How about Opie Taylor's?" I haven't been there in a while.

"Opie Taylor's?"

"It's a cool little restaurant on the square. The food is great."

"As long as there is food, I'm in."

We drove the short distance downtown. Parking could be a real bitch downtown and around IU, but I found a spot only a couple of blocks from the restaurant without too much difficulty. Soon, Caspian and I were inside Opie Taylor's, sitting in a huge booth on the right side of the restaurant. We ordered drinks and browsed the menu.

"I usually get the special when they have it," I said. "It comes with the burger-of-the-day, a side, and a drink and it's only $8. The burgers here are great!"

We both ended up ordering the special, which was a basil burger, and we both selected fries as our side. We gazed around Opie's as we sat in the booth. There were televisions high up on the walls, including a big-screen TV on the back wall, all tuned to the same sports channel. I liked the old Bloomington photos and autographed pieces that decorated the wall. There were a couple of flyers signed by John Mellencamp on the wall in our booth. Mellencamp lived in the country near Bloomington, I wasn't exactly sure where.

"So..." I said. I don't think I realized until just that moment that I knew almost nothing about Caspian beyond the tragedy that brought him to Bloomington and the fact he was Percy's nephew.

"So, are you into Goth-type music or..."

"I like a lot of different kinds. From Alanis Morrisette to Marilyn Manson to, and I'll kill you if you tell anyone this, the *Glee* cast."

"That is quite a range. I'm all about *Glee*, but I like a lot of pop artists and even some classical, especially Joshua Bell."

"He plays the violin, right? What? Don't look at me like that. You think I don't know anything about classical?"

"I'm just surprised. Yeah, he is one of the most talented violin players *ever*. Guess where he went to high school?"

"Hey, I know some things about classical music. I'm not a trivia expert. How should I know where he went to high school? I do know he's kinda hot."

"He went to *our* high school. He graduated from North."

"Now you're just making things up to see if I'm gullible or not."

"No, he grew up in Bloomington, went to North, and attended IU. He's a Bloomington boy."

"Is that why you like him?"

"No. I started listening to him before I knew he was from Bloomington."

"Maybe you can play me some of his stuff sometime."

"Sure."

Caspian knew a little about classical music. I was shocked.

"Hmm, what books do you like to read?" I asked.

"I'm into the Percy Jackson books right now. How about you?"

"Well... my favorite author is your uncle."

Caspian rolled his eyes.

"I think you have a crush on him."

"Well, he is kind of hot..."

"Dude!"

"I'm messing with you, Caspian, mostly. I do think Percy is very attractive, but I don't think of him like that. He's like another dad to me. I'm so glad he's dating my dad. They are perfect for each other. Have you read any of your uncle's books?"

"Nope. I'm not a big mystery fan. That's mostly what he writes, isn't it?"

"That's mostly what he writes under the name Percy DeForest Spock. He writes under other names too. Ever read anything by Mark Roeder?"

"Never heard of him."

"Well, that is your uncle, too."

"Writers are a sneaky lot, aren't they? I didn't know Percy had a secret identity. It's too bad he's not something cool like Spiderman instead of a boring, unknown writer."

"Hey, that's my favorite writer you're talking about."

"He's my uncle so I can say anything nasty about him I want. Let's talk about something else. I do not want to spend my time talking about my uncle."

"Fair enough. Have you ever dated anyone?" I asked.

"Yeah, right! You?"

"No, I haven't. It's kind of hard to date when you want to keep your private life on the down low."

"Why are you so secretive?"

"You're one to talk about secretive. It wasn't long ago you acted like a complete homophobe. You had everyone fooled."

"Okay, maybe I lost myself in playing the part of a bad ass, but most of that wasn't acting."

"So, you're saying you're naturally a jerk?"

"Yes. I told you that already." Caspian began to laugh and his laugh was contagious.

The waitress arrived with our food. I took a bite of my basil burger and it was delicious. The basil added an extra touch of flavor to an excellent burger. I liked the fries at Opie's too; they were steak fries, rather than thin fries. I liked them good and salty.

"Do you really hate Dylan?" I asked Caspian after a while.

"I don't hate him. He's just annoying. I don't like him hanging on me. I don't like being touched and he's way too touchy-feely. Well, I don't like being touched unless it's by someone I want to touch me."

Caspian surprised me again by reaching across the table and taking my hand. I looked down at our clasped hands for moment, then back up at Caspian. He withdrew his hand after a few moments more and looked uncharacteristically awkward and shy. The boy was full of surprises.

We began talking about teachers at school, which ones we liked and didn't like. We talked about the food in the cafeteria, which guys we thought were hot (a new area of discussion for me, but one I loved), and who we thought might be getting head from Dylan. I didn't mention the one I knew for sure because that was Caleb's personal business and I didn't divulge confidential secrets to anyone.

Caspian and I talked and laughed in the way I'd hoped we would that first day when I picked him up to take him to school, before everything got weird and Caspian began acting like such a jerk. I could feel a lot of hidden pain from Caspian, but then how could he not be hurting? His parents had recently died and he'd lost everything. He wasn't going to get over that in a few weeks.

He'd never completely get over it. I knew I'd never get over losing my dad if it happened. Time might make it easier, but it would never make it okay. Caspian had lived out my nightmare. I tried not to even think of the possibility that Dad might not always be around.

I pushed the unpleasant thoughts out of my mind and enjoyed my time with Caspian. I enjoyed eating, talking, and laughing with him as if we were friends, which meant we *were* becoming friends, and maybe we could even become more. I had a slightly nervous, but not unpleasant feeling in my chest when I realized I could fall for Caspian. That realization filled me with both elation and fear. The world had truly gone mad... or perhaps it was just me.

Percy

Caspian returned from eating out with Tyler with a smile on his face. Seeing that smile was worth more to me than I can express. Caspian looked like he was about to tell me something, like he was bursting to tell me something, but then he closed his mouth, went into his room, and closed the door. The fact he didn't slam it was promising. I also didn't hear him lock it. Something was up with Caspian. He was acting very peculiar and I was certain Tyler had something to do with it.

Life with Caspian improved greatly over the next few days. He wasn't talkative or cheerful, but he was more pleasant and polite that I'd ever seen him. It wasn't so much the presence of pleasantness or courtesy that I noticed, but the absence of belligerence and rudeness. Caspian revealed nothing to me about what was going on his in life, but he did answer in full sentences instead of clipped, one-word answers that told me absolutely nothing. As curious as I was, I didn't pry. He wasn't communicating much, but he was communicating. It was as if a switch had been flipped from off to on. If I was patient, Caspian might begin to open up.

Autumn tightened its grip. The leaves turned to brilliant yellows and oranges and began to fall. We had entered October and Halloween was creeping nearer. I loved this season with its crisp air and chilly nights, but it meant it was nearly time to garage the Shay for the winter. A roadster without side windows was not a car to drive in the colder months. I did have side curtains for the Shay, but visibility was so poor with them attached I thought it unsafe to drive. Soon, I'd be back to driving a "normal" car like most everyone else. I sighed. It was the price I had to pay for the scent of fallen leaves and the coming holiday season.

I loved this time of year. To me, fall was walking in showers of crimson leaves, reading ghost-stories as cold rain tapped against the window panes, buying pumpkins and colorful squashes and gourds at the farmer's market, sipping hot tea to drive away the chill, eating pumpkin pie, sipping apple cider, and snuggling with my boyfriend on the couch. I was sorry to see summer depart, but I loved all seasons in turn.

Caspian and I had survived our first few weeks together. I hadn't strangled him and he hadn't knifed me in my sleep. He no longer glared at me or slammed doors. He'd once even hugged me and cried on my shoulder. He would not mention his parents and I knew better than to do so myself, but he was getting on with life. He was hanging out with Tyler and hopefully he was making other friends. Caspian was a troubled boy, but his friendship with Tyler gave me hope. One good friend could make all the difference.

I sensed a deepening closeness between Caspian and Tyler. It was almost as if they were, or were becoming, more than friends. They were both gay but any serious intimacy between them seemed highly unlikely. Then again, the way they'd been at each other not so long ago made *any* form of friendship between them unlikely. Friendship could often give the appearance of more. Sometimes, there was very little difference between the intimacy of friends and that of more-than-friends. Of the two, I was betting on the former, even though my heart leaned to the latter.

Caspian was more comfortable with my relationship with Daniel. At least that's the impression he gave. There were no more rude comments, but that might have had something to with the fact he'd come out. He couldn't very well go off on me for being gay when he was gay himself. Then again, Caspian's arguments had rarely followed any logic. Completely gone were Caspian's insinuations that Tyler was my boy toy. That was undoubtedly due to his growing friendship with Tyler. I guess there was no need to analyze the situation. Things were improving between my nephew and me and that's all that mattered. We had a long, long way to go, but the situation no longer seemed impossible.

Daniel and I had settled into a comfortable relationship. He was often busy with work, but I needed time for my own life and I wasn't one of those who needed to spend every moment with their significant other. I smiled as I thought of Daniel as my "significant other." I'd feared that our twenty years of separation had changed us both beyond recognition, but my fears had not been justified. We had changed, but even more we'd remained the same. I could see the boy I'd fallen in love with when I gazed into Daniel's eyes. He had the same compassion and kindness that had drawn us together long ago. I wished now I could go back in time and comfort the teenage version of myself and let him know that he hadn't lost Daniel, that he only had to wait and he'd be with him again. I'm not sure how my teenage-self would have reacted to a twenty-year wait. It was easy enough now to have romantic thoughts about being reunited with a long, lost love, but when I'd lost Daniel it had all but destroyed me. I couldn't go back in time, but I could enjoy the present. The present, after all, was what was important. It was eternity.

Tyler

My date with Caspian at Opie Taylor's marked the beginning of a week of happiness. I wasn't sure it was a date until after it was over, but the next day Caspian sat right beside me at lunch. When I turned to look at him, we were pulled together by an irresistible force and kissed right there in front of all my friends.

"Get a room, please," Jesse said.

"And invite me over for the three-way! I'll be the middle of a naked boy sandwich," Dylan offered.

Jesse picked up Dylan's chicken sandwich and shoved it in Dylan's mouth to shut him up.

"Is it just me or do Tyler and Caspian seem to be getting along better?" Caleb asked.

"They don't seem to be fighting as much, unless they're trying to suffocate each other with their tongues," Tyreece said.

Caspian stuck his tongue out.

"So... are you guys an item?" Caleb asked. "Can I inform the rumor mill?"

"We're..." I paused, turning to look at Caspian. I had to fight myself to keep from going in for another kiss. "We're..." I wasn't quite sure what we were.

"We're casually dating," Caspian said.

"I'm not up on the gay dating scene," Jesse said. "Does that mean you're just getting to know each other or that you just haven't discovered which one of you is the bottom and which the top?"

I could feel myself turning red.

"We're feeling things out," Caspian said, then realized he'd opened himself up with a poor choice of words. "I mean we're going out on a few dates to see how we work out!"

"I think we just witnessed a Freudian slip," Tyreece said.

"I think Tyler just wants to date Caspian because he can get him into movies for half-price," Caleb said.

"Hey!" Caspian and I said at the same time.

"Well, he is a lot younger than you, Tyler," Jesse said.

"He's only three years younger," I said.

"Yeah, you're eighteen and he's fifteen, doesn't that make sex between the two of you illegal?" Jesse said with a smirk. "Tyler is a felon!"

"We haven't... I mean... Oh, just shut up, all of you!"

"If you were getting some you wouldn't be so testy," Dylan said.

I just stared at Dylan, but all he did was grin. He was almost impossible to intimidate.

"Do you think we should see if we can turn Tyler completely red or should we stop?" Tyreece asked the table.

"Let's stop for now," Caleb said. "Let's think of some really good material for tomorrow, then we can let him have it."

"Some friends I have," I said.

"If you're going to rob the cradle, you have to pay the price," Tyreece said.

I growled in frustration.

"If Caspian doesn't work out, maybe you kind find a nice boy at the grade school to date," Jesse said.

"Why are you suddenly talking so much?" I asked. "Go back to being self-absorbed."

"Oh no. Opportunities to pick on you are too rare to pass up. If you were a slut like Dylan, I wouldn't bother. I can pick on him anytime, but you... no, this is a rare chance to give you a hard time."

"Hey! I resemble that remark!" Dylan said, giggling.

"No one will argue with that," Tyreece said.

"That's right," Dylan said.

"Give Tyler and his little boyfriend a break, Jesse," Tyreece said.

"I'm not little! I'm a big boy," Caspian said, "*very* big."

Dylan perked up.

"How big?" he asked.

Caspian just grinned.

Lunch was an ordeal and yet it felt good to be teased. I wasn't sure where the relationship between Caspian and me was going, but we were causally dating as Caspian put it and it felt like we might soon get serious. Was I living in the Twilight Zone? None of this felt quite real.

Caspian met me at my locker after school and we walked to my car together. We both just assumed he'd be riding with me now. We made plans for meeting up at the nearby Taco Bell for supper. Caspian didn't seem to want Percy to know we were getting into the "more than friends" stage and I felt secretive about the two of us as well. I don't know why I didn't want Dad or Percy to know about us just yet, especially since there wasn't that much to know.

We sat across from each other in a booth in Taco Bell on 6th Street and North Walnut. We both went crazy and ordered a $2 meal deal with a Gordita Supreme, Doritos, and a drink.

"Your face turned really red at lunch today," Caspian said.

"I'm not accustomed to the guys teasing me like that, especially about... stuff."

"Sex?"

"Yeah."

Caspian laughed. "You're really... I don't want to say naïve or innocent, but... you seem so... well you do seem innocent when it comes to talking about personal things."

"I'm not exactly innocent, I'm just reserved."

"I'm not!"

"Yes, I know that, Caspian. I would classify your personality as *in-your-face*."

"You say it like it's a bad thing."

"I like it, now that you've turned from the dark side."

"Who says I've turned?" Caspian said with a smirk.

"Well, at least you've toned it down a bit."

"I'm just letting you and your friends see my nicer side. It doesn't mean I'm not a bad ass."

Caspian spoke with sincerity. He was a bad ass. I found that attractive, as long as he wasn't being an asshole as well.

"They could be your friends too. I think they mostly like you now."

"Now that I'm not calling them a freak-show?"

"That is a plus."

"Well, Dylan is a freak show and Jesse... I seriously cannot believe that dude is not gay."

He's not. If Dylan can't seduce him, he's not gay."

"It's too bad. Jesse is hot."

"It's so weird to hear you say that. It's... completely out of character."

"No, it just doesn't match with who you *thought* I was."

"You shouldn't be so hard on Dylan. I know he gets on your nerves, but he's a good guy," I said.

"He's also the school's biggest slut."

"Well..."

"He is. If half of what I've heard is true he's a total slut and he didn't deny it when Jesse said he was a slut. I think he's proud of it."

"Seducing straight boys is an accomplishment."

"I bet seducing horny jocks isn't *that* difficult. I bet they'll stick it anywhere when they get worked up enough."

"You are way too worldly. You make me feel like I'm younger than you."

"I'm from California! Anyway, about Dylan... He's too much like a girl. I like guys who are tough."

"I'm not tough," I said.

"You aren't girly. I remember the day Tyreece had to hold you back when you wanted to pummel me."

"Yeah, I vaguely remember that too."

"You scared me that day, but I didn't let on. I was afraid you'd escape and mess me up."

"I think we both know you would have kicked my ass."

"Well... yeah, but you would have hurt me, pretty bad I bet."

"I don't know. I'm not a fighter."

"We can't all be perfect and you did well when we tangled."

I liked the ease with which we were communicating. We sat there and talked a long time, through several soda refills. There were some big differences between us, but I still liked Caspian.

I walked Caspian home, close to home anyway. Neither of us said anything, but we were both feeling secretive. Before we got too close Caspian pushed me up against a tree and shoved his tongue in my mouth. We made out for a couple of minutes and then parted. Caspian smiled when he saw the bulge in my pants.

Caspian and I spent a lot of time together after that. We began studying together in either my room or his. We kept the door open whenever we did to avoid suspicion. We were hot for each other, but there were places to explore away from the prying eyes of Dad or Percy.

Caspian and I went out in the middle of the next week. We grabbed something to eat at the Pita Pit on Indiana Avenue, right across from campus, and then drove to a secluded area to park. I stopped the car and Caspian and I pulled close. We began to make out. His tongue was so silky and smooth.

My breath came harder and faster. Making out never failed to get me worked up. I ran my hands over Caspian's slim, hard body and even let my hands wander down over the front of his jeans. His hands were just as busy and it drove me crazy.

"I want to keep going, but..." I said, or rather panted between kisses.

"Yeah," Caspian said.

We pulled back for a few moments. I had to stop or I would keep right on going. Instinct was kicking in and my instinct was to go all the way, right there in the car.

"I think we should decide on how far we want to go and how soon," I said.

"That's probably a good idea. I want to get it on, but..."

"Me too, but this it feels a little weird," I said. "It feels good, but weird. Percy is like a dad to me and you're his nephew so..."

"Isn't incest accepted in Indiana?"

"Not funny. Dad and Percy may get very serious. We could be living together someday. If Dad adopted you, you'd be my step-brother."

"Kinky."

"Seriously! Think about it."

"You are talking about something that may never happen. Even if we all lived in the same house why would your dad adopt me? Even if you were my step-brother it wouldn't be the same as if you were my brother. There is no reason for your dad to ever adopt me. Even if he does, he hasn't yet so I'm not your step-brother. We can sit here forever and worry about stuff that is never going to happen, but it's a total waste of time. You think too much."

Caspian made a move to pull me to him, but I resisted.

"Let's just go slow. Let's ease into this. Part of me wants to do it all right now, but I'm trying to think with my head and not my dick."

"So you're saying we should keep it in our pants?"

"I think that's a good rule for now. Anything goes, but we keep it in our pants and keep our pants on. We can talk about going further later when we're not both worked up."

"I can live with that, for now."

"Where were we?" I asked.

Caspian pulled me to him again and we made out while our hands explored. I wanted to forget about the idea of waiting, but I forced myself to maintain control. I discovered there was a certain tortuous pleasure in getting all worked up and not going beyond groping. Maybe I was just a masochist. I grinned at that idea.

We kept at it until the windows were totally steamed up. We were both panting when we pulled apart and Caspian had a glazed over look in his eyes. I felt wild and nearly out-of-control just then. I wiped the window clear with my shirt-sleeve and started up the car. I thought it best to avoid more temptation just now. Caspian had no idea how close he was to being ravished.

That was only the first of several make out sessions. I wanted to break our rule and I'm sure Caspian did too, but we held to it. Whenever I was alone and thinking rationally I knew the decision to wait was the right choice. In the heat of the moment I was ready to do just about anything. I don't know how we managed to control ourselves, but then our make out sessions were so intense they almost seemed like sex.

I thought of Dylan and his promiscuous ways. I didn't judge him, but I wondered if sex was something special to him or just another recreational activity. We didn't talk about his exploits much, but I had once voiced my concern about the risks he was taking it. Dylan assured me he always used protection. That was a relief, but he was still taking a risk. Then again, we all took a risk every time we crossed the street or even when we stepped out the front door. All of life was a risk. Still, I intended to play it smart and part of that meant not going too far with Caspian too quickly. We'd be safe if we went all the way, but condoms offered no protection against emotional risks. I tried to imagine how I'd feel after we did the deed, but I think it was one of those things that just has to be experienced. I wanted to do it in the worst way, but I was afraid of the risk, afraid of how I'd feel *after*.

I was hesitant because of Caspian's age too. He seemed older than me in many ways, but he was fifteen. I was pretty sure sex between us was illegal. I thought that was pretty stupid, but people went nuts when sex was involved. They absolutely freaked out. I wasn't even sure Dad and Percy would approve of Caspian and me having sex. I could almost hear them advising me to wait until he was sixteen. That actually might not be a bad idea. How long could it be before he turned legal anyway? Surely we could wait. We could do a whole lot without going all the way.

Dad didn't seem too suspicious, but he was happy that Caspian and I were getting along better. If only he knew how well we were getting along… Percy was another matter…

Percy

"Four, five, six, damn!" Caspian said as he landed on the Reading Railroad.

"You can afford $200, Caspian. You're the one with hotels on Board Walk and Park Place," I said.

"I shall bankrupt you, bah-ha-ha-ha," Caspian said.

"We'll see. It's your turn, Tyler."

I was surprised when the boys asked me to play Monopoly with them, but not as surprised that they'd been getting along so well, or that Caspian had all but dropped his belligerent attitude. He was still a little smart-aleck and a smart-ass, but I could easily tolerate that. He reminded me a little of myself at his age. He was also immature in a lot of ways, but he was fifteen.

I couldn't explain the sudden change in Caspian, but I was grateful for it. I didn't let it lull me into a false sense of security. With a boy like Caspian, there was always trouble ahead.

I had spoken to Tyler alone about Caspian and he couldn't explain the change in his attitude either. He seemed almost hesitant to talk about it, but Tyler had told me Caspian was now sitting with him and his friends. Perhaps just making a few friends was enough to explain the change. Being lonely and feeling like an outsider can affect anyone deeply.

Tyler laughed at me when I landed on Illinois Avenue and had to pay him a hefty sum. He put his hand on Caspian's for a moment, but then drew it back quickly. A glimmer of fear crossed Tyler's features but was masked in an instant. I wouldn't have thought much about it, but on top of the other things I'd noticed the touch and the fear made me wonder...

A couple of days before I'd looked into Caspian's room as I walked past. The boys were studying on Caspian's bed, but at the moment I passed they were gazing into each other's eyes. It was nothing in itself, but another time I'd caught Caspian gazing at Tyler with an expression that could best be described as tenderness. That emotion didn't fit Caspian at all and didn't fit with the relationship between Tyler and Caspian, at least not with the relationship as it had been. It wasn't all that long ago they'd been in a fist fight. The bruises hadn't even all healed yet.

Was something going on between Tyler and my nephew or was I just seeing things that weren't there? Most likely my writer's imagination was at work, but... maybe not.

Tyler seemed slightly uncomfortable during the rest of our game, but I tried not to read too much into it. Did it really matter if my suspicions were correct? Would it hurt if Caspian had a crush on Tyler? Would it be a problem if his feelings were reciprocated? Caspian was a little young for Tyler. Three years was a significant difference at their ages. Then again, who could I trust with my nephew more?

"Yes!" Caspian yelled as I landed on Boardwalk later in the game. "That's $2,000, but wait... you don't have that much do you? I'll just take everything you've got."

"You'd think he'd have some pity on his uncle," I said to Tyler.

"Pity my ass!"

"Okay, I'm out. Would you boys like something to drink?"

"Could I have a Coke please?" Tyler asked.

"Yeah, make that two," Caspian said.

I went into the kitchen and prepared the boy's drinks as they continued their game. I returned to the living room and sat in my comfy chair browsing a *Country Living* magazine. I enjoyed sitting there, listening to the boys talk and laugh in the background. Who would have thought I'd someday be sitting in the living room listening to "my" kids. Tyler was as much man as boy, but he felt very much like my son. I had grown closer to Caspian, too, and for all practical purposes he was my son. At just that moment I felt very content and happy. The only thing that would have improved the evening would have been for Daniel to be sitting across from me. I'd see my boyfriend soon enough. Just knowing he was a part of my life made me feel all warm and cozy inside.

Tyler

Jesse glanced at me nervously and then looked away. He shut his locker quickly and hurried down the hallway. I stopped for a moment, trying to figure him out, but then some kid who was texting and walking plowed into me, sending me stumbling forward.

"Sorry."

I continued walking. It had been such a beautiful weekend that I was sorry Monday had arrived. Caspian and I had spent a wonderful Saturday walking all over campus, making out among the falling leaves of Dunn's Woods, and then pigging out at the Scholar's Inn Bakehouse. I couldn't remember being so happy or seeing Caspian so happy, either. Things had changed so much, so quickly, that it was hard to believe it was real, but the look in Caspian's eyes told me he *really* liked me. The feeling was mutual. If someone had told me a few weeks before I'd fall for Caspian, I would have told them they were out of their freaking mind. I was glad now that Tyreece had kept me from strangling him on the day I'd wanted nothing more than to wrap my fingers around his neck and squeeze and squeeze and squeeze.

Had it only been a week since Caspian and I had started dating? It seemed longer, but maybe that was just because my friends had teased me about him so much or maybe because we'd spent so much time together. Time did pass more quickly when I was having fun.

I knew Caspian and I were just getting to know each other. We weren't in love, but we were definitely in like. Was this what it was like for Dad and Percy all those years ago? Did it all start out slow and then build? I knew it hadn't been love at first sight between them. I didn't have the whole story of their romance, but Dad had told me Percy all but ignored him in the beginning. Were Caspian and I at the beginning of a meaningful relationship, or was it just a temporary fling? Either way, I liked the way I felt when I was with Caspian or just thinking about him. I liked making out and feeling up too.

I worked the combination on my locker, opened the door, and then sorted through my backpack. I carried as few books to my classes as possible, but I didn't like to return to my locker between every class, so I usually carried books for two classes with me. That gave me time to hang out a bit between classes and catch up on recent events.

"Okay, you need to just keep calm. Don't go nuts."

I turned at the sound of Tyreece's voice.

"Think before you act, Tyler. You know how Dylan is. Kicking his ass will only get you suspended."

I just stared at Tyreece.

"What are you talking about?" I asked.

Tyreece suddenly looked like a deer caught in the headlights of a speeding car. I'd never seen that expression on his face before.

"Um..."

"Wait a minute... Jesse just about tripped over his own feet earlier trying to avoid me, now you're trying to calm me down. What is all this about?"

"Shit. I thought you'd heard. Everyone is talking about it. Well, not everyone is talking about it, but word gets around fast about this kind of thing and a lot of people were at that party on Saturday night."

"Will you just tell me what's going on?"

"Don't fly off the handle, okay? I know it's bad, but you know Dylan. He has no control and..."

"Just tell me!"

"Dylan gave Caspian a blow-job at Cory's party on Saturday night. I wasn't there, but apparently they weren't too careful and a couple of girls saw them. I'm really sorry, Tyler. I know you and Caspian have been getting close."

All the color drained from my face. I shook my head. It didn't make any sense!

"No," I said.

Tyreece gazed at me with such compassion that it terrified me.

"No!"

Caleb wheeled up and looked back and forth between Tyreece and me. I just stood there; shaking my head, tears began to roll down my cheeks.

"Why would Caspian do that to me?" I looked at my friends; desperate for an answer they couldn't give.

"We're here for you, Tyler," Caleb said. "I don't know what we can do to help, but we're here."

"It can't be true," I said. "I was with Caspian Saturday. We had the best time ever! The whole week was... we're closer than ever and he... he wouldn't do this to me! I thought we were..."

"Maybe he got drunk or..." Tyreece's voice trailed off. He knew there was no way to make what Caspian had done okay.

"Are you absolutely sure?" I asked.

Tyreece nodded.

"Yeah. I talked to Brice Parker. He was there. He didn't see it, but he was there when the girls came out and started talking about it. Caspian and Dylan got out of there plenty fast. There were probably afraid they'd get their asses kicked. I'm really sorry, but it happened."

"This doesn't make any sense," I said, rubbing tears out of my eyes. "Everything was so good between us. Hell, if Caspian wanted... I would have... why?"

Tyreece and Caleb stood there gazing at me, helpless. There was nothing they could do to make this better. Nothing. I couldn't believe Caspian had cheated on me. It didn't even make sense. We'd barely started dating! This was like the old Caspian, not the one I'd been hanging out with recently. As I stood there my pain turned to anger.

"Where's Dylan?" I asked.

"Tyler, no," Tyreece said.

"I'm going to kick his ass."

"That's not going to make anything better," Caleb said.

"I can't believe that little shit sucked off my boyfriend!"

I was talking too loud. My classmates were listening. I didn't care.

"Just calm down," Tyreece said.

"I'm gonna rip his nuts off and shove them down his fucking throat!"

I slammed my locker door shut, but before I could step away Tyreece firmly grabbed my upper arms and held me up against my locker.

"Let go of me, Tyreece."

"Not until you calm down."

"I'll calm down after I kick his fucking ass!"

I was breathing hard and tears were rolling down my cheeks again.

"You have every right to be pissed off, but you'll just get yourself in big trouble," Caleb said.

"It will be worth it, now let me go, Tyreece."

I struggled, but Tyreece was way too strong for me. If he had been a bully holding me up against the wall I would have kneed him in the nuts, but I couldn't do that to Tyreece and he knew it.

"I'm your friend, so I'm not letting you go," Tyreece said. "You thanked me after I kept you from attacking Caspian that day he pissed you off."

"You should have let me kill him."

"You need to calm down and think before you act," Tyreece said. "Don't do something stupid that will get you in trouble. If you want to go off on Dylan, fine. If you want to go off on Caspian, fine. Do it with words, not your fists."

"It will feel so much better if I do it with my fists!" I said, struggling to free myself. I only managed to move away from the lockers a couple inches before Tyreece pushed me back again.

"Tyler, wait twenty-four hours," Caleb said. "Promise us you won't physically attack Dylan or Caspian for twenty-four hours and we'll let you go. If you're still determined to kick some ass after that, we'll help you."

I looked at Caleb. I knew what he was doing. He figured I'd calm down and no longer be hot to kick ass if I waited that long.

"You can promise to wait twenty-four hours or I can just stand here and hold you that long," Tyreece said.

I scowled at my friends.

"All, right! I promise. Now get off me!"

"Say it," Caleb said. "You're a writer. We know you're tricky with words."

"Okay, I will not physically attack Dylan or Caleb for twenty-four hours."

Tyreece let me go. I shot my friends a sullen look, but I couldn't really be angry with them. I knew they were just looking out for me.

"Later, guys," I said and walked toward my first period class. I wanted nothing more than to track Dylan down and pound his face until he was unrecognizable, but I'd promised. I could break the promise, but Tyreece and Caleb knew I wouldn't. I didn't break promises I made to my friends, even when I *really* wanted to, like now.

My anger began to ebb, but I wasn't sure that was a good thing, for the pain of betrayal immediately replaced it. Dylan was my friend and Caspian my boyfriend. Okay, maybe boyfriend was stretching it, but he felt like a boyfriend and he wasn't far off from being my boyfriend. I did not understand how either of them could do this to me. I could kind of see Dylan thinking with his dick and going down on Caspian without allowing himself to think of the consequences, but Caspian... everything had been going so well between us. There was no sign of trouble. If he really needed a blow-job he knew I would have given him one. We could have discussed it and... I didn't understand how he could do this to me.

Everyone was looking at me. There were whispered conversations all around me. Everyone knew. I was humiliated. I'd been uncomfortable about my classmates thinking about Caspian and me having sex, but having them know he'd cheated on me was even worse. Word was probably flying around that I wasn't any good at giving head and so Caspian had gone elsewhere. That's just what I didn't need; a reputation as a homo who was lousy at sucking dick.

As I sat down in my first period class, I tried to block out all thoughts of my cheating former boyfriend and lousy son-of-a-bitch ex-friend, Dylan. I wasn't very successful.

There was way too much whispering going on. It probably wasn't all about me, but I was willing to bet that the Caspian, Dylan, and Tyler triangle was the major cause. I hated being the center of attention, especially when it was something so humiliating.

I spotted Dylan just after my first class. I clinched my fists, glared, and started toward him before I remembered my promise. At least Dylan had the decency to look ashamed of himself. If he had looked smug I'm not sure I could have held true to my word, especially since Tyreece and Caleb had forced me to promise.

I didn't see Caspian anywhere and that was likely for the best. I didn't think I could stand looking at him. He had hurt me and I didn't understand why. Now I understood why he acted weird when I drove him to school. He'd barely spoken and I'd even wondered if he was mad at me. He'd seemed almost belligerent and wouldn't talk about it when I asked him what was wrong. It also explained why he said he couldn't hang out on Sunday.

I spotted Tyreece, Caleb, and Jesse more often than usual. I saw all three of them after second period and Caleb and Jesse after third. It was obvious that Tyreece or Caleb had told Jesse about their before-school discussion with me. They were watching me to make sure I didn't get myself into trouble.

I always valued my friends, but they were especially important to me now. They didn't judge me. They just cared about me. Just knowing they were there for me made me feel better. Knowing that I could go talk to any of them about what had happened was a relief. I didn't know if I wanted to talk about it, but knowing I could was comforting.

My first Caspian-sighting came at lunch. I had just sat down by Caleb, Tyreece, and Jesse when I saw Caspian coming out of the serving line with his tray. Our eyes locked for a moment. He looked sad, but then his expression changed to a smirk. I clinched my fists and fought to keep the tears out of my eyes until Caspian had passed by. I didn't sob out loud, but tears rolled down my cheeks. Jesse moved from his spot on the other side of the table to sit beside me. He wrapped his arm around my shoulders and squeezed. I got myself under control and grabbed up a chicken nugget.

"At least Dylan had the decency not to show his face," I said.

My friends looked at each other.

"It's okay," I said. "We all know what happened. You guys can talk about it. We don't have to tip-toe around it."

"In that case, I'm really surprised Dylan did this," Caleb said. "We all know Dylan is... well, I'll say it... a slut, but I'm shocked that he'd hook up with Caspian when he knows you guys are dating."

"*Were* dating," I corrected.

"It really isn't like him," Tyreece said.

"No, but he did it. I thought he was my friend, but... I lost a friend and Caspian in the same day," I said sadly. "I thought Caspian had changed. I thought I was getting to know the real Caspian. I guess I already knew him. I guess he really is a jerk. Good riddance... I guess, but still I've lost two friends."

"We're still here and we aren't going anywhere," Caleb said.

"Yeah, and none of us will ever hook up with any boyfriend you have in the future," Jesse said.

Tyreece punched Jesse in the upper arm.

"Oww! Too soon?" he asked.

"You know, that would mean a lot more if you weren't all straight," I said. I couldn't help but smile. "Seriously though, guys, thanks."

I noticed a few kids looking at me as they walked by. I also noticed Jesse, Tyreece, and particularly Caleb glaring at them to frighten them away. I'd lost two friends, but those who remained were awesome.

I intended to avoid Caspian and Dylan until my twenty-four-hours was up. I wasn't sure if I ever wanted to talk to Caspian again and I wasn't sure I could keep myself from punching Dylan in the face.

Dylan thwarted my plan to avoid him by waiting at my locker at the end of school.

"We need to talk," Dylan said.

"Why would I want to talk to you?"

"Please? I... we just really need to talk, but not here."

Dylan looked around. All eyes were watching us, probably waiting for a fight. I wanted to punch Dylan in the face so bad I couldn't stand it so a fight was likely, despite my promise.

"Please, Tyler. I know I have no right to ask you for anything but... please."

Dylan's eyes were rimmed with tears and one slid down his cheek.

"Yeah, you're right. You have no right to ask me for anything."

"Please, I'm begging you."

"Fine! Come with me. We'll talk in my car."

And I'll take you somewhere remote where no one will hear you scream and no one will be likely to find your dead body.

I smiled to myself. It was an enjoyable fantasy, but the real reason I wanted to talk to Dylan in the car was that I didn't want to provide more drama for the rumor mill.

"So start talking," I said, none-too-kindly, as Dylan and I buckled up and I pulled out of my parking space.

"I'm really sorry, Tyler, but Caspian is soooo hot and..."

"This doesn't sound much like an apology. Your excuse for sucking off Caspian is that he's hot?"

"I'm... I'm sorry. I know it was too soon and I didn't mean for it to happen, but... well he is incredibly hot. I fantasize about him when I..."

"What do you mean 'too soon'?"

"Too soon after you guys broke up. I was going to wait, I swear. I'd even planned to ask you if I could..."

"Whoa! Whoa! What do you mean too soon *after* we had broken up? You blew *my* boyfriend *while* we were dating, you fucking slut."

"But... Caspian said..."

"Caspian said what?"

"He said you guys had broken up. I swear! He said you had an argument and that you were guys were over."

"Are you lying to me, Dylan? If you are fucking lying to me I'm going to pull over and beat the shit out of you right here."

"No! I even asked him if he was sure. I thought maybe you guys were pissed off at each other but that you'd get back together. I didn't want to do anything with Caspian if that was going to happen. You're my friend, Tyler. I wouldn't do that to you."

Dylan had a horrified expression on his face when I spared him a glance.

"I'm so sorry, Tyler. I swear I didn't know you guys were still dating! Caspian told me you were finished. Oh God, no wonder the guys have been looking at me like they have. Tyler, please, you have to believe me. I didn't know. I've been feeling so guilty all day for hooking up with Caspian so soon after you broke up with him, but I really thought it was after! I never thought for a second Caspian was lying to me. Please. Please forgive me. I'm soooo sorry!"

Dylan started bawling, right there in a passenger seat of my car. We were far enough away from school that there was no one there to see it. I'd never seen Dylan so upset. I wanted to slug him a few minutes earlier, but now I felt more like holding him.

Dylan had never lied to me before. True, I hadn't known him all that long, but he'd never lied to me. One thing that hurt so much about his betrayal was that it came as such a shock. I couldn't believe it at first and maybe I'd been right not to believe it. I also couldn't believe Caspian had cheated on me, but that was an established fact. Caspian had gone back to his old ways. Not only had he cheated on me, he had lied to Dylan so Dylan would give him head. It didn't make sense. Caspian didn't even like Dylan very much, but there it was. It was just too bizarre to be true, but it looked like that was what had happened. Damn, I had been so delusional. I'd even began to think of Caspian as my boyfriend. What was I thinking? I must have been out of my freaking mind.

"It's okay," I said. "I forgive you, Dylan."

Dylan slowly calmed down.

"I'm so sorry, Tyler."

"I know, and I forgive you, Dylan. I believe that you didn't know Caspian and I were still dating when you hooked up with him. What you did wasn't cool, but it's not nearly as bad as what I thought you did."

"That explains why Caleb was so harsh with me," Dylan said. "I mean, I knew I'd done something bad but he ripped me a new one."

I actually laughed out loud for a moment.

"We'll have to talk to the guys and explain."

Dylan whipped his head around to look at me.

"Does that mean I can still sit with you guys?"

"Yes. You used poor judgment, but you didn't betray me. I'd be a lousy friend if I didn't forgive you. I'm sure the others will understand."

"Thank you. I thought you all hated me. I've been so upset all day. You guys mean so much to me."

"Maybe you should think a little before you act, Dylan."

"I know, it's just so hard when I'm around a hot guy, no pun intended. When I see a guy like Caspian I want him so bad it's like my entire body is on fire. I *need* sex."

"We all need it, Dylan, but you've got to exercise a little self-control."

"I'll try."

We were silent for a few moments.

"Wow, now I'm glad that Tyreece held me up against my locker this morning and made me promise not to kick your ass for twenty-four-hours."

"You were going to kick my ass?" Dylan asked, swallowing hard.

"Oh yeah, when I found out what you'd done with Caspian I was so mad I couldn't think about anything but pounding my fist into your face. If Tyreece and Caleb hadn't stopped me... well, I'm just glad they did."

"Me too," Dylan said, his eyes till wide with fear.

I drove Dylan to his house.

"So, we're really cool? I would never betray you, Tyler. Never!"

"We're cool, but dammit, try to think before you act once in a while! I'll see you tomorrow, Dylan."

"Bye, Tyler!"

Dylan shut the door and ran toward his house. He was back to his old self as if nothing had happened at all. I pulled away from the curb and drove toward home.

Dad was there when I arrived. I tried to keep my tone of voice upbeat as we spoke, but I kept our conversation brief. I knew Dad would try to help me if he sensed something was wrong and I didn't feel like talking about Caspian just yet. Dad didn't even know Caspian and I were a couple—make that *had been* a couple; our relationship lay in ruins now. I escaped to my room, dumped my backpack, pulled on a hoodie, and headed out to Miller-Showers Park to walk and think.

I thought more clearly when I walked and I had a lot to think about. Dylan hadn't betrayed me. That made sense. Dylan was boy-crazy, but I never dreamed he would try to seduce my boyfriend. His betrayal had hurt me nearly as much as what Caspian had done and it was a relief to discover he hadn't betrayed me at all.

Caspian had betrayed me. There was no denying it. It was true. Not only had he cheated on me, he'd lied to Dylan so Dylan would hook up with him. The thing is, Caspian's actions didn't make sense. Caspian and I had experienced a wonderful Saturday together and the whole week before that had been great too. He hadn't given the slightest hint he wasn't happy with our relationship. Our time together had been near perfect. I couldn't even imagine a better day than Saturday, so what had happened? What took place between my date with Caspian and Cory's party?

I walked around the long, oval, asphalt path as I tried to work it out in my head. I stopped at the northern end to look over the railing and watch the stream disappear into the culvert. The stream looked much the same as always as it rushed through the grasses and over the rocks, but it was never the same. The water flowed continuously so it was impossible to gaze upon the same stream twice. I turned from the racing water and took time to admire the flowers and the large sculptures before moving on.

I neared tears several times, but I fought back the pain of betrayal and tried to make sense of what had happened. Had Caspian been toying with me all along? The transformation from homophobic jerk to kind and loving boyfriend had been a little too sudden to believe. Was the change an act? Was our relationship just a long-term game plan to hurt me? I didn't think so. If Caspian had been faking all of that, he was one incredible actor. When we had spoken of intimate things I could feel the emotions deep inside him. When he shared his pain I could feel the turmoil within him. No, our relationship had been real. I was sure of it.

Maybe I was pushing it when I thought of Caspian as my boyfriend. Had we ever put what we had in those words? Maybe not, but that didn't make Caspian's betrayal any less painful. What we had, whatever it was, was real. Why then had Caspian cheated on me? It was as much his idea as mine to move slowly. If Caspian was that desperate for sex surely he would have talked to me about it instead of hooking up with someone he wasn't even into. None of it made sense!

I walked and thought and thought some more. Slowly, an idea began to form in my head. I considered it carefully, making sure I wasn't deluding myself or merely seeing what I wanted to see. There was a real danger of that. I was hurting so bad inside I was willing to grasp at straws. I ran my theory over and over in my head. If I was right maybe all wasn't lost. If I was wrong... well, I didn't even want to think about that.

Percy

My work was interrupted around 2:30 by a phone call from North High School. I was asked to come in and speak to the principal about Caspian. There had been an *incident*, as the secretary put it.

I sighed as I pushed the disconnect button. I saved my work, powered down the computer, grabbed a jacket, and headed for my old high school. I wondered what awaited me. This parenting thing wasn't easy.

I experienced an odd sense of déjà vu as I entered my old high school for the first time since graduating in 1990. Weird; 1990 didn't seem that long ago and yet nineteen years had passed. The older people around me had always said that time passed faster as one aged. Did this mean I was getting old? I was sure Caspian would think so.

My nephew was sitting with arms crossed and a sullen look on his face as I entered the outer office. He was sporting a fresh black eye. He looked up when I announced my name to the secretary. I gave him a sympathetic smile and received a disgusted "you're just too stupid for words" glare back. I paused for a moment. I hadn't seen that look for quite a long time. The secretary pressed a button on her phone and announced my arrival.

"Principal Maclaine will see you now."

I stepped into the office and stopped short as the secretary closed the door behind me. I immediately regained my composure and reached out to shake Principal Maclaine's hand.

"You look surprised," she said.

"It's just that when I attended North, our principal was a rather ancient and stern old man, at least we thought of him as ancient then. He was probably all of fifty."

The principal who sat behind the desk was an attractive woman in her mid-30s.

Principal Maclaine laughed.

"About Caspian..." I said.

"Please have a seat, Mr. Spock."

"Call me Percy."

"I see from Caspian's file that he enrolled less than two months ago."

"Yes, he's my nephew..."

I went on to explain about my brother's death and my new role in Caspian's life.

"I've read through the file I received from his former school. Your nephew has quite a record."

"Unfortunately true, but what did he do today?"

"He picked a fight with two older, bigger boys because they "looked at him funny" according to your nephew. I've spoken with both the other boys involved and they couldn't explain why he attacked them. They seemed rather bewildered in fact. Neither of them has been in any trouble in the past. I'm inclined to believe them, mainly because they seemed genuinely perplexed as to why Caspian jumped on them. They did fight back, but the teacher who witnessed the altercation said their actions were clearly self-defense. Of course, we don't tolerate any fighting here, but the other boys did use a minimum of violence to protect themselves. The fight didn't last long. The teacher on duty broke it up within seconds."

"I'm very sorry about this," I said. "Caspian has been through a lot recently, but that isn't an excuse for what he did. I wouldn't have been too surprised if this has happened a month ago, but now... he's been doing so much better."

"You're his sole guardian now?"

"Yes."

"How are things between the two of you at home?"

"They've been very strained, but our relationship has improved lately. We were thrown together rather suddenly. It's extremely difficult to get him to communicate, but that has also improved. I think a large part of it is that he's just being a teen, but I'm sure losing both his parents so recently and suddenly is causing a lot of the difficulties."

Principal Maclaine looked thoughtful for a moment.

"It's difficult being a single parent. I speak with quite a lot of them. I can tell you are genuinely concerned about Caspian. When I spoke with him earlier he wasn't cooperative or commutative. He was quite combative, in fact. He couldn't or wouldn't give me any excuse for his behavior beyond his "they looked at me funny" defense. He also told me he won't be around long, that you don't care about him, and that you can't wait to get rid of him."

I rubbed my head in frustration.

"I thought we were making progress, but he sounds like the Caspian who first showed up on my doorstep. It's as if he's reverted to his old self."

"After speaking to you I'm quite sure his portrayal of you is inaccurate. You are definitely not the uncaring and heartless individual he described."

"I do care about him very much and, despite the difficulties of integrating a fifteen-year-old into my life, I'm actually quite glad to have him."

I thought for a moment.

"This fight doesn't make any sense. Let me run a theory past you," I said.

We talked for several more minutes. It was a relief to speak to someone knowledgeable about adolescents. Principal Maclaine wasn't a bureaucratic pencil-pusher, but rather someone who genuinely cared about her students.

"Okay, bottom line, can we avoid a suspension?" I asked after our discussion.

"Physical violence is something that can't be tolerated in a public school. Taking into consideration all the factors, however, I think suspending Caspian would only aggravate the problem. I'm assigning him a Saturday detention instead."

"I think that's very fair, even generous. I also agree that suspending him would only make things worse. He can be quite combative."

"I'm well aware of that," Principal Maclaine said with a grin.

We spoke a few minutes more then I walked back into the outer office.

"Come on," I said and walked out into the hall without waiting to see if Caspian followed or not. I heard his footsteps behind me and slowed so that he could walk side-by-side.

"This place brings back a lot of memories," I said.

"Spare me. We studied the 1950s back in middle school. So... she kick me out?"

"No, you have Saturday detention."

Caspian looked surprised.

"That's bull-shit!" he said, a beat too late and with forced hostility.

I didn't respond. We walked out to the car and then drove home in silence. Caspian eyed me now and then, trying to figure out how I was reacting. I purposely gave him no indication.

We were back at our small Victorian home in a few minutes. Caspian made for his room, but I grasped his shoulder.

"We need to talk."

"Get off me!"

I released Caspian's shoulder and motioned for him to lead the way into the kitchen. He shot me a resentful glare, but didn't resist.

"Sit," I said, pointing to one of the kitchen chairs.

I grabbed us both Cokes from the refrigerator and put one down in front of Caspian.

"Drink it."

"Been a control freak long?" Caspian asked.

I just sat there and looked at him, letting the silence build. His hostile glare turned to one of uncertainty and he glanced around the room as he sipped his Coke. Finally, he couldn't take it anymore.

"So, should I pack my bags or what?"

"Do you expect me to kick you out?" I asked.

"If you had any fucking sense at all you would. Don't you get it? I'm a thug. That trip to the principal's office is only the first of many. Next time I will be suspended or I'll be put in some juvenile facility. This is only the beginning."

"Why?"

"God dammit! Stop with the questions! You even answer my questions with questions! That fucking pisses me off!"

"Okay, here's a statement instead of a question. There was no reason at all for you to attack those boys today."

Caspian started to protest, but I held up my hand and he closed his mouth.

"You attacked them for no good reason and you did it in full view of the teacher who was on hall duty. We both know you are far too intelligent to do something so stupid."

"Maybe I didn't see the teacher, okay?"

I just gave Caspian a look that said, "please."

"You wanted to get busted. You wanted to get suspended. You wanted me called into the school. I thought we had progressed beyond this point, but I was wrong. There is quite obviously an issue we haven't dealt with yet. You got yourself into some serious trouble on purpose, not as serious as you were shooting for, but still serious. We both know why."

Caspian turned away for a moment, angry tears forming in his eyes.

"I know you don't fucking want me here! I know you don't care about me!" he screamed at me from across the table.

"You can't know those things because neither of them is true," I said calmly. "You don't even believe those things; you're just terrified that they *might* be true. I've told you I care about you and that I want you here, but you still don't trust me enough to believe me. I've tried to be here for you and show you that I care. I thought you were beginning to understand that, but something inside you won't let you believe. You're terrified that I don't care about you and don't want you.

"You don't have to be afraid, Caspian. This is your home. I'm not going to kick you out now, or ever. If you cause trouble I'll ground you. I'll take away your cell phone and your computer. There will be consequences when you get into trouble, but I will never kick you out and I will never stop caring about you. I've been trying to show you that for weeks now, Caspian, and I think I've demonstrated it fairly well. Obviously not well enough or we wouldn't be having this conversation, but understand this: I will not give up on you, now or ever. No matter what you do, I will not send you away. This is your home and it *always* will be. I love you, Caspian, and I'll never stop loving you."

Tears were flowing down Caspian's cheeks. It was only the second time I'd ever seen him cry. I stood up, walked around the table, and took a big risk. I put my hand on Caspian's shoulder and squeezed. He was up out of the chair in a moment, crying into my chest. I wrapped my arms and held him, just like I had on that day that now seemed so very long ago.

"I'm sorry," he said.

"It's okay. I love you, Caspian."

Caspian's arms tightened around my waist and he hugged me close.

"I love you, too."

I just stood there with tears running down my cheeks and held him as he cried.

Tyler

It was lunch-time again. Dylan had moved back to his usual spot at our table. I'd explained to the guys what had happened. Dylan was still partially in the doghouse with my friends. I wasn't at all happy with what he'd done, but it wasn't nearly as bad as what I thought he'd done. I'd forgiven Dylan, and in time I'd even forget.

"Excuse me," I said.

I could feel my friends watching me as I walked toward Caspian's lonely table. Caspian eyed me fearfully as I approached. I just stood there for a moment and looked at him. He didn't look like a bad-ass now, just a frightened boy.

"Meet me on the west side of the stadium, by the big guns, at 4."

I turned and left without waiting for a response and walked back to my friends. I sat down and didn't even look in Caspian's direction. Jesse, Dylan, Tyreece, and Caleb were all looking at me, but I didn't offer an explanation. This was between Caspian and me.

The minutes ticked by slowly until the end of the school day. I headed home a little after three. I changed into jeans and a red IU hoodie. Shortly before four, I walked over to the stadium.

The parking lot was busy. A lot of IU students parked at the stadium and rode the campus buses. One of the buses pulled out as I crossed Dunn Street. Across the parking lot, I could see a blond figure sitting on the wall, right by one of the big howitzers or whatever they were.

Caspian stood up as I climbed the stairs. In moments, I was standing only three feet from him, facing him.

"I'm here, so... is this where you punch me in face?" Caspian asked.

There was no smirk on his face and no hint of sarcasm in his voice. He looked sad and resigned.

"When I first found out you'd cheated on me with Dylan I wanted to punch you in face and kick his ass. The guys made me promise not to touch either of you for twenty-four hours. They figured I'd calm down and they were right."

"They should have just let you hit me."

"Slugging you would have felt *really* good, but then I would have gotten the worst of it. We both know you can kick my ass. Beating the crap out of Dylan would have been very satisfying as well, but I talked to him instead. I wasn't so mad at him after I found out you'd tricked him."

"Yeah, I tricked him. I knew he wouldn't do it if he thought we were still dating. I'm a bastard as you've probably figured out."

"I've figured a lot of things out, Caspian. You've never expressed that much interest in Dylan. You think of him more as a pest then anything. It doesn't make any sense that you'd hook up with him."

"I was horny and a mouth is a mouth. He does have a reputation for giving great head."

"You weren't very careful about where you did it, either."

"When I think with my dick, I don't consider the details."

I shook my head.

"I'm not buying it, Caspian."

"What's to buy? I cheated on you."

"Yeah, you cheated on me, but it doesn't make any sense. Just like your arguments about Percy wanting to molest you never made any sense."

"Why do you have to analyze everything?"

"To understand what really happened."

"Dylan sucked my dick, that's what happened. I cheated on you."

"I also analyze things to figure out *why* they happened."

"It doesn't matter why. I did it. I fucked up everything. You don't like me anymore and there's no reason you should."

Caspian's eyes were moist. He was drawing closer to crying.

"No, why you did it matters a lot. After I calmed down I got to thinking about it and none of it made any sense. You don't particularly care for Dylan and you had no obvious reason to cheat..."

Caspian started to open his mouth but I held my hand up.

"I don't buy that you got horny and threw caution to the wind or that you were thinking with your dick. I've thought about this a lot. Things were going really well between us. I think you got scared because things were going a little too well. I think you began to feel something for me and it freaked you out. Maybe you even started to fall in love with me and you couldn't handle it. You were afraid of getting close, of getting hurt, and of losing me. I think you were afraid because you were getting close to Jesse, Caleb, Tyreece, and even Dylan. You were afraid because things were going well at home too. You were just waiting for something or someone to come along and mess it all up because you just couldn't believe everything was working out. You couldn't stand the pressure of waiting for the ax to fall. You couldn't deal with waiting so you intentionally sabotaged it all."

Caspian stood there, looking down at his shoes. He didn't say a word. After a few moments, his body began to tremble slightly, and hot tears began to fall and drip onto his shoes. When he looked up at me his eyes were red and tears ran down his cheeks.

"I just brought about the inevitable. None of it was going to last. I'm sorry. I never meant you hurt you. I should have kept my distance from the beginning, but... it doesn't matter. I'm sorry," he said, and began to walk away.

I grabbed his upper arm and twirled him around so that he was facing me again. He grimaced, obviously waiting for me to punch him in face, but making no move to protect himself. I grabbed his chin in my right hand and used my left to pull him close to me. I leaned in, pressed my lips to his, and kissed him. When I pulled my lips from his he just stood there looking at me, tears still streaming down his cheeks.

"You're not getting away from me that easily, Caspian."

"I'm so sorry," he said and began bawling.

I pulled Caspian close and held him. He wrapped his arms around me and held me tight. I held him and let him cry, ignoring anyone and everyone who might be watching two boys standing in front of the stadium, holding each other.

Caspian quieted after a few minutes, but still held onto me. After a few minutes more he raised his head up and looked into my eyes.

"You were right about what you said. When I moved here I was scared and so lonely. Everything was so different and... things started to get better, but I was still so scared. It's like you said. I couldn't stand waiting for everything to be ruined, so I went ahead and made it happen... but... it hasn't worked out like I thought. First Percy, now you; neither of you shoved me away like I expected."

"I heard about the fight. You tried to get in trouble so Percy would kick you out, didn't you?"

Caspian nodded

"Only he didn't. I thought I was clever but he saw right through me. You know what he did? He told me he loved me."

"He does love you, Caspian. I told you that. I told you Percy wants you here. Why can't you believe there are people who love you?"

Caspian began to cry again.

"Because I don't deserve to be loved."

"Caspian, everyone deserves to be loved."

He shook his head and sobbed even harder.

"I used to do a lot of bad stuff. I got in trouble a lot. My parents... they loved me but I didn't appreciate them. I went ahead and did things and..." Caspian had trouble getting the words out through his sobs. He couldn't speak at all for a few moments. "I did all that bad stuff and..." Caspian sobbed so violently he scared me. "I did so much that... God took my parents away from me!"

Caspian totally lost it. I grabbed him and held him close.

"It's my fault they died! It's my fault our house burned down! It's all because of me!"

Caspian bawled. Great, heaving sobs welled up out of his chest. My shirt was soaked with his tears. I held onto him tightly.

"Caspian. No. What happened was an accident. You didn't cause it. God didn't take your parents away from you because you didn't appreciate them or because of what you did. You aren't responsible for that happened, Caspian. You didn't make it happen. Sometimes, horrible, horrible things just happen. My mom died when I was two. I don't even remember her. She died and it's not because of anything I did. It just happened. The same is true for you. I don't care what you did or how little you appreciated your parents. They didn't die because of anything you did. They didn't."

Caspian was crying too hard to answer. I didn't know if I was getting through to him or not. I was crying my own tears. I couldn't imagine how horrible the guilt was for Caspian. I knew he'd gone through terrible things. I knew he lost his parents, lost everything, but I never knew he blamed himself for it. No wonder he acted like he did.

I don't know how long I stood there holding him. Time lost its meaning. Pain poured out of Caspian, first in racking sobs and then with gentler tears. When he pulled away his eyes were red and his face puffy.

"Some bad-ass I am. I've been crying like a baby all the time lately," Caspian said, wiping his eyes.

"I think even bad-asses are allowed to cry sometimes."

Caspian smiled for a moment, but his eyes were still filled with pain. I took his hands and held them in mine.

"Caspian, I can't make you believe this just by saying it, but what happened to your parents was not your fault. I don't know everything you did, but there are tons of kids who get into all kinds of bad shit and nothing happens to their parents. I know kids at school who were close to their parents and then lost them. Maybe there is such a thing as Karma, but there is no way you caused the death of your parents. As far as not appreciating them, I don't think anyone appreciates their parents enough. Of course, there is nothing to appreciate with some parents, but I don't even appreciate my dad like I should. I appreciate him, but a lot of the time I don't stop and think about all he does for me."

"Please! You're like the perfect son."

"I'll admit I get along great with my dad and I appreciate him, but even I don't appreciate my dad enough. You weren't a bad son, Caspian, you were just a son."

"I miss them *so* much."

I squeezed Caspian's hands as I held them.

"I know. I can't pretend to understand the pain you're in. You are facing my greatest fear. If I lost my dad... I don't even want to think about it. I miss my mom, even though I don't remember her. I was too young when she died to understand that I'd lost her. I know that losing Dad would be so hard I don't even want to think about it. Nothing I can say will make what has happened to you okay, but you can't push away love because you're afraid of losing it. If you do, you'll never have love. You'll always be alone. You'll bring about what you fear.

"I can't promise that you'll live happily-ever-after with Percy. Life isn't a fairy tale. I do know that he'll stick by you and he'll do whatever he can to help you. I can't promise that you and I will work out. Maybe we won't get along as boyfriends, maybe we will. Do you really want to throw away all the fun we can have together just because you fear things won't work out? Think about it. What if we don't work out? What if we date for a few weeks and then we have a messy breakup and never see each other again? We will still have had good times together—making out in Dunn's Woods, eating together at Opie Taylor's, smiling because we spotted each other in the hallways at school, eating lunch together in the cafeteria with our friends. We'll still have all that, just as you still have all the good times you had with your mom and dad. Chances are we aren't going to date forever. I'll start college next fall and you'll still be in high school. We'll probably date other people after that, but that doesn't have to take away from what we can have now. If we do get pissed off at each other and break up we can probably still be friends. There is no way we can know what's going to happen. The only sure way to ruin it all is just to give up and turn our backs on what we could have because we're afraid of what *could* happen."

"I'm afraid, Tyler."

I could tell that admission cost Caspian a lot.

"I know you are. We're all afraid sometimes, Caspian. Just don't mess up your life because you're afraid. Don't let the fear win. I won't call you lucky, because some of the worst things I can imagine have happened to you, but there are good things in your life, Caspian. You have Percy and he'll be there for you no matter what. You have friends, if you'll only let them be your friends. Immodestly, you have me, a boyfriend who cares about you very much and is pretty sexy, too."

Caspian grinned.

"I don't have any guarantees for you, Caspian. My dad told me long ago that life doesn't come with guarantees and he was right. Life is *life*. It's what you make out of it. I want you to be my boyfriend, Caspian, but you've got to be brave enough to take a chance. You have to be willing to go out on a limb and risk getting hurt."

Caspian pulled me in close and kissed me deeply. When he pulled back he was smiling.

"I'm feeling pretty brave right now," he said.

I took Caspian's hand in mine and we walked down the steps and out across the parking lot.

"You won't tell anyone at school about all the crying I did, will you?" Caspian asked.

"What crying?"

"Thanks. It would be hard to keep up my rep as a bad-ass if everyone knew I bawled like a baby."

"It would make you seem a little less fearsome."

Caspian grinned again. He was so cute when he grinned. My heart swelled with happiness.

"No more secrets, okay?" I asked. "I'm your boyfriend and your friend. I want to know when you're hurting. Don't try to be brave and handle things alone. I'm here for you, Caspian."

"No secrets," Caspian said. "The same goes for you. I want you to share your pain so I can at least try to help. Are you okay, Tyler? We've only been talking about me."

"We've been talking about us. I'm okay—now." I smiled at my boyfriend.

"Promise?"

"I promise. No secrets."

Percy

Daniel, Caspian, Tyler, and I took the Shay out for one last spin before I garaged it for the winter. The boys sat in the rumble-seat and Daniel and I sat up front, holding hands. The crisp October air was perhaps a bit too chilly for a ride in a roadster, but the heater provided some warmth for our feet up front and the boys were entwined in the rumble-seat, making their own heat. I gave them the glance of a worried father in the rear-view mirror, then forced myself to relax. Tyler was a mature eighteen-year-old and Caspian... while not so mature would undoubtedly follow Tyler's lead. I couldn't think of anyone I wanted to date my nephew more.

Caspian dating... and dating a boy! It was going to take me a while to get used to that idea. There had been hints, some of them rather large, like Caspian kissing Tyler at the end of their fight. I'd witnessed some signs of closeness between the boys, but still I wasn't prepared when they walked in together and told me. Maybe age didn't made one smarter after all.

Tyler, Caspian, and I had had a long talk and then Caspian and I spoke alone even longer. I finally had all the pieces of the puzzle. Everything made sense now. I wish I could have figured it all out for myself and much sooner, but life doesn't come with easy or quick answers. I was fortunate that Tyler and Caspian had become close. Without Tyler, I would still have been guessing.

I was sure our troubles weren't over. Caspian was fifteen and any fifteen-year-old was trouble just waiting to happen. We had reached a significant turning point and one I thought would make a tremendous difference. Only time would tell.

The drive to La Charreada on North Walnut was short. We could have easily walked, but I just had to drive my roadster once more and Daniel and the boys loved riding in it. We parked, then walked inside and were given a booth where Daniel and I sat side-by-side across from the boys. I glanced up at my menu for a moment as everyone else was browsing and savored the moment. I'd be waiting for this moment for so long. Here we were, all together, a family. I didn't know if Caspian and Tyler would work out as a couple. I didn't even know if Daniel and I would for that matter. As my nephew had recently told me; there are no guarantees in life. Here and now we were together and now is all that matters.

Books by Mark A. Roeder

Listed in suggested reading order

Outfield Menace
Snow Angel
The Soccer Field Is Empty
Someone Is Watching
A Better Place
The Summer of My Discontent
Disastrous Dates & Dream Boys
Just Making Out
Temptation University
The Picture of Dorian Gay
Someone Is Killing The Gay Boys of Verona
Vampire's Heart
Keeper of Secrets
Do You Know That I Love You
Masked Destiny
Altered Realities
Dead Het Boys

This Time Around
Phantom World
Second Star to the Right
The Perfect Boy
The Graymoor Mansion Bed and Breakfast
Shadows of Darkness
Heart of Graymoor
Yesterday's Tomorrow
Boy Trouble
Christmas In Graymoor Mansion

Also by Mark A. Roeder

Homo for the Holidays: A Collection of Mostly Gay Christmas Tales

Made in the USA
Lexington, KY
29 February 2012